THE GESTURE THAT FIT

THE GESTURE THAT FIT

a novel

LINTON TAYLOR

Dedicated to Je'vardo and Grandma.
To the wholeness of their love.

"For the Wages of Sin is Death…"

Romans 6:23

PART I

CHAPTER 1

They were inescapable. Paned in glass, the steel sky-scrapers made a deep cut into the sky that was as open and free as the buildings were precise and measured. The soft pink and orange hues of the setting sun bled onto the protruding structures like a melted popsicle running down its wooden stick. The scene made me uncomfortable, but I didn't know why—maybe it was the violence that unfolded in heaven as it did here on Earth or the audacity of these manmade structures attempting to bring nature to heel. Whatever it was filled my thirteen-year-old self with transient feelings of dread and longing, yet the most prominent feeling was that of being trapped.

"Jay, do you want to *call* her again?"

"Sure."

I called her cellphone again. Silence was followed by a soft click and then, "Please leave a message after the beep." Jaw clenched, I avoided Ms. Turner's piercing stare that drilled into the back of my head. I hung up and then tried the home phone. It rang… and rang… and rang.

"Hello?" A voice said sleepily on the other end.

"Christian!" I responded. Ms. Turner sighed with relief and murmured, "Thank God," just loud enough for me to hear. "Where's Mom?"

"In the kitchen, you wanna talk to her? Where are you?"

"No," I answered, relieved to hear his voice but a little annoyed at his offer to put her on. *Of course, she forgot. She didn't even notice I was gone.* I closed my eyes and pushed the thought away. "Tell her I'm back from my trip, and she gotta pick me up from school. They won't let me walk home."

"She's on her way," I said, handing the cellphone back to Ms. Turner. She painted a smile onto her face like a last-minute addition to a portrait—hesitant, as if the artist couldn't pinpoint where they had seen the gesture but still sure that this was where it belonged. A belabored sigh escaped through the gaps in her teeth, and then she returned to her steady gait, pacing to the streetlight at the corner and back to the school mural of little Black kids holding hands in a pasture. There was a prevailing joke that if she ever stopped moving, she would tip over and fall. Middle school kids could be cruel.

Ms. Turner waddled past on her phone. "You said the movie starts at 8 o'clock, right? ... I know that's in fifteen minutes. I've been waiting for forty-five." She glanced at me, then lowered her voice to a whisper. "But she's on her way. I'll probably miss the previews..."

My friends were the ones who started the joke. I didn't find it funny but laughed when they did. It seemed like the gesture that fit.

6:35 AM

"Chaperones, please make sure that everyone in your group gets on the bus," Ms. Turner bellowed.

Eric held his arms out and rocked side-to-side, mimicking Ms. Turner while she paced the line. He made mooing sounds and then stopped moving, tipping over until he fell. Herb and Mason's snickers turned to boisterous laughs.

"You good?" Herb asked, noticing my absent stare.

Smile! I reminded myself.

"I'm good! Just a little tired," I said, smiling.

"Good shit gettin' here early, Jay," Eric said, adjusting the drawstring bag on his back. A crucial part of my plan was to secure the seats at the back of the bus, so I had insisted on arriving early to hold our spots. My heart raced at the thought of what awaited us on the bus ride. I wiped my sweating palms on my shorts.

Smile!

I acknowledged his gratitude with a nod and steered the subject.

"I've never been to Baltimore before. Wonder how different it is from Philly. I went to D.C. once at my old school. It's not as big as here. Maybe Baltimore is simi—"

"Yooo!" a voice interjected suddenly; silence followed as heads swiveled to find the source.

"Demetrius! What did I tell you about yelling like that?" Ms. Turner asked, intercepting Meat on his way to join us at the front of the line.

"My bad, Ms. T! Just excited." He grinned, putting his braces on display. Demetrius—or "Meat" as the students called him—was as oblivious as he was goofy. He added a present lightheartedness to the group that balanced out Mason's rigidity, Eric's insecurity, Herb's supervision, and my veiled aloofness. As the class clown, he often found himself in trouble with the teachers but rarely faced any severe punishment. Why? Although funny, goofy, and oblivious, more than anything, Meat was charming. Armed with an unflagging joviality and a boyish grin, he could win over any boy, girl, teacher, principal, or parent.

"Don't let it happen again," Ms. Turner said, for what must have been the fiftieth time this year and certainly not the last time that day.

"Yo!" Meat repeated at a tempered volume. "Y'all ready?"

"I was just about to tell them about the aquarium in Baltimore," I responded. "It's supposed to be one of the biggest in the country, and you get to touch some of the fish and stuff."

"That's not what I'm talkin' about, little guy." Meat tussled my hair, and I pushed him off. In one fluid motion, he took off his backpack and reached into it. "Y'all got yours?" He held a blue plush blanket in his hand: speckled with white bubbles, on one side was SpongeBob SquarePants; and on the other, his pineapple home. Strange it was to imagine Meat once a fan of cartoons. It rendered a kid-like image of him my mind couldn't make sense of. Stranger, however, was that he chose this blanket for the trip–the impending collision of childhood innocence and sexual pleasure made me uncomfortable and sympathetic to what SpongeBob was about to witness.

"I got mine," Eric said.

"Me too," Mason added, reaching his arm behind his back to pat his bag and confirm his statement.

"Oh, shit. Fuck! Hold on." I took my backpack off and searched for a blanket that I knew wouldn't be there. "Fuuuck. I think I left it in the crib when I was rushin' to get here." I put my hand to my forehead and sighed, "and I know exactly where I left it too. Anyone bring an extra one I can borrow?"

"I got you," Eric said. "Y'all know I be gettin' cold easily."

He pulled the spare blanket out of his bag and handed it to me. *Fuck.*

"You would think all this would keep you warm," Mason responded, patting Eric on his belly.

"Damn, dickeater," Eric snapped back.

"You laughin' hard as shit, dickhead," Mason said to Meat, who became the new focus of his derision, "with those dumbass braces in your mouth."

"You just mad your teeth fucked up," Meat rebutted. "I'm cute as shit with these jawns and pull mad bitches."

Eric laughed as Mason's face got red. "Bro, you don't get any bitches. And my teeth—"

Their voices became muted as I willed myself invisible and faded into the background. "Good look," I squeaked out from a distant place where no one could hear or see me, through a contrived smile and panicked thoughts. *Fuck, fuck, fuck. FUCK!* I squeezed my eyes shut and hoped this was just a bad dream, but when I opened them, the world remained unchanged, and Herb was staring at me. *Shit, why is he looking at me? Smile!* With his blanket tucked under his arm and some urgency, he said he was going to go ask his dad when we would be getting on the bus.

"Ard," Mason said while surreptitiously running his tongue over his teeth. "Who y'all sittin' with? I'm next to Lea."

"I'm with Taylor," Eric responded.

"Aniya," Meat added, rapidly moving his middle finger back and forth. Mason and Eric joined in miming the movement and recounted past experiences of fingering girls, ending their stories with exaggerated moans.

"Brianna," I said, laughing while I unraveled alongside the threadbare blanket in my hands.

Herb returned and draped his arm around my shoulder. "I just spoke to my dad. He said we're about to get on the bus." Herb must have felt me trembling because he squeezed me lightly to steady the tremors—it worked. Even though Herb and I were the same age, he treated me like his little brother, which I didn't mind because proximity to him meant safety. This had only been my first year at Blanche Creek, but Herb had welcomed me into the group as if our relationship were picking up from where it ended in a previous life. With the newly discovered friendship came a circle of friends that was there for each other—something I had never experienced before but for which I had longed.

"Who you sittin' with, Herb?" Mason asked.

"Evey."

"I can't wait to get on this bus." Meat pulled his dick out and slapped it against his hand. "I'm so fuckin' horny, bro!"

"Nigga, you so fuckin' gay," Eric said, laughing and covering his eyes.

Having witnessed this "joke" many times, Mason sneered and turned his back to Meat.

"See somethin' you like?" Meat asked, grinning. My face grew hot as the spotlight turned on me. I quickly looked away, ashamed and embarrassed. Herb scolded him and told him to put it away.

"Alright, we're about to start boarding," Ms. Turner yelled. She took a cursory look at her clipboard, nodded to Herb Sr., who walked towards us, and then paced the line one final time. He tapped me on the shoulder, so I shimmied from under Herb's arm and out of line. Herb glanced at me and then returned to talking to the guys.

"What's up, Big Dub?" I asked cheerfully, ignoring the discomfort on his face.

I had met Mr. Wynpark—or "Big Dub" as the guys and I called him—several times, yet his stature always caught me off guard. As I craned my neck to meet his eyes, I again remembered how much Herb looked like his dad or, to be more accurate, a younger version of his dad. I had seen pictures of Mr. Wynpark when he was younger, and it always made Herb laugh when I couldn't distinguish who it was. Both had autumn eyes that contrasted with their summery skin, and at thirteen, Herb was almost his dad's height. Looking at Mr. Wynpark now, though, felt eerie. Here he stood, a glimpse into the future, while a past version of him stood behind me.

"How you doing, Jay?" Mr. Wynpark asked, replacing his discomfort with a warm smile that resembled Herb's. I answered that I was "good," but he had already started talking again, "so, there's been a last-minute change…"

"Oh. What's up?"

His warm smile wilted into a straight line, and the look of discomfort returned. "Uhm… you know what, let's go find Ms. Turner. She can explain better." Nodding, I attempted to alert the guys I would be right back, but before I could, Mr. Wynpark placed his arm around my shoulder and led me away.

After some equivocation by Ms. Turner about why I had been switched, she told me I was in Xavier's group, which consisted of just him and his dad, Mr. Reid. Before going to find Xavier, I decided I should tell the guys what had happened, but as I got closer to the front of the line, they began to board the bus. Pushing through the clamoring crowd, I called to Herb as he got onto the bus, but he didn't respond, only glancing at me with what looked like disdain and condemning me to the surge.

———

For years I had begged my mom to let me switch to the neighborhood public school, but each time I asked, her response was the same. "The education is better at a private school." This was true given the tuition fees and funding from the archdiocese; however, I had become fed up with the orthodoxy of Catholic school and wanted out. The forced attendance at mass every month despite my not being Catholic; the pressed button-down shirts, maroon cardigans, and khaki pants; the strict adherence to norms; and the doling out of punishment for the violation of said— all of this created an environment that stripped you of your spirituality and identity while replacing it with prayer beads and a measured sense of self. When I got kicked out of Catholic school at the end of sixth grade— unintentionally, but who was I to question how God answered prayers?—I transferred to Blanche Creek Middle School.

At the beginning of seventh grade, I tested into the gifted program, which was where I met Xavier. I found his wit, sarcasm, nonchalance, and preference for discussions about music theory or history attractive—most of our peers preferred talking about sex and sports. This had earned him the label of "weird" around the school, so he stuck to himself with a book in tow. And he was weird—so was I when held to these standards—but there were rumors about him, things said that were more difficult to ignore and more pernicious to be, that made me avoid associating with him for fear of being labeled the same. That was until a few weeks into the school year when Mr. Castor, our teacher and director of the gifted program, assigned us as partners for a project.

Mr. Castor asked that we write a conversation between

two artists discussing the privatization of public spaces in a manner commensurate with their writing style. I chose Edgar Allan Poe, and he chose jazz singer Nancy Wilson. While I had Poe speak to the inextricable connection between man and nature and the oxymoronic relationship between the commons and individuality, Xavier complemented Poe's romantic tone with lyrics from one of Wilson's love songs, "The Masquerade Is Over." In a resolved yet sad tone, Wilson decried that her lover had changed in a way that made him unrecognizable to her and their relationship now felt contrived, leading to the end of their love. The pairing of Poe's romanticism with Wilson's literal romance, or lack thereof, led to our getting an A and becoming friends.

As the school year went on, my friendship with Xavier grew, as did my relationship with Herb and the guys—and thus my popularity—which deterred any move to have a friendship with Xavier outside of class. While I ate lunch with them, Xavier sat with a book in a library corner or in Mr. Castor's classroom. Many times while walking through the halls with the guys, we would frequently encounter Xavier, who always greeted me with a "hi." In the beginning, I would return his greetings with the same level of enthusiasm. But when the guys started mocking me for this, my hellos slid into tepid smiles and then imperceptible head nods, until I eventually stopped responding altogether. I felt bad about it and expected Xavier to confront me, but he never did. With each class, we would talk and laugh as though the previous day never existed, and we had the opportunity to create a new one just for ourselves.

Still, a part of me existed that wanted to merge the two worlds, so I proposed a way for Xavier to get in good with the guys by watching WWE. In my early days of hanging out with them, I adopted their viewing habits, and although I wasn't a huge fan of wrestling, it helped me to bond with them. When I told Xavier this, he asked me why I watched the show even though I didn't like it, and I responded by explaining the practical effect it had on my relationship with them. He then asked if it was worth feigning an interest in something I didn't like just to make friends, to which I had no response. After that, I never brought the guys up again. So, our friendship grew, sheltered in a world made new each day, cloaked in the understanding of who he was and how others perceived him, yet with no desire to change either.

Now, here we were, released from the shadows and unburdened of responsibility. I didn't choose to be in Xavier's group; I was *assigned*. We greeted each other—me doing so with less enthusiasm and a cognizant distance between us in case others were watching—and then boarded the bus. We sat up front, while my friends were in the back with their blankets wrapped around themselves and their female counterparts. Xavier and his dad sat together across the aisle, speaking excitedly about the aquarium and the prospect of touching the fish and stuff. I looked out the window and watched the school fall away as the bus rumbled down the road. Knowing the alternative, I was grateful for the empty seat beside me.

7:58 PM

"Jacob," Xavier called. His voice sounded sweet and far away, as if it were coming from beyond the clouds. "You ok?"

"I'm good," I responded, a bit surprised to see him but happy. "I thought you left."

"No, we weren't going to leave until your ride came. I would've come over sooner, but I was on the phone with my mom."

"Catching up?"

"That too. But mainly we talked about the itinerary for when I visit." Xavier sat down on the steps next to me and looked up at the sky. "Where do you think that plane's going?" His finger traced the contrail until the plane disappeared into a cloud.

"I don't know. Somewhere far, I hope."

He waited for the plane to reappear, but when it didn't, he allowed his hand to fall to his side. "Yeah, me too."

"Anything fun planned for the visit?"

"Of course."

"Fun *and* cryptic," I added. He smiled.

The sounds of the city pulled us back to the ground, and he stiffened with each car that honked or slowed down as though he didn't want the next one to be mine. This thought made me smile and assuaged the anxiety I had been feeling. Now that he was with me, I also hoped to prolong our time together.

He cleared his throat and then asked, "Do you need a ride home?"

"No, my mom will be here soon. But thanks."

"Cool," he said and then turned to face me. "I had a good time."

"Me too."

"What was your favorite part? I didn't get the chance to ask you."

I paused and then responded, "The captain letting us steer on the riverboat city tour. He got *so* mad when we made the boat go over the speed limit that he gave us. What was it? Like forty mph? That, and when we got to the aquarium, the sharks—"

"Forty *knots*," he said with an arrogant grin.

"Right, *knots*… you couldn't just let me have it?"

"Well, what kind of friend would I be if I let you be wrong?" He smiled, and I felt my heart slip into my stomach. *Friend.* The word made me feel ashamed—he regarded me as a friend, despite how I had been treating him—however, shame was a feeling I was familiar with, and so I did with it what I always had when it reared its head. I buried it.

"Whatever," I said. "I think we hit like sixty *knots* on that jawn."

Xavier laughed, and the richness of his voice felt like it could pull the clouds apart. Even so, it invited and empowered me to join in before acquiescing to the cricket songs. The streetlights flickered on, casting an orangey hue reminiscent of the June-time sun. A shallow representation—the light wasn't warm but pallid and cold and made the impending darkness starker and more violent.

"Can I tell you something?" he asked.

"Sure."

"Well, it's actually three things. Ard, so the first one. Don't get mad, but I'm kinda glad you got switched and were with me instead of your friends."

That word again, *friend*. His usage of the word felt like an indictment, like he was accusing me of not being a good one. It annoyed me. I wanted to tell him he was also my *friend*, although I had to pretend he wasn't, but I decided against it because even in my head it didn't sound great. Whatever response that would've been acceptable got stuck in my throat—choked up by that word *friend*—so I just smiled.

"That's a little fucked up."

"Maybe, but this is the first time we've hung out outside of class."

"Yeah… that's my bad." He looked at me expectantly, waiting for my justification for why that was, but I had an inkling that Xavier already knew my reason and just wanted to hear me say it, so I left it at that. "What's number two?"

He smiled and placed a hand on my knee. "I won the Har—"

"Hold on, I think my mom's here." Panicked, I picked myself up off the step and shook his hand from my leg as I investigated the forest green sedan at the stoplight. "It's her. My bad, you were saying?"

"I'll tell you later. I'll just skip to number three." He stood up to face me and rocked back and forth on his heels, as if being swayed by whether to tell me. "Ard, promise you won't get mad."

"Yeah, hurry up and tell me."

"Do you know why you switched groups?"

"No… well, Ms. Turner said that there were a lot of us in that group and that she wanted to make it smaller and more 'manageable.'"

"Sure, but why only switch out one person? And why you?"

"I don't know. Probably because we're both in the gifted program? Why do you care so much? I thought you were happy I got switched."

"I was. I am. But I overheard Herb asking his dad to get you put into another group. I wasn't sure if I should tell you, but I—"

"So, why *are* you telling me?" I asked.

"Because it's the truth and we're friends, so—" he began but my mom's honking interrupted him.

Friend. What had begun as an indictment that sparked guilt, the word now felt like a premise for intrusion. The timing of my removal from the group wasn't lost on me; I knew Herb had me switched. Still, the change had benefitted me, so I avoided the rationale for why and denied the truth. Regardless of what Xavier had said, his justification for telling me had nothing to do with truth or friendship, at least not ours. He had said it himself—he was "happy" I had been switched—this was him trying to drive a wedge between me and them.

"No, we're not," I said, throwing my shoulder into Xavier and sending him stumbling backwards. "I gotta go."

6:50 PM

We filed out of the bus and clumped into groups outside the school.

"Seven A, do not leave before checking in with me," Ms. Turner yelled. "I need to see your parents before they pick you up. Chaperones, please don't leave until all members of your group have been picked up."

"That was fun," Xavier said.

"It was," I agreed. "I thought it would be like D.C. because it's close, but Baltimore seemed… a little empty."

"I know, right! I enjoyed it, though. I think my favorite part was touring the ships. I had read about the one that had been used in—"

He continued to speak, but I couldn't hear him. Truthfully, I had stopped listening, though not from a lack of interest. Instead, my focus had inadvertently shifted to his lips, which continued to form mute words. In the crowd's bustle, we didn't stand out, existing together in a space that wasn't shrouded in darkness. The Dead seized the opportunity. From their graves, their lurid whispers seeped into the external world, changing the density of the air and bending the light of the raging sun so that it shone on just us two. A small piece of me—the inextricable piece bound to nature that shielded the Dead even as I prayed for their destruction—hoped this wasn't a mirage and the happiness they whispered about wasn't borne of a desperate thirst. But the Dead had led me astray before.

The moment ended as the guys walked by, and the reality of our circumstances came roaring back.

"Hey," I said to Xavier, "I'll be right back." He nodded, and I disappeared into the current.

"Yo, how was the bus ride?" I asked coyly with a smirk on my face.

"You tell me!" Meat put me in a headlock and held his fingers beneath my nose. It was pungent and smelled faintly like vanilla. I grimaced at the scent, and they all laughed while Herb watched stone-faced.

"Get the fuck off me, pussy!" I yelled, pushing him off.

"Calm down, I'm just fuckin' with you!" He continued to laugh as he walked away, taking a long whiff of his index finger. "I'll see y'all tomorrow."

"I saw you talkin' to the weird ass boul," Mason said with a sardonic smile. "That's your bro now?"

"Who? Xavier? Nigga, stop playin' with me. I was only talkin' to boul because I got switched to his group."

"I ain't even notice you wasn't with us until we got on the highway, to be honest. What happened?" Eric questioned.

"I don't know." I glanced at Herb, who looked away. "She just said she was puttin' me in boul's group."

"That's ass," Eric responded. "Taylor told me that Brianna really wanted to sit with you, too. But I'll get at y'all later. My mom's here. Mason, you need a ride?" Mason answered "no," and Eric peeled off from the group.

"Sounds like y'all had a good time," I said.

"You know she likes you, right?"

"Brianna? Yeah, I know."

"You like her?"

"She's cute."

"Would you fuck her?"

My throat tightened as if the question had gripped it and wouldn't let go until I answered correctly. I looked to Herb to intervene, but he, too, held his breath in anticipation of my answer. "Of course," I said with confidence to mask my fear. Herb exhaled and then placed his arm over my shoulder, but something felt different.

"Bet. Herb is gonna ask his pops if he can have a party for his birthday next month. I think she would come through if you went. You can talk to her there, maybe get some pussy."

"Don't get your hopes up," Herb said, finally interjecting. "I need to see if my mom is cool with it. And you know Jay's mom is strict as hell. Who knows if she'll let him come?"

"Still, if he does come, she'll definitely pull up." Speaking to me now, he added, "Just don't tell your mom."

"You know you're volunteerin' them to fuck in my bed, right?" Herb forced a laugh to lighten the mood but caused the tension to set in heavier.

"Change the sheets afterwards," Mason said, grinning. "Listen, I'm just tryin' to help my bro." He dapped Herb and me up. "Ard, I gotta go. My mom's callin' me. I'll see y'all tomorrow."

"Walk me to the car," Herb said. Without waiting for a response, he walked towards the car, shepherding me with the arm around my shoulder. "How was the trip? Did you touch any of the fish or whatever? I know you were excited about that."

"It was ard. I touched one of the manta rays."

"Lucky. We just barely saw the aquarium. We spent so much time in the cafeteria because all they wanted to talk about was the bus ride. Lunch took almost two hours!" He laughed to himself. "You ain't miss nothin'."

"How *was* the bus ride?"

His arm tensed. "It was ard... Evey and I just talked for most of it... like I said, you ain't miss nothin'."

"Right. And this party you havin'?"

"Still gotta ask the folks. But I'm thinkin' the day after my birthday. I'll let you know. And what Mason said... don't worry about it."

"What you mean?"

"Nothin'." He had a smile on his face, but it served to mask the same look of discomfort Mr. Wynpark had had.

I wanted to ask him why he had me switched, but I was afraid of what his answer would be. Had he seen the truth behind my smiles and laughter? Was this a show of compassion before my excommunication? His arm still around me, I could feel in his now perfunctory touch he was trying to pretend that everything was normal, but something had changed. Herb lightly squeezed my shoulder and then climbed into the passenger seat of the car.

"Glad you had fun, even if it was with Xavier. It sounds like you had a better time than we did. I'll see you later."

"See you," I responded. It was the first time I had heard him say Xavier's name.

When I went to find Xavier, he was gone. The groups had disappeared, and I was alone.

8:11 PM

I sat in the car and waited for my mom, who was talking and laughing with Ms. Turner. I couldn't decide with whom I was more upset: Ms. Turner—who had mumbled for the past hour about my mom's cavalier attitude for being on time—or my mom, who had won her over, nonetheless.

"Ok, dear! Have a good weekend!" my mom shouted to Ms. Turner as she crossed the street to the car. "Hey, how was the trip?" she asked, putting the key into the ignition. The engine coughed and hacked until finally turning over.

A knot formed in my stomach as she pulled out of the parking spot and onto the empty street. For the next seven minutes, we would be two lone travelers on the same road, but even so, I didn't feel comfortable opening up to her. More than anything, I wanted to tell her about what had happened: how I got switched to Xavier's group; how Xavier and I steered a boat in the bay of the Patapsco River; how Mr. Reid and I trailed behind Xavier as he read every plaque in the maritime museum; how we touched a manta ray at the aquarium and then had lunch along the waterfront; and how I was happy I spent the day with Xavier, even though I couldn't let the guys know that. I wanted to tell her about how I had "forgotten" a blanket to avoid having to finger anyone on the bus, but Eric had an extra one; how Herb was the one that asked for me to be switched; how I didn't know why, and now his touch felt different and that scared me; how he may have a party and Brianna would be there, and

I would be expected to have sex with her; how I couldn't; how I wasn't ready to do so, but how I had no choice if I wanted to keep my friends and the safety and belonging that came with them. There was a chasm between us, and we couldn't bridge it until she realized it was there as well. However, the only word I could muster was, "fine."

"That's good." She smiled at me and placed a hand on my shoulder, gently squeezing. The touch felt like one of resignation, like she wanted to know more but was too tired or frustrated to prod, so she just accepted my answer. It made me feel guilty, so I shrugged her hand off and looked out the passenger window. I loved her, I did. I loved her more than anything and anyone in the world, including myself, but I had long accepted the fact that we would never have a relationship because she would never know me. To the best of her knowledge, she taught me what it meant to be a man. Ironically, that meant being cold, being hard, and hiding the dead body of the boy she once knew.

I looked out the window and watched the houses blur into a gray stone tapestry. With stillness, the weight of the day finally settled in, and I drifted off to sleep. The Dead quietly murmured their desires as I thought of Xavier's hand on my knee, but I was too tired to push them away. In my dreams, the Dead would soon roam unfettered.

CHAPTER 2

There was this one time in February when the seventh-grade class went on a field trip to Jamz, *the* local roller-skating rink. I stayed behind because I didn't like to skate, and Meat also skipped the trip, but he wouldn't say why. Not going on a trip wasn't an acceptable excuse to miss school—not for my mom and not for the school—so often they assigned older students to a teacher of a lower grade to help with their class. Meat and I were assigned to Ms. Yolanda's kindergarten class, which, besides staying home, was the best situation if one had to miss a trip. Ms. Yolanda was funny, she was loud, she was caring and passionate and real, and she had a regality that commanded respect, even though you were obliged to give it without coercion. The older kids, however, loved being assigned to her class because of the unwarranted trust she placed in us. They believed her to be naïve, but to me, she saw in us our innocence, unwarranted or not, and for that, I cherished her. After reading to the kids and doing some painting, we helped with lunch, and then it was nap time. Ms. Yolanda relieved us and said that we could use some of the hour to read in the library or go to the computer lab. It was on our way to the computer lab that we ran into Nina.

Her full name was Regina, but when her baby sister was younger, she couldn't say this and pronounced it, "Wenina," which was then just shortened to Nina, and the name stuck. Because of the size of the seventh-grade class, students were split into two sections that rotated through classes on an alternate schedule. Meat and I were in Seven A along with the rest of the guys. Nina was in Seven B, as were Xavier and Brianna, and a few other people who were among the cool kids. Nina didn't run in our social circle. Like Xavier, she had been branded with a label that made her a social pariah, so she stayed to herself.

According to the guys, though, Nina was once a part of the upper echelon of middle school society. Being among the select few individuals who had been there since kindergarten, the "popular" kids exuded an air of ownership. It wasn't a title that was given to them but rather established through sheer collective thought, like the invention of fiat money. This currency had no intrinsic value, but by their own authority, they had made it an enviable commodity.

According to the guys, Nina was going out with a guy named Iman. The two had been dating for most of sixth grade, the story went, which for middle school was a long time.

According to the guys, Iman had the house to himself

for a few hours while his parents were at the *masjid*. They started on the couch and, after some convincing, moved to Iman's parents' bedroom.

"Why his parents' room?" I asked as they told me the story one random day at lunch.

"Bigger bed," Meat replied, adding in the sounds of squeaking bedsprings.

According to Iman, he lasted about twenty minutes.

"That nigga was lyin'," Mason said. "We all watched the video. It was like forty-five seconds long. But he tried to say that his phone died, so it got cut short."

"Wait, why did he videotape it?" I asked.

And responding again as if the answer were obvious, Meat replied,

"So that we could watch it."

According to the guys, the video leaked, but no one knew who had leaked it. Although Nina didn't know she was being recorded, the other girls—those whom she believed were her closest friends—were afraid of also being labeled as a "whore" shunned her.

According to Nina, they were in love.

"That nigga did not love her," Mason said.

According to the guys, Iman's parents found out about the video and subsequently sent him to live with his grandparents in Jersey. Nina, unable to escape the peering eyes and relentless whispers, finished the rest of the school year at home. When she returned, she no longer hung out with the popular kids, the value of her currency having fallen to zero.

Meat and I raced on top of the chairs to the back of the empty auditorium while Nina sat on the stage and refereed.

"I win again, dickhead," I jeered.

"Let's run it back," Meat said, smiling.

"Nah, you said best two outta three. Plus…," I checked my watch, and the small rectangular face faintly read 2:30. "We need to go back to Ms. Yolanda's class soon to get the young bouls ready to go home."

"Ard, hold on," he said with a sly smile on his face, "watch the door real quick."

"Watch the door for what?"

The slight downward slope from the back of the auditorium to the stage forced Meat to tiptoe, and he bobbed up and down like a paper boat floating down a stream. He lifted himself onto the stage to sit next to her and whispered into her ear. However, from the back of the auditorium, anything less than shouting might as well have been a whisper. She made a sound that was akin to a laugh and then playfully pushed him away.

I watched the door from the last row in the auditorium, passing the time by doing random calculations on my watch—which also doubled as a calculator—and thinking of how to alert them if someone was coming. I couldn't see through the window embedded in the door, so any signal would've been moot as soon as someone walked in, but I still thought of ideas to get their attention. Maybe whistling, but then I remembered I wasn't too good at that. I considered a bird call, and even rehearsed it in a small voice, the result of which had me chuckling to myself in the back row. Finally, I settled on just "RUN!" It was concise, effective, and prescriptive—what more could one ask for?

"STOP!" Nina shouted as she hopped off the stage. I paused mid-calculation to see what was happening.

Meat leapt off the stage after her, grabbing her arm and pulling her back into the auditorium as she left through the side door. "Where you goin'?" Meat asked, not yelling, but loud enough for me to hear clearly. "I was just playin'!" Her face was hard to decipher from where I sat, but it hovered somewhere between disgust and fear. She tried to pull away from him, but his grip never loosened.

"NO, I'M NOT DOIN' THAT!" She tried to use her right hand to pry his hand off her arm.

"Chill!" Meat said. I couldn't see his face, but I could tell he was smiling because with each second that passed her struggling acquiesced until it stopped altogether. It was like watching a snake charmer soothe the violent serpent back into the basket. "Ard, you don't have to do that. I'll let you go if you just touch—" Meat's voice dropped back to whisper levels.

"No!" she exclaimed, resuming her attempt to break loose.

"Why you bein' like that?" Meat's voice took on an uncharacteristically solemn tone. "If you don't, I'll te—" he whispered something in her ear, and the fight went out of her. As Meat unbuckled his pants, it was clear now her face had shown both disgust *and* fear.

2:45. Meat and Nina sat in the front row of the auditorium. Low moans echoed throughout the empty auditorium, traveling delicately on the dim lighting of the sconces that lined the walls. Nina's left hand moved up and down vigorously while she looked at the side door and plotted her escape once this detached body part was done with its task. I had thought of leaving but knew if he got caught, I would be to blame. More than this, however, something powerful anchored me to the seat and dared me to go further.

The Dead whispered from their graves—

She needs help.

Move closer.

She doesn't want to be here.

Move closer so you can see it.

I stood up, and the old wooden chair creaked as the seat snapped upright and reverberated until coming to a stop. They must have forgotten I was there because their heads shot back to look at me.

"Yo, bro," Meat sat up straight in the seat and pulled his shirt down to cover *it*. "You want parts?" He looked at Nina, who looked at the door for escape. The Dead went silent. As usual, they got me into situations they could not get me out of. Their only suggestion: **RUN!**

"Bet. Let me just make sure no one's comin'," I said. They watched me as I exited through the rear of the auditorium into the deserted hallway. I peered through the window to see if they were still looking, but all I saw were the rapid up-and-down movements of Nina's arm like a firing piston.

I waited in the bathroom until the bell rang before heading back to Ms. Yolanda's class, preferring that Meat lied to her about where I was and not the other way around. When I finally went to get my things, she only asked if I was ok with a look of concern on her face and then thanked me for helping. Later that day, Meat regaled the guys with how Nina jerked him off in the auditorium and how he got her to put it in her mouth. Even though there was a moment when they were alone in the auditorium, I knew that this was a lie, but I couldn't call him on it. He neglected to mention that I was there, not that he forgot, but because I posed a risk of exposing him. Equally, my being there exposed me to questions about why I didn't participate, so I remained silent. We both held versions of the story, but only one of us knew the truth, and no one would believe her. He smiled that charming smile at me, sealing our unspoken agreement, and then finished his story.

I woke up an hour before my alarm but not by choice. Beads of sweat clung to my forehead, and my shirt was drenched. Across the room, I saw Christian sprawled out on his twin bed, his shirt half off as if he had tried to undress mid-sleep and never quite finished. The air conditioner had been turned off. My mom hated when we ran it all night and argued that we only needed it to cool the room down before going to sleep. I often rebutted that our carpeted, sun-facing room was subject to intense heat, but logic wouldn't keep the energy bill low, so she often ignored it. Still, I felt refreshed. The events of the prior day—blanket-gate; Herb switching me out of his group; spending the day with Xavier, and his betrayal; Herb's pending party. It all felt like a vivid fever dream, the contents of which I steadily forgot as my body awoke. I loved how sleep felt like it could fix anything or at least dull the nervous system enough to recognize that things would be ok.

It was the last day of school and the end of my first year at Blanche Creek Middle School. Remembering this wasn't the first time I had sidestepped a precocious expectation placed at my feet, I had confidence I could avoid this one as well.

"Great job on your final essays," Mr. Castor said, weaving through the desks as he returned papers. The heat of the day hadn't fully set in, but it was sweltering in the classroom. All the windows were open—but if anything, this only made things worse—and the solitary standing fan at the front of the room did little but push the hot air around. In his usual get-up, Mr. Castor cooly moved through the rows in his gray wool suit.

"While you all did well, I hope you don't stop here. I encourage you to swap papers with your peers to read about which American holiday they analyzed and to continue to ask questions about your reality. There's a story behind everything." He returned the last paper and then leaned against his desk. "But the stories that are obscured, and those done so purposefully, illuminate deep truths, not just of our nation but also of ourselves and our responsibility as citizens." A wave of intermingling conversations swelled and drowned out Mr. Castor as we discussed our grades. With a single clap, the sea of chatter ceased. "I have one last announcement. As most of you know, the HPA Scholarship allows a handful of top-performing students from the School District of Philadelphia to attend Harbor Park Academy, covering tuition, room and board, and other expenses from eighth grade through high school. I am extremely proud to announce that, for the first time, a Blanche Creek student has been selected as a winner for this year's cohort." His eyes fell on Xavier, who was seated at the front of the class instead of at his usual spot next to me. Xavier's light-brown face rouged, the dark speckles on his cheeks becoming stars set against a sunset. "Xavier, congratulations on your hard work." The class erupted in applause and cheers, and although I smiled and clapped, a feeling of grief grew heavy in my heart. "Whether he chooses to accept or not is his choice, but I'm proud, nonetheless." His eyes roved the classroom, connecting with each of us individually. "To be clear, however, I'm proud of all of you. While attending Harbor Park Academy is an amazing opportunity, I truly believe that all of you possess the skills to succeed despite, and in spite of, the barriers stacked against you. It was an honor to be your teacher this year. Have a wonderful summer and be safe. I look forward to seeing you in September."

The bell rang, and a rush of students poured into the hallways, cascading down the steps with whoops and flooding the schoolyard. A few students had stopped to congratulate Xavier, so I repacked the same notebook over and over, waiting for them to leave. I didn't know what I would say to him but felt like I needed to say something. It was the last day of school, and with him going to Harbor Park, I wouldn't see him again. I had to make things right.

The remaining students said their goodbyes and left. Mr. Castor, who was cleaning the chalkboard, announced he was going to the bathroom and stepped out as well. This was my chance.

"Congrats," I said, standing over his desk.

He glanced up at me and then returned to gathering his things. "Thanks."

"Seriously, you deserve it. I know you worked hard and that it's something you've wanted for a while now."

"Yup."

"You think you'll go?"

"Did you want something?" He stopped packing his bag to look at me. Really, the bag had been packed—I saw him remove the same black water bottle and put it back several times—but he was waiting for me. I felt like I should apologize, but that cold, hard thing deep within me prevented it.

"Yeah," I swung my bag off my shoulder and pulled out my essay, "here. Mr. C said we should switch." Xavier looked at the paper in my hand and scoffed. "I think you said you were gonna write yours about Columbus Day, right? Here," I said, forcing the papers into his hand, "I wrote mine on Valentine's Day." He pulled his essay out of his bag and handed it to me.

"Was that it?"

I'm sorry. I'm sorry. Say it. I'm sorry. Say it. Say it!

"Yeah, I guess," I responded. "Oh, how can I get this back to you?"

"Keep it. Have a good summer, Jacob." He adjusted the strap of his satchel on his chest and then left the classroom.

"Have a good summer," I heard Mr. Castor saying to Xavier in the hallway.

I crumpled Xavier's essay in my hand and then started out. The guys would be waiting for me outside.

"Have a good one, Mr. Castor."

"You too, Jay." With everyone gone, his cologne lingered in the humid air. From the filing cabinets, he pulled out papers; books, including a King James Version of the Bible; several bars of soap and deodorant, which he discretely provided to students who needed them; and packs of pens, pencils, and other things and placed them on the top of his desk. He assessed how much he had to pack, and with a sigh, placed things into boxes. "Hey," he called out to me as I left the room, "are you and Xavier ok?"

"Yeah, why?"

"You two have been inseparable in this class all year. You think I wouldn't notice the last-minute seating change? I also noticed that when I announced he had won the scholarship, you seemed a little surprised, so I'm guessing he didn't tell you." He placed a stack of books into a box labeled "Am. Hist / Greek Mythology."

"How long has he known?" I asked flatly, attempting to show my contrived disinterest in the subject.

"I told him on Monday when I found out. He said he would tell you, but it seems it didn't come up." I didn't know what my face was doing, but it prompted Mr. Castor to stop packing. He walked over to me and placed a hand on my shoulder. "I know you're happy for him. It's also ok for you to be sad. But just because he's going to a different school, it doesn't mean you two must stop being friends." *Friend*— that word again. I thought of the crumpled paper in my hand, and it made me think of the torn pieces of Spiderman paper with What's-His-Name's number on it. That pang of loss struck me anew like lightning, and I could feel the tears being held back by the same cold, hard thing that held an apology at bay. "I guarantee you Xavier is having mixed feelings as well. It hasn't been easy for him here these past few years, so it was very encouraging when you two became friends. I know your friendship means a lot to him, and I can tell it means a lot to you, too." He squeezed my shoulder and then started packing again. He grabbed the bars of soap, deodorant, tubes of toothpaste, and toothbrushes and put them in the box labeled "Donation." "I don't know what's going on between you two, but you have a whole summer together. Don't let it end like this."

"Have a good summer, Mr. Castor."

"You too, Jay."

CHAPTER 3

On the last day of school, the first few hours of the morning were used for administrative purposes, and then they released us into the schoolyard for the summer carnival. It wasn't extravagant, but there were hot dogs and burgers and cotton candy and water ice and soft pretzels; and the girls played Double Dutch or hopscotch, while the boys played kickball or basketball or "tuggah-war." We personified the little Black kids holding hands in the school mural, exhibiting quantities of joy, of freedom, and of love that only exist in that brief period between blissful ignorance and the knowledge of right and wrong.

"Yo!" Herb called as I approached the group. "Where you been?"

"Just got outta class."

"Damn, I guess the smart niggas got more to learn than the rest of us, huh?" He laughed.

"Yeah… I guess. How long y'all been out here?"

"Like twenty minutes. Ms. Bryson let us out early. We were waitin' on you and Meat, so we can play football."

"Oh. Where is he?"

"That nigga takin' a shit," Mason said, and everyone laughed. "He was fartin' the whole day because he thought it was funny. He went to do it and almost shit himself, and *then* it became funny." The guys laughed again, but I just smiled. It was surprising how childish they could be while still purporting to be men.

"Did y'all want me to QB for both teams?" I asked.

"That was the plan, but—" Herb began to say before Eric cut in.

"The eighth graders wanna play us." Eric spiraled the football straight up into the air with his right hand and then caught it with his left. "They been talkin' shit all day, but we about to buss they ass!" We high-fived each other in agreement—as though nothing had happened the day before—then Herb put his arm around my shoulder, and the safety I had once known returned.

"What's that?" Herb asked.

Xavier's essay crumpled in my hand. "Nothin'," I said, "just a paper from class. I should throw it out."

"Yo, tell him the good news," Mason said to Herb.

"Oh… right." Herb's arm tensed. "My—"

"Yoooooooo!" Meat bellowed, running up to us with a painted-on grin. He tried to jump on my back, but I trapped him in a headlock before he had the chance to catch me.

"Ard, you got me." He tapped my forearm, and I set him loose. "So, what we doin'," he asked, fixing the collar on his shirt.

"Eighth graders want to play us," Eric responded.

"Bet, what we waitin' on then?"

"Nigga, you!" Mason said.

"True," Meat said, laughing, "we about to buss they ass!" He signaled for Eric to throw him the ball and tore across the schoolyard as Mason chased behind him. Eric lobbed the ball high and far. They climbed over each other to catch it, but Meat came out the winner, cheering as he ran circles around Mason with the ball in his hand—"Mossed him!" Eric jogged towards them, clapping and signaling for them to pass it back.

"We cooked them dickheads," Eric said, tossing the ball to me. It bounced out of my hands and hit the floor.

Meat scooped the ball up, "and that's why you're the QB." I gave him the finger, and we laughed.

"And a good one too," I added. Meat nodded in agreement and tossed the ball back to me. I caught it this time.

"You had some good plays," Eric said, "like that play when you ran the ball to get the first down or the last jawn when you told everybody to go long and—"

"Let me tell it," Mason interrupted, "you not even tellin' it right."

"How am I not tellin' it right?" Eric asked, embarrassed and frustrated. Eric and Mason were cousins, and although Eric was larger than Mason, Mason knew how to make Eric feel small.

Without acknowledging Eric's question, Mason picked up where he left off. "He told Meat to go out because Jason was stickin' him and Meat's taller, so if he had to throw it to Meat, he could get over him. He told you to go deep, but you can barely catch, so he probably was never gonna throw you the ball." Mason's words were calculated and sharpened to a razor's edge as if his tongue was a whetstone. Eric chewed on what was left of his fingernails, pretending not to hear Mason yet flinching with every word as they prickled his skin. Mason looked at me for confirmation, but I knew better than to get involved. A heaviness hung in the air, not to be confused with the humidity of the day.

"Remember when Herb ran the ball," Meat chimed in, "and the boul, 'Taye, was on his ass, but Herb juked him, and he damn near broke boul legs." Meat widened his stance to imitate Taye's wobbling legs, which resembled a baby deer learning to walk, and the group erupted in laughter. The air grew lighter.

The girls walked by and stole glances at us over their shoulders.

"I think I fucked my ankle up, too," Herb said suddenly, wrapping his arm around my shoulder and putting all his weight on his right foot.

The girls walked by again, and we watched them in silence.

"Her ass so fat, bro. I'm gonna fuck the shit outta her one of these days," Meat said of Aniya. "I ran into them before we started playin' football. I told them to meet us in Eastern. I think that's where they headed now."

"You been sayin' the same shit all year," Mason contended with some annoyance. "If you could've fucked, you would've by now."

"You really a hatin' ass, nigga, bro! Like damn! But, bet. Let's put bread on it. Promise you I can fuck her by the end of the summer."

"Bet," Mason said, shaking Meat's hand.

"I got money on Meat," Eric added, dapping him up.

Mason called Eric a "dickeater," and they started arguing as Meat heckled and mediated from the sidelines. They began walking, and Herb held onto me and limped toward Eastern.

"Eastern" was the name of the stairwell on the far east side of the school. The stairwell was out of use due to perpetual repairs, so the entrances were cordoned off with yellow "caution" tape. Isolated and poorly lit, Eastern had become the designated hangout spot for some of the older cool kids. While they risked getting caught, it was low. In my time at Blanche Creek, only three students had ever been caught, and it happened because the smell of cigarettes filled the second floor. Overall, teachers avoided it to reject any responsibility for what they might see and to avoid having to acknowledge their inability to effectively do anything about it, and students used it for whatever we could.

"You don't wanna go to the nurse?" I asked.

"Nah, I'm good. I think it's just sore. Plus, school about to be over anyway," Herb responded. The guys walked ahead of us and looked back often to see how far behind we were. "Y'all can go 'head," Herb yelled, but they continued to take small steps, throwing the ball back and forth to each other.

Although I was sure they were dragging their feet so

that the girls wouldn't think they were too eager, I couldn't ignore their loyalty to Herb. Knowing each other since kindergarten, their shared history calcified their bond but also precluded my full acceptance into the group. Even as Herb held onto me, I knew to them I was just a crutch. Had I been the one that had gotten hurt, I believed that there wouldn't have been a hesitation to go ahead without me; concern for my wellbeing would have started and stopped with Herb.

As we neared Eastern, the sun became more intense, as though the Earth were moving closer to it. I had been to Eastern several times before—several times with the girls, in fact—and nothing ever happened. Yet with the events of yesterday, despite things seeming to be back to normal, something felt as if it had been unearthed and couldn't be undone, much like Adam couldn't un-eat the apple.

"Wait, what was the good news?" I asked as we stood outside the entrance to the stairwell.

"Oh, yeahhhh!" Mason said excitedly. "Tell him!"

"My mom said I can have a party for my birthday," Herb responded in a flat tone.

"Nah, nigga, the *good* news," Mason replied. Herb shrugged. "Fuck it, I'll tell him. We told the girls that Herb havin' a party, and Brianna said she would come. You can get at her at that jawn."

"Young boul finally gon' get his dick wet," Meat said.

"Our little guy's growin' up," Eric wiped a fake tear from his eye, and they all laughed. I laughed too out of habit but could only think about how bright the sun was: so bright that it felt like I could pluck it out of the sky and hold it in my hands; so bright that I was convinced my dark skin had become transparent, and one could see my racing heart and the fear coursing through my veins; so bright that the rays reached into the deep recesses of my mind where the Dead were buried.

They're going to find out.

Who knows what'll happen in there.

You can't go.

Herb looked at me and retracted his arm. In his eyes was the same look of disdain I had seen as he boarded the bus.

"Ask her when we get in there," Mason added as he opened the door.

"That's weird as shit," Meat responded. "Don't listen to him. He don't know how to talk to girls."

"Bro, what are you even talkin' about? I get way more bitches than you."

Meat looked at the ground and then the sky and then spun around. "Where they at?"

They laughed as they one-by-one disappeared into the stairwell. I stepped toward the door, but Herb placed his hand on my chest and stopped me. "Could you do me a favor?"

"What's up?" I asked.

"I thought my ankle was just sore, but it's startin' to hurt now. It might be sprained."

"You want me to walk you to the nurse?"

"Nah, she's just gonna make me sit there until the bell rings and then send me home. But I could use some ice. Can you go get me some from her office?"

"I got you," I said, moving toward the door. A cool draft came out of the entrance, carrying with it the sound of giggling and sweet nothings.

"No," Herb said, grabbing my arm, "go around to the other side. It'll be quicker."

"It'll take the same amount of time if I walk around the buildin' to another entrance versus if I cut through here." I wrested my arm away from Herb and felt a sense of apprehension as he positioned himself between me and the door. I didn't think that Herb would hurt me, but I couldn't shake the impending feeling of danger.

"I was gonna ask if you could grab me a burger, too," Herb said. "Wasn't hungry when we got out here, but now I'm starvin'." He smiled to ease the sudden tension, but it only made me more aware of his strange behavior. His reason didn't make sense, but I acquiesced anyway.

"I got you."

Herb said, "Thanks," and gave my shoulder a firm squeeze—his touch was cold and detached, as if given by a ghost of himself, a confirmation of the danger ahead— and then he disappeared into the darkness. The heavy metal door slammed shut behind him, the metallic ring echoing through the emptiness on this side of the schoolyard.

The sun's intensity remained the same and followed me across the concrete desert as I made my way to the nurse's office. In truth, I had no intention of going back because I knew I wasn't welcomed. The guys had rejected me while clunkily laying out I needed to fuck Brianna to be one of them; and Herb... well, I was still unsure what was happening with him, but he was pushing me away. Yet, the journey quieted my dread and made me feel like I still had purpose, so I continued the search for ice in a desert. Heat waves rose from the asphalt and shaped the air into his image—was this another mirage?

"Hey," I said. Xavier glanced up from his book and then flipped the page. Seated underneath a tree that reached across the fence from a neighboring house, Xavier was in the one place in the schoolyard where the sun couldn't reach us. "Can I join you?" Without looking up, he sidled to make space on the small ledge. "What're you reading?" I sat down next to him, our thighs pressing together. He closed the book enough for me to glimpse the cover but not long enough to read it, so I didn't catch the title. "What is it about?" He sighed, indicating the title of the book was information enough and then started to pack up his things. "Wait." I reached into my bag and pulled out his essay. "I skimmed it, but if this is the last time I'll see you, I should probably give it back now. I do have to say, though, that 'your analysis of Columbus' mistake in where he landed being spun into a serendipitous event was insightful.'"

"I thought you didn't read it," he said, turning his head to look at me.

"I didn't," I pointed to the red text on the paper, "but I did read the comments Mr. C left," I chuckled.

Xavier smiled briefly and then pulled his smile into a straight line as he scanned the schoolyard. "Why aren't you with your friends?"

"I am. I was just on my way to the nurse's office when I

saw you sitting here, so I wanted to give this back to you." Xavier examined me. "Herb sprained his ankle—I'm grabbing him some ice." Xavier resumed surveilling the schoolyard. "If you're looking for them, they're not out here. After I get the ice, I'm meeting them in Eastern. Some of the girls are over there, too. And I know you wanna ask, 'Why you?' I think it's because he trusts me more. Imagine if he sent Meat," I chuckled, "all this food out here, he would never come back. Oh! Herb's also having a birthday party, and he invited me. It's gonna be fun. So… yeah, things are going well. Just because I'm not with them doesn't mean anything is wrong. I don't have to spend all my time with them. You know?… What're you even looking for?" I followed Xavier's gaze, and on the far side of the schoolyard I saw a football spiral into the air and then land in Herb's arms. Herb held the ball tight and pretended to juke one of the girls.

"I'm heading inside." Xavier stood up and grabbed his things. "You can come if you want."

———

The sconces lining the auditorium flickered and hummed what sounded like spirituals. The warm lighting painted the walls a custard color while they pulsed slightly, exhaling secrets of past experiences—quiet moans, pleas for mercy, requests for encores, scripted recitations, and somewhere in the chatter I could recognize laughter, but it was faint. Instead of secrets, it occurred to me that maybe the walls were casting spells—their sultry incantations enchanting those who sat in these seats, seducing them to adulthood and swindling them out of their innocence, an irretrievable substance. That was it. We had been cursed. Somewhere beyond these custard walls, some ancient figure had crafted images of us, like dolls or puppets placed on an altar, and influenced our actions through the very strings we were given to hang ourselves.

Xavier suggested we relocate to the auditorium, citing the heat as the reason for his decision. I had asked him why he chose the auditorium instead of the cafeteria or his usual spot in the library, both of which were air-conditioned, to which he responded that it was quieter here. Indeed, it was quieter, but the Dead hinted at other motivations while they quivered in their coffins.

We sat in near darkness, but Xavier still attempted to read his book, holding it inches from his face as he squinted to read the words.

"It's hot," I said.

"Did you say something?"

"It's hot," I repeated, shifting in my seat to face him.

"You can head out if you want. I'm probably gonna stay here until the bell rings, though," he said, never looking away from his book. "Didn't you need to meet your friends anyway?"

"I did. I do. I thought you wanted to talk to me about something, though, and that's why you brought me here."

Xavier put the book down and looked at me with a piercing stare. "I didn't *bring* you anywhere. I extended an invitation, which you could've denied, an invitation I can easily withdraw if that's what's keeping you here—or is there something *you* wanted to talk about?"

Again, Xavier looked at me expectantly, waiting for the words he felt I owed him, but I only responded, "Nah, but I don't really feel like moving… I'll just stay here." He nodded indifferently and then returned to his book. I repositioned my body to face the stage, and silence descended on us. I thought Xavier had forgiven me. I came over and talked *to* him, left the guys *for* him, and I was there in the auditorium *with* him. Was all this not enough? He was waiting for an apology, but the cold, hard thing within me persisted.

Sitting there, my eyes gradually became accustomed to the low lighting, and shapes and figures manifested in the waning light. The shadows took form and moved across the auditorium like ethereal players, existing only in stark contrast to the undulating dimness. They moved in familiar ways. Across the stage, a few leaped like ballerinas. At the far end, one recited a soliloquy while others hurried to their places, shifting their form to fit the setting—a streetlamp, a gun, a pair of sneakers tied together by the laces, a casket, a butterfly, a tree, a lump of clay, a shallow grave, a stump, a minefield, a tap dancer.

The hum of the sconces turned into a violent rattling, like the clicking of broken hair clippers, as they got brighter. I looked over at Xavier, who sat still with the book pressed against his face. The minor characters receded, except for one, and two figures took center stage. They sat at the stump across from each other and, for a while, did nothing. I leaned closer to Xavier to ask if he saw them too, but when

I looked over, he was gone. Panicked, I tried to leave but couldn't stand. And as if sensing my fear, the figures ran to the edge of the stage.

The rattling turned into the blare of a trumpet, raising the Dead from their graves.

The roof lifted off the building.

Sunlight spilled into the auditorium.

And against the sharp edges of the light, the figures became recognizable.

The boys held hands, then collapsed and died.

An unwilling participant, I watched as the stump morphed into a mirror and the body of one boy liquefied into a puddle that quickly evaporated in the heat. I tried again to flee, but the blood in my veins had chilled into concrete. Without warning, the remaining boy stood up and observed himself in the mirror. He lifted his right hand, then his left, but the image didn't respond; his actions were his alone. He tried to speak, but the air grew stale in his lungs, so he opened his mouth and let out the wailing of his frozen heart. The howl shattered the mirror and, to no avail, the boy cut himself on the pieces as he tried to reassemble his reflection and then disappeared.

The blaring of the lights turned into blood-curdling screams that vibrated throughout my body and shook the frost off my limbs. I covered my ears and squeezed my eyes shut against the blinding light.

"Hey, are you ok?"

"Huh?"

Relief washed over me as my eyes adjusted to the low

light of the auditorium.

"Are you good?" Xavier's silhouette asked again.

"Yeah, why?"

"Because—,"

Kiss me.

"What?"

"I said—,"

Kiss me.

Xavier's lips were moving, but the voice wasn't his.

Kiss me. Kiss me. Kiss me. Kiss me. Kiss me! the Dead chanted.

Xavier placed his hand on mine, and I felt myself getting hard. He waved the other in my face, but I was focused on his freckles that formed constellations and guided me to my destination—his lips, which silently outlined their wanton desires.

Kiss me!

Concise. Effective. Prescriptive.

I puckered my lips and leaned closer to Xavier as the resonance of their voices propelled me towards the night sky.

"What're you—?" Xavier asked, his voice finally cutting through the chatter.

"Attention staff and students, we are experiencing a blackout," Ms. Emily, the office secretary, announced over the loudspeaker. "Please remain in your classrooms. Teachers, the bell will ring shortly. Please escort students to the schoolyard and dismiss them from there."

The thick darkness draped over us and quieted the Dead. Realizing what I had almost done, I gathered my things and ran out of the auditorium.

"Wait, where are you going?!" Xavier's voice called after me.

RUN!

CHAPTER 4

"Christian! Jacob! Get up!" She called from the hallway as heavy footsteps climbed the stairs. "I'm not telling you all again."

It was Sunday. And like every Sunday over the past year, we were going to church. It hadn't always been like this, though. My mom had always been religious—a product of her Jamaican upbringing—but we had only recently begun to go to church. After I got kicked out of Catholic school, my mom only had to pay tuition for my brother, so she reduced her hours, freeing up her Sundays. I hated it.

"Hate" was a strong word, but it was precise, if not accurate.

Imagine an omnipresent, omniscient being that knew your every thought—whether or not it had been vocalized or acted upon—and these thoughts in their fleeting, unformed state were grounds to be considered a sin.

Imagine sermons that peddled shame and explicit promises of spiritual violence through the threat of eternal damnation.

Imagine the core of who you were being considered the seat of sin—this inextricable bit of nature, though you've tried to extract it through rigorous prayer and physical punishment—unlovable by the standards set forth by your creator, thus by your creator Himself.

Imagine being told to "hate the sin, not the sinner," but when the two were the same, where did that leave the sinner?

Detestable. Damned. Unworthy.

Maybe "hate" was accurate.

Whatever the word, I had a strong aversion to going to church. The only redeemable part of Sundays was dinner. As was tradition, special dishes were had on Sunday. Oxtail, curry goat, or fish, served with rice and red peas. Today she was making oxtail, my favorite, and the smell wafted into the room as Christian opened the door to go brush his teeth.

"Jacob, get up," he said, his voice drowsy.

"Five more minutes," I uttered after reading 8:00 AM on the clock.

The sound of errant honking woke me from my power nap. It was 8:40 AM. *Fuck!* Although church didn't start until noon, my mom insisted that Christian and I arrive three hours earlier to attend Sunday school. As a result, she had added us to the route of the church shuttle that picked up a few of the other unlucky kids and teenagers in the area, as well as some elderly shut-ins who couldn't make it out on their own. The heels of Christian's dress shoes clacked rhythmically as he pranced down the stairs, contrasted by the soft padding of my bare feet as I all at once brushed my teeth and my hair while putting on my freshly pressed dress clothes. With one shoe on, the other in my left hand, and my Bible under arm, I darted down the steps and raced to the front door. My mom waved at Brother Simon, and he responded with two honks before accelerating down the road. She gave me a look that said, "You know what to do." I sighed, slipped on my other shoe, grabbed something to eat—since I was no longer in a rush—and started walking.

The church was about a mile away, but the walking wasn't the worrisome part. The path weaved through several of my friends' neighborhoods, so the chance of running into someone I knew was not unlikely. It's not that I was ashamed of my "church life," but there was a desire, a need, rather, to keep it separate from my social one. I was one of the popular guys, and that fickle status was rooted in looks, athleticism, promiscuity, and secularism. Of course, we were all "Christian"—except for Meat, who was ostensibly Muslim—but it wasn't a declaration or something to be claimed. It was a given, like heading home when the streetlights came on. It was something you invoked when someone sneezed. It was reminiscing about that one time you went to church with your grandma when you were seven and being scolded for emulating the woman who fell to the floor in a fit of seizures when the pastor touched her forehead. It was apologizing when you exclaimed, "Oh my God!" because you used the Lord's name in vain. It was the prayers spoken over your brother's casket after being shot dead on the basketball court. It was a secret, like those thoughts that excited you but made you ashamed and angry. It was by inheritance, not by choice, that we were Christian.

Going to church wasn't cool.

My lilac shirt became polka-dotted with dark purple in places drenched with sweat. I had jogged the few blocks close to Herb's house and now assumed a casual walking pace to steady my breath and prevent further sweating. It was a nice morning. One of those summer mornings that made you want to smile at a stranger or help an old woman cross the street. A summer morning that made you believe this was truly the City of Brotherly Love and made you forget the echoes of gunfire that would fill the streets every evening following sunset. I unbuttoned my shirt to let in the cool breeze, which fluttered my sleeves like the plumage of a bird, and I held the large leather-bound Bible above my head to shelter my face from the sun. Printed in what looked like 30-sized font, the Bible resembled an ancient tome with its rumpled leather face and crinkled pages, a few of which clung on to the withering spine through sheer will. My mother said it used to be Grandma Junie's, so I carried it in her memory, although the text meant little to me.

A sudden gust of wind forced my eyes closed, and then I heard it. *Rrrip* and several pages freed from the deteriorating binding went flying.

I gathered what I thought had been all the pages and continued walking.

"Hey!" a voice called out from behind me. Its familiarity was like a jolt, forcing me to pick up the pace. "Hey!" it called out again. The exclamation traveled on the sound of impending footsteps until the words were being spoken directly into my ear. I knew the voice; however, I hoped that by not acknowledging it, it would go away. A strategy that had not worked before, but the laws of probability implied that its success was right around the corner. The sound of the footsteps quickened, and then a hand landed on my shoulder to turn me around. "I think this is yours."

I snatched the pages from his hand and hastily placed them in the Bible as though the motion would erase this memory of me from his mind.

"I only go because I have to," I blurted out. He looked me up and down, and then his face softened. "What are you smiling for? I usually don't walk. I stayed up watching movies and playing on the computer, so I slept in late, but then the—" His sudden laughter made me pause.

"Look at your little tie," Xavier said, running the satin fabric through his fingers.

"Shut up," I responded, laughing.

***

"You didn't have to walk me," I said, hoping Xavier would receive this as a cue to leave.

"The papi store is on the way. Buying some milk."

"Cool... I didn't know you lived around here. Herb's place is pretty close, actually," I added, feeling an urge to reaffirm Xavier of my friendship with Herb.

"I know."

"Oh. Wait, how—,"

"Why'd you run off the other day?"

"When?"

"Friday… the last day of school… we were in the auditorium. The lights went out, and then you took off."

"I don't think I *ran*. I *casually* left because I had to use the bathroom."

"And you couldn't say that?" he asked, his tone suddenly solemn.

"It was an emergency!" I laughed.

"Right. But before you 'casually left,' it seemed like you were about to… do something?"

"No idea what you're talking about."

He remained silent, watching his feet intently as though he were trying to avoid the cracks in the sidewalk.

We walked in silence for a few blocks, and then the church came into view. After what had almost happened in the auditorium, I decided it would be best if I never saw Xavier again. Of course, I wasn't expecting to run into him, which made what I needed to do a lot harder. We crossed the street and came to the doors of the church. The shuttle sat in the parking lot, and I vowed that this would be the last time I missed it.

Xavier lifted his eyes to meet mine, and I stared into them, examining myself in the brown still lakes. I shouldn't have spoken to him after class. I shouldn't have spoken to him in the schoolyard. I shouldn't have followed him to the auditorium and allowed the Dead to lead me astray. He wanted an apology, but I couldn't find the words to apologize because I wasn't sorry. He had tried to drive a wedge between my friends and me, and I corrected him. If anything, he owed me an apology. I followed this line of reasoning like breadcrumbs, but at the end of the trail there wouldn't be a house or whatever the fuck Hansel and Gretel wanted to return to. There would be nothing. A cold, hard *nothing*. A hole. The emptying and absence of compassion, of kindness, of love, of grace, and of light—a black hole that couldn't be seen but whose gravity was significant and measurable. A cold, hard *nothing*. But it was *something*—it was what made me a man.

The image of myself in his eyes rippled as they watered; the person looking back looked familiar. I felt a displaced anger move through me, boundless and without cause, and I tried to focus this growing ire on Xavier. I thought about the perfect day that we had spent together and how he had ruined it. *This is all your fault. This is all your fault. This is all your fault.* I repeated to myself, while steadily forgetting who the subject of my reproach was. I clenched my jaw and followed the breadcrumbs but upon reaching the end of the trail, the cold, hard nothing that was something was not where I had left it—the breadcrumbs had led me to a place I had once known but had since become foreign.

The image in Xavier's eyes made one last plea as he took my right hand in his.

"Have a good summer," he said in a placid tone, shaking my hand. His cool demeanor belied the dejection drawn in the stars on his face.

"Hold on," I said, still holding on to his hand. What I had felt in the auditorium—exposed, wanting, bare—now poured into me like a warm liquid and replaced my anger. "I'm sorry. I didn't mean what I said. I was just angry that

I got switched and took it out on you." The front door to the church was clear, and through it I could see the occasional Brother Such-and-Such or Sister To-Whom-It-May-Concern peering at us, which prompted me to let go of Xavier's hand. God had eyes everywhere, and often they weren't His own.

"What're you doing tonight?" Xavier asked, his eyes widening with what looked like joy or skepticism.

"Nothing," I responded, unsure whether he was still mad or not.

"Bet, I'll text you," he said and then left without waiting for a response.

God's eyes receded as I climbed the steps to the church. "Good morning," an usher said. I answered with a listless smile and entered the sanctuary.

***

I nestled into my usual seat at the back of the church. Pastor Hooks sometimes made the joke that kids started their religious journey in the front rows, and as they got older, they sat further and further back until they were out the door and only on occasion seen again. No kids my age sat in the row. There were some high school boys scrolling on Facebook and texting; parents with babies rocking them gently and eyeing exits should the baby begin to cry; plain-clothes attendees new to the church yet familiar with the common refrain, "come as you are," who came as they were; however, feeling unwelcomed by the modest suits and adorned hats, the newcomers sat close to the door. Then there was me, not a member of these groups, yet equally transient.

People arrived in steady waves and filled the sanctuary with hushed chatter resembling the static between radio stations and drowning out the murmurs of the Dead, who attempted to push Xavier to the forefront of my thoughts. The wayward droning of the organ and the soft brushing of the steel brush on the hi-hats gained form as the praise and worship leaders assumed their place at the front of the church. Attendants filed into the pews, clearing the aisles and assuming the pomp and circumstance obliged of a church service.

A "reverence for the Holy Spirit" enveloped the room as the praise and worship leaders began singing. The first couple of songs were jaunty and upbeat, permitting the congregation, who held their breath in earnest anticipation and fear, to exhale. With permission and encouragement, the crowd clapped in unison and tapped their feet to the beat. I even found myself nodding my head surreptitiously and silently mouthing the words as I followed along to the lyrics on the screen. The "praise" section ended with applause and roaring amens. The lead singer whispered, "Hallelujah," repeatedly, lulling the sanctuary back into reverent silence.

> *All the way my Savior leads me;*
> *What have I to ask beside?*
> *Can I doubt His tender mercy,*
> *Who through life has been my Guide?*

Hands went up across the church, which the lead singer

attributed to "God's Spirit moving through the sanctuary." Feeling some conviction, the teenagers in my row abandoned their phones and got on their feet.

Heav'nly peace, divinest comfort,
Here by faith in Him to dwell!

In unison, the congregation swayed side-to-side. The Dead squirmed in response to the overt spirituality. Another reason I didn't like church was this level of connection with God seemed unattainable. I felt an unquenchable shame that could only be slated—yet was caused—by a relationship with a god who didn't, and, being the quintessence of holiness, *couldn't* love me. The sin was the sinner.

For I know, whate'er befall me,
Jesus doeth all things well.

The lead singer, still in her solo, repeated the verse.

In Sunday school, we learned God created us in His image, so either God was gay or someone was lying. *Gay.* The word was disgusting. It was abrasive on the soft palate and bitter on the tongue. It was a word of disrespect, a diss with no comeback, a cause for violence, and a reason for death. It was a cussword, a basis for censorship, and was to be treated as such—g*y. The thought of God being g*y made me chuckle, but recognizing the blasphemy, I promptly asked for forgiveness. And this was our relationship—an endless bartering of apologies for forgiveness. I rued the day when the value of my good wouldn't be enough. On that day, what more would I be able to offer?

All the way my Savior leads me,
Cheers each winding path I tread,

I wrestled my attention back to the service. Surrounding me were avid worshippers. The Holy Spirit even overtook the newcomers, shouting and frantically waving as if hailing a taxi. It seemed unfair.

> *Gives me grace for every trial,*
> *Feeds me with the living bread.*

I felt my face get hot with anger. It was unfair that on their first visit, they were having this spiritual experience. I had been coming for a year and had had no such thing. Hours of praying and entreating did nothing but elicit feelings of frustration and guilt that ultimately surrendered to that cold, hard nothing, that black hole, to avoid being overwhelmed by them. I was ashamed to have these thoughts and had sinned by envying others, so I asked for forgiveness. My anger turned to frustration and then to sadness as I again remembered our transactional relationship. *Please forgive me. I'm sorry, God. I'm sorry. Please forgive me. Please forgive me.*

The music swelled, and the Dead railed against their coffins in response.

> *Though my weary steps may falter,*
> *And my soul athirst may be.*

The other singers joined the lead and their voices in harmony cut through the errant hallelujahs and wailing that had filled the church. The piano and organ intensified as the choir repeated,

> *Though my weary steps may falter,*
> *And my soul athirst may be,*

Cries for freedom rang out from the graves of the Dead

as their drumming intensified in tandem with the music. I closed my eyes and did as the others did. My hands shot up into the air, and the words I had silently mouthed now found a voice. Burying my concerns about how others might perceive me, I sang the lyrics like a member of the praise and worship team, unhindered and empowered by a feeling of victory.

> *Gushing from the Rock before me,*
> *Lo! a spring of joy I see,*

All the shame and guilt I was feeling came to the surface and evaporated under the white-hot lights; I felt weightless, like I was soaring, and from that great height, I yelled, "Hallelujah!"

> *Gushing from the Rock before me,*
> *Lo! a spring of joy I see.*

The music acquiesced, the voices of the praise and worship team became softer, and as quick as this feeling had come, it went. I opened my eyes to see familiar faces staring at me and felt embarrassed. I didn't take a beat to register what their faces were conveying; instead, feeling very aware of my body and the space I was occupying, I told my legs to walk as I hurried to the bathroom.

When I returned, Sister Lani, dressed in a red skirt suit and a matching red hat adorned, was at the front of the church reading the weekly announcements. She made some joke about the news and then rattled off deadlines and dates about events happening in the neighborhood; I heard nothing other than the sponsored spot to attend youth camp hadn't been claimed, and it was the last day to sign-up. My cluttered mind prevented me from understanding what had just happened. It was like sitting at a messy desk, knowing where all the papers and pens go, yet being paralyzed by the decision of what to put away first. I slunk down into my seat. I couldn't shake the feeling that everyone in the church had witnessed it and was now staring. Even though they were all focusing on Sister Lani, God's eyes were on me. A weariness—borne of my lack of sleep, the fullness of my thoughts, and my growing apathy to address the latter—blanketed me, and I fell asleep.

I awoke to the irritated nudging of a teenager. Still in a fog, I saw him gesturing for me to take the collection plate, and inpatient with the speed of my response, he nudged me again with the silver plate, forcing it into my hands. I groggily pulled a dollar out of my pocket, placed it on the plate, and then passed it to the person on my left. *Please forgive me*, I prayed, apologizing for falling asleep.

The tithing portion of the service ended, and then Pastor Hooks was introduced to deliver the sermon. My eyes were still heavy with sleep, but the service was almost over. I needed to stay awake for only another hour. The approaching end of the service eased my anxiety. Soon God's eyes would be cordoned off and what had happened consigned to oblivion. Pastor Hooks instructed the congregation to open their Bibles to a passage I didn't catch. I flipped to the Book of Revelations and began reading.

Revelations was my favorite book of the Bible. There was something fantastical about glimpsing into the prophe-sied end of the world and what that end would look like. It made me wonder what the point of anything was; we were barreling towards an inevitable end that could be sprung on us at any moment. Whether that end be a good old-fashioned natural cause or celestial warfare, death, like God, was omnipresent. "Jesus is coming," they would say with a righteous contempt, stopping just short of actual salivation, as though the end of the world would not only vindicate all the violence they enacted in God's name but reward them for it with eternal life and heavenly riches. This "indignation" for non-believers presumed a moral superiority that placed everyone on a playing field with no explanation of the rules and full condemnation for breaking them. In truth, I didn't think the goal was to save anyone—for in lieu of preaching God's unconditional love, what they spread was a polarizing message of fear and hatred that entrenched those meant to be saved—the goal, it seemed, was to recruit as many people to the team as possible, hope this religion was the right one, and then deride others with a, "I told you so," from Heaven, or if God was indeed fair, from Hell.

As I read about the moon turning to blood and whores riding dragons and stars falling from the sky, I wondered what Xavier would think about this. Xavier's deep interest in history encompassed a vast knowledge of apocalyptic traditions and their cultural contexts, so I was sure he already knew of the Christian apocalypse. I imagined he would say something like it not being his favorite because the story was too predictable or the metaphors were too on the nose. I would see him tonight—the thought, which only a few hours before propagated in the shadows of my subconscious like ivy on a building, now bloomed with fervent expectation. I braced for the Dead to conjecture what I was eagerly anticipating, but they had been quiet. No words and no movement.

I had read through the first half of Revelations when the sermon ended, and Pastor Hooks invited people who weren't saved to the altar to receive Christ. A handful of the newcomers walked up the center aisle to the front and were welcomed with applause from the church. Pastor Hooks asked if they believed Jesus was the Son of God and if they accepted Him into their hearts. They responded "Yes," and he declared them saved. The church applauded again, and then Pastor Hooks opened the altar up to those who were sick and needed healing, or who needed to be set free from something, or who wanted to rededicate themselves to God. I watched as the altar filled with people. Some eagerly rushed there, and others waited for a crowd to form so that they could blend into it. A steady melody played in the background, underscoring the scene as Pastor Hooks drew crosses on their foreheads with olive oil. The sanctuary overflowed with the sound of impassioned pleas that grew more ardent as the lone piano played louder.

I clenched my eyes shut and searched for the confidence—or the desperation, whichever came first—to go up to the altar. If the Dead were gone, this could be my chance to get rid of them for good. I stood up and shimmied out of the row. I was sitting close to the center aisle, but whatever I had found deep within to propel me forward wasn't enough to face the stares, so I walked up the side. I hesitated at first, but with each step, I became emboldened as their silence persisted. If I could make it to the altar, that would be the end of them; I just needed to seal the deal.

As I neared the altar, my heart slipped into my throat as a vibration worked its way up my legs, but I smiled with relief when I realized it was just the musicians. I exhaled and took my final steps to join the crowd when I heard—

Xavier plays piano. Ask Xavier about the apocalypse. I wonder if he read the paper. What's at Snake Hill? Alone at night. I can't wait. Xavier. Xavier. His lips. His eyes. His freckles. His touch.

Stop! Fuck, I'm getting hard.

The Dead's whispers coalesced into a rushing river that swept me up in a young man's fancy and refused to set me down. I wanted to yell—maybe a hallelujah would shut them up—but when I opened my mouth, a chuckle escaped. I turned around and hurried back to my seat, putting my head in my lap. Naturally, the Dead had returned; it had been too easy to get rid of them. I thought about how naïve I was to think I had won and chuckled again. My thoughts then shifted to God being g*y, and my chuckle turned into full-blown laughter. Those sitting next to me must have thought the Holy Ghost caused my convulsions, but my God was a comedian.

Altar call ended, and Pastor Hooks issued the benediction, bringing the service to a merciful close. The air of seriousness lifted, and indiscriminate conversation once again filled the sanctuary. Attendants shuffled out of the pews to tell Brother So-and-So and Sister Did-You-Hear-About goodbye, but I remained seated with my head in my lap for a few minutes longer.

Please forgive me, God. I'm sorry, I'm sorry, I'm sorry. Please, God, please forgive me. Please, I'm sorry, I repeated, as laughter racked my body.

CHAPTER 5

I had forgotten I was supposed to hang out with Xavier until he texted me and said to meet him at Snake Hill at 7 PM. I arrived at 6:59. After the brief cessation of the Dead and their sudden return, my faith in God went the way it always did. There would be a brief period of dormancy while I debated His existence. Then fear and shame would set in, and my faith would come roaring back as I prayed for forgiveness. It was a spiritually exhausting cycle and draining to think about, so I didn't. Besides the soft trickle of the water, it was quiet. I tossed pebbles into the flow and wondered why I had never come here before.

Snake Hill, which got its name from the winding path that slithered up the side of the hill opposite that of the stream, was in Cobbs Creek. Away from the basketball courts and playgrounds, the picnic areas and asphalt, there was a piece of wilderness that was untouched. Perhaps even unknown. Given how pristine it appeared, I may have been the only visitor in a while.

The hill stretched above the surrounding trees, enveloped at its base by tall grass. But on the riverbank where

I sat, the ground was bare, littered with smooth pebbles that in a few short eons would become fine sand. I picked up a handful of them and one-by-one flung them into the stream: *He loves me…He loves me not…He loves me…He loves me not.* I smiled at the idea of love being dictated by something as random as the number of pebbles I had in my hand. As the pebbles became fewer, I sighed with relief, recognizing that I had scooped up an odd number: "He loves me," I uttered as I tossed the last remaining pebble into the slow-moving water.

"Hey," Xavier said, emerging with his satchel from an opening in the trees, "sorry I'm late, I lost track of time debating with my dad." He sounded out of breath, and his forehead glistened with sweat.

I picked myself up and brushed the dirt off my shorts. "Anything interesting?"

"I read your paper about love in society and was telling him how I agreed with you that Valentine's Day isn't about love but just buying stuff. And I added how our collective understanding of love is this commercialized version propagandized through films, through ads, through music, etc. and how—"

"Commercialized? Propagandized?"

"Commercialized means—"

"I know what they mean… well, now I know. I had to look them up after class. They're the same words Mr. C used in the comment you're quoting."

Xavier's face turned red, and then he smiled. "Ard, you got me. I may have passed the comment off as my own to my dad, *but* I do agree with the thought. I'm glad you stopped me when you did, too, because I kinda forgot what they mean. I was going to bluff my way through a definition."

We laughed.

"Let's not rush past the 'you agree with me' part, either."

"Don't get used to it." He chuckled and then touched my elbow lightly for me to follow him up the hill. "My dad agreed with the argument—mostly. He liked your point about the focus on Valentine's Day being on gifts but disagreed that it wasn't about love. He said that although advertising promotes gift-giving as the main way to express love, it still inspires people to reflect on those they love. He then said something about how two things can be true at once and how things aren't always black and white. Then I said something about music, which I realized was a mistake as soon as I said it because he's a musician. Wait, did I mention my dad is a jazz musician? Well, he is, and 'as a jazz player,' his words, he harped…"

I watched his mouth form words, but I couldn't hear them over the Dead, who schemed to recreate the conditions of the auditorium. Xavier licked his lips and renewed my desire to touch the stars. I turned my attention to the steeply rising hill, placing my feet carefully to avoid slipping. The climb felt familiar, or at least the action of climbing felt familiar. I had never been here, yet I couldn't shake this feeling of déjà vu.

"… I'll have to show you the song sometime. Anyway, his main point being we're too young to even know what love is and—" Xavier stopped talking. I imagined to catch his breath. "Sorry, I've been rambling. Moral of the story is that I liked your essay."

"Thanks. And yeah, you will," I responded, not knowing what song he was referring to but enthused about the opportunity to spend more time with him.

We reached the summit, and he pulled a blanket out of his satchel to spread on the ground. He sat on the blanket and patted the space next to him.

"Not too much longer now," he said, looking up at the sky.

"Until what?"

"You'll see."

As the sun set, the gentle stream became more violent, and the sound of rushing water combatted the aimless wind. I stole glances at Xavier when he wasn't looking. The sunlight framed his head in a fiery orange-red halo; he seemed like something from another world. The wind moved through the trees unnoticed, stealing away the scent of pinecones, and rustled his curly hair. He caught me staring, and we both looked away. The pounding of my heart intertwined with the movement of the Dead—I was unsure of which was which yet wanted neither to stop.

"Do you think that we're too young to be in love?" Xavier turned to look at me, propping his body up with his elbow.

"What?"

"My dad said we're too young to know what love is. Do you think that's true?"

"I don't know. I don't think so." I lifted myself onto my arm to mirror him. "No. I think you can experience love at all ages, even a young one. For example, at my old school, there was …," I paused. The Dead urged me to continue, but I ignored them. "Remember when we read *Romeo and Juliet* for class in the fall? They were teenagers in that play."

"Sure, but that's a story. Isn't the whole point of your paper that culture spoon-feeds us this artificial version of love?"

"Yes, but I don't think Shakespeare wrote *Romeo and Juliet* with ad-placements in mind… unless for some reason he was trying to drive up the price of poison."

"Funny."

"You know what I mean. I think the point of the play is to show that love is supernatural; it's destined, it's—"

"'Fatal'," Xavier jumped in, "that's the word Mr. C used."

"Exactly. It's fate. Think of the parents you're born to, the family you're born into, the person you're born as, and all the chance encounters that happen in a lifetime. Think about Romeo and Juliet. So much had to go right and, equally, go wrong to be in love. I don't think age is part of that function. I also think there's a difference between 'loving someone' and 'being in love,' but anyone only ever talks about being in love."

"I think I…agree?"

"Wow, is that two in a row?"

"Shut up. So, have you ever been in love?" His cheeks flushed with color, not red, but brown, as if a million more freckles appeared on his face.

I thought of What's-His-Name from my previous school

and shuddered from the cold whispers of the Dead on my neck. "I… do you think your dad was right about us being too young?"

"Hmmm. I do." He took a long pause and then started again. "I think we're too young to know what love is, but I don't think we're too young to experience it."

"That's just semantics."

"Think about it." He sounded both annoyed and eager to explain his point. "Babies can experience desire and toddlers can experience anger. And at any age, one can experience sadness, happiness, jealousy—what makes love any different? There's no age threshold to experience emotions, but I do think it takes time to identify them and even more to understand them." He paused again to allow me to interject, but I remained silent, shifting from my side to my back. He followed suit, and we both watched as the orange sky acquiesced to black. "I think you're right, too, though."

"Have you been in love before?"

"I don't know, maybe. But I don't know what 'being in love' feels like, so I don't know if I've experienced it or not."

"Why'd you say 'maybe,' then?'"

"I used to come here all the time. But I haven't been here in a while because of something that happened between me and the friend I would come with. I don't know if I've been in love before, or if it's just an emotion reserved for romance, but I've experienced heartbreak…, so that's why 'maybe.'"

A switch flipped and darkness fell. It was profound, such that I couldn't see my hand when held in front of my face, such that I would have forgotten Xavier was next to me if not for the warmth of his body pressed against mine.

"What happ—"

Xavier sprung to his feet. "It's time!"

I held the flashlight steady on the black pieces of metal in Xavier's hand. He assembled them, attaching one piece lengthwise onto the other, until they formed a single metal tube. He uncapped the end of the tube and revealed the lens.

"It's way too bright for that." I looked up at the night sky that was ashen with the sickly, yet sterile, white glow of Philly's skyline.

"Trust me," Xavier said and screwed the telescope onto the tripod. The telescope assembled, he made a few adjustments and then instructed me where to look. "It's bright, but there's a small patch of sky where you can see the stars." The luminous haze of the city coated the sky, but he was right—the small patch seemed invulnerable to the light. "It's cool, right?"

"Cool" wasn't the first word that came to mind. It was odd, eerie, and sparked a feeling of dread that made me afraid, yet underpinned by excitement. I wanted to respond to Xavier, but the patch was like a portal into another realm, and I had already stepped through.

In this alternate dimension, I imagined Xavier wouldn't take the scholarship, and instead he would decide to stay here with me. I imagined we would finish middle school and high school and then move far away to attend college, where we would share a dorm room. I imagined what we would be like there. Were we seen? Were we heard? Did we know love, even if we were 'too young' to understand it?

Xavier's hand grazed mine as he reached for the telescope, yanking me from that distant world and bringing me back to Earth. I tried to envision a future in which he took the scholarship and what that would look like for me, but all I could see was the inky darkness engulfing us. I yearned for this other life—our life together—but the darkness persisted. He turned a knob and the patch went out of focus, then he turned another and the stars became clearer than they had been before.

"It's cool, right?"

"Yeah, it is."

"When do you leave?"

"Mid-August."

"Why so soon?"

"Time to move-in and get settled, meet other scholarship winners, orientation and stuff. We also have to do a 'catch-up' program to make sure that we're ready when classes start."

Xavier and I lay on our backs, our heads nestled in our hands and watched the silver clouds billow across the sky like smoke signals—the clouds slammed the portal shut and swallowed the moon and stars, still, the version of me that existed through the portal continued to communicate possibilities of our future. The light of the skyline reflected off the metallic clouds but did little to alleviate the darkness that swaddled us. It felt as if we existed outside of time.

I could witness all my past experiences, one stacked on another, inseparable from the present that once had flowed from them. I could see the wind move around us and the warm breaths that left our body as we exhaled. I could feel a cool relief in my lungs as I inhaled the sounds of the violent stream. Beneath us, the earth pulsed tenderly with our heartbeats, grounding our mercurial desires even as our instincts compelled us to take flight. Above us, I could sense God watching, but I didn't care.

"That's cool… Mr. C said you knew for a while you'd won the scholarship. How come you didn't tell me?"

"I planned to… remember when I said I had three things to tell you? Well, this was supposed to be number two."

"Why'd you skip it?"

"I needed to say number three."

"What good that did."

"We wouldn't be here if I didn't, so lots of good, I think."

He loves me, the Dead uttered.

"Are you excited to leave?" I asked, nervous about how he would answer.

"I am."

He loves me not, I thought to myself.

"…but I don't know. What if I'm making the wrong decision? What if I don't make any friends? What if I hate it there?" Xavier inhaled deeply as if all the pondering had taken his breath away.

"Sure. But what if you love it? What if you make a ton of friends? You're gonna get there and wonder why you ever doubted going. You're gonna get there and forget all about me—us… all of us." I held my breath to listen for Xavier's movements. Silence. "Besides," I exhaled, "if you don't like it, you can always go to high school somewhere else. I'm thinking of going to Central. You could come with."

I could feel Xavier's smile permeating the darkness. "Sounds like a plan."

———

"My mom has been blowing me up," I said as Xavier packed up his telescope.

He laughed. "Are you gonna get in trouble?"

"Probably. But I'm mad at her." I folded the blanket and handed it to Xavier.

"How come?"

"She signed me up for some bullshit church camp today and didn't ask me. And when I told her I didn't want to go, *she* got mad. I wish I could leave… like, *really* leave."

"Why don't you?"

"Where would I go?" I looked up at the patch hidden behind the clouds. "I wish I could, though, you know? Just vanish and come back as something new, someone different. But even that feels like a pointless wish sometimes. If I disappeared, the person they knew would still exists in their eyes. They'd always be looking for him. Always staring. And over time, those stares—I feel—would shape me back into the person I was. So, would anything really change?"

These thoughts were once just tangled ruminations

I only shared with the Dead and voicing them breathed life into the Dead. Still, there was comfort and freedom in knowing that Xavier would be leaving—even if he was too afraid to believe it—and carrying my words with him. Xavier placed a hand on my shoulder. I wanted him to hug me but was too afraid to ask. I imagined that the other version of me wasn't a coward and got what he wanted.

"Why?" Xavier asked.

"Why what?"

"Why do you care if they stare?"

"For the same reason you feel you have to prove you're the smartest in every room."

He frowned but then said, "Here," taking my forearm into his hand. He took a black marker out of his bag and scribbled on me.

"What are you doing?" He finished and then did the same to himself. "I can barely see. What is it?"

"Something to remember each other. For if I accept the scholarship. For if you disappear and come back as something new."

"*If* you accept? Not when?"

"If," he replied.

He loves me.

"Hey, what do you think of Revelations?"

"What?" he responded, laughing.

"The Book of Revelations."

"A bit predictable. But that's to be expected in standard apocalyptic tradition. Everyone back then basically took the same story and added their own twist, like a game of doomsday telephone. It's ok. Not my favorite. Metaphors are way too on the nose for me. Like, come on, the moon turning to blood? How much more direct could you be about—"

Without giving myself time to second-guess it, I wrapped my arms around Xavier and hugged him. I must've been squeezing him hard because his breath came out in short spurts, but he didn't say anything. Instead, he hugged me too, and we embraced each other under the watchful eyes of God.

My phone vibrated steadily. It was my mom calling me to figure out where I was. I let it ring. Xavier and I awkwardly stumbled down the steep hill, out of those sacred woods, and back onto the Philly streets. We agreed to hang out again and then parted ways.

From a distance, Xavier yelled: "SO, WE'RE GOING TO CENTRAL, HUH?" His laugh poured into the empty streets like a sweet elixir, healing the ravaged buildings and damaged roads.

He loves me.

Under the wan streetlights, I could see what Xavier had hastily drawn on me. I smiled at the triangle missing a third side and the crude circle filled with tiny specks floating above—it was Snake Hill and the patch in the sky. My mind wandered, thinking of the world through the portal, but I looked at my new tattoo and accepted that this was our reality. And for the time being, it was enough.

CHAPTER 6

Five Weeks Before Camp

Mason: swear to God, bro, I thought you was in this jawn already.

Me: it's cool

Eric: forreal thought you was in here, bro. Herb said he was gonna add you

Herb: I thought I added him and he was just quiet lol. My fault, bro

Me: it's cool

Meat: deadass thought you was in here the whole time, bro. You do be quiet as fuck XD!

Mason: XD.

Eric: forreal! XD

Me: it's cool… LOL

Meat: wyd?

Meat: y'all tryna go to the courts?

Eric: I'm down

Mason: What time?

Herb: ^

Me: damn, I'm on punishment. Can't leave the stoop

Meat: like 3?

Eric: bet

Mason: I'm down.

Herb: ^

Herb: what happened? @Jay

Me: some bs. I was out late last night. Was supposed to be home when the streetlights came on. Now she trying to take my phone away because she was calling to see where I was and I wasn't picking up so she said I must not need it

Me: it was only like 11:30. She was mad and yelling and shit when I got home then she started drawling about the phone

Me: looked like she was crying too

Meat: crying?! 11:30 not even late! I be out until 1 in the morning sometimes and my mom don't be saying shit

Eric: she still gonna let you go to Herb party?

Me: idk. I ain't ask her yet

Mason: your mom be drawling frfr. That's why I said don't even tell her about that jawn. Just say you at my crib or something and pull up.

Meat: nigga, his mom definitely gonna say no. She don't like you rofl. The one time she met you, she told you to watch your mouth and tuck in your shirt

Eric: XD!

Mason: stop dickeating.

Meat: ahhhh you mad as shit dickhead lmao. Jay tell her you staying at my crib. She loves me ;)

Me: stop fucking playing with me

Meat: XD! My bad bro lol

Herb: where was you at? @Jay

Me: wym?

Herb: last night. Where'd you go?

Me: oh

Meat: he was probably with one of his hoes. Let's goooo!

Mason: doubt it.

Mason: Speaking of, you fuck Aniya yet?

Meat: nigga it's only Monday…school just ended on Friday.
I got a whole summer. Why you so worried about my dick?

Mason: stfu. I'm not, but you always talking and don't be
about nothing fr.

Meat: you fucked Lea?

Mason: no, but I can.

Meat: whatever, nigga, but bet. If I fuck Aniya before you,
I win. If you get Lea first, you win

Mason: ard, we got until the party. I don't need the
whole summer.

Mason: @Jay you in this too.

Meat: say less

Herb: lol don't listen to them @Jay

Me: XD

Eric: I still got my money on Meat

Mason: bcuz you a dickeater.

Eric: and you a hater

…

Three Weeks Before Camp

Two weeks had passed since they'd added me to the group chat.

In the initial days of being added, my phone buzzed with constant chimes of plans to meet, discussions of the NBA playoffs, and goals for Herb's party. The notifications slowed some after the finals and the guys busied themselves with their summer plans, but even in the lull, the bet remained a trending topic. Each chime—regardless of the content of the text—was a reminder of what needed to be done and my inability to do it; so, after a week, I told them that my mom was taking my phone, and I turned it off. The future could wait.

Two weeks had passed since the night at Snake Hill with Xavier.

While I was avoiding the guys, Xavier and I began to spend more time together. It was rainy in the subsequent days, so we didn't return to Snake Hill, but I carried the memory on my forearm, which I renewed every day with a black Sharpie. We spent our days—planned over the house phone or in person—at the library or at Xavier's house, watching movies, listening to his dad's records, and talking about everything. The future, though, was off limits. I had even started to miss the church shuttle so Xavier and I could walk together. After a speedy jaunt through Herb's neighborhood, I would meet up with Xavier for a stroll through University City before parting ways for church. We sometimes fantasized about going to Penn as we passed students on the street but agreed that Philly was too small, so it would be better if we went to school elsewhere:

"How about this place, McGill University?" I had once asked, browsing the internet.

"Never heard of it. Where is it?" Xavier had responded while flipping through channels for something to watch.

"Montreal, in Canada."

"Huh… why Canada?"

"I heard two men can—"

"Oooo, how about this? It's a classic zombie movie."

"Sure."

"Sorry, I cut you off. What were you saying about Canada?"

"Nothing… a dumb joke. Seems like a cool place, though."

Overall, my favorite thing to do was to sit and listen to Xavier play the piano. Mr. Reid had an extensive collection of jazz records from which Xavier drew inspiration, and I loved the moments when he invited me over to showcase a new piece. Before playing, he would preface, "It's my first time doing this one, so it might be a little rough," and then play as if he had been practicing for hours—I was sure he had. I concluded that the disclosure was to excuse potential mistakes or make me more impressed if there weren't any, but even the discordant notes seemed to fit. When he finished, I would present a bouquet of fictional flowers, and he would bow as if he had just played a full concert at Carnegie Hall and was met by the applause of adoring fans. After my standing ovation, Xavier's wide smile slide into a solemn line as he spoke about the jazz musician whose piece he had just played. "Did you know …," he would say with deep reverence and gratitude as if speaking at their wake. Inevitably, the eulogy would balloon into a broader history lesson, followed by a, "wait, how did we get here?" and laughter.

On the night before he left to visit family in Chicago, he gave me a card and told me not to open it until my birthday.

Two Weeks Before Camp

With a week left in June, I would leave soon for camp. With Xavier gone and me avoiding the guys, I turned to Christian to stave off my boredom. He was almost three years younger, and we had once been close, but over time, we had grown apart. Now, in attempting to reconnect, I realized how different we were. Where he preferred to play sports, I wanted to stay inside and read. When watching movies, he cringed at the excess violence of the slashers I put on, while I rolled my eyes at the cheesy romcoms he enjoyed. When speaking of our futures, I spoke in hopeful terms that always seemed to outline what I had seen through the portal, while Christian could say with specificity what he wanted to be when he grew up (entrepreneur), what he would buy first when he got rich (a new car for mom and then season box tickets for the Sixers), where he would live (Lower Merion because that's where Kobe went to school), how many kids he would have (four: three girls, one boy, or all girls, for a reason I couldn't remember, but it made me laugh), and even the name of his wife (Aaliyah, after the late great). In pushing my baby brother to grow into a man, he had become a person separate from me, complete with his own personality and desires—I didn't know he would grow into a stranger.

Yet despite how much we had both changed, some things remained the same. For example, our love of Kung-fu movies. *Kung Fu Hustle* was our favorite, and after each rewatch, we would emulate the moves with me as the grand master and Christian, my student. Our love for video games also never wavered, and we spent many nights, which often turned into early mornings, playing them. My baby brother—even with aspects of his being unknown—I soon realized was no more of a stranger to me than I was to myself. His smile was familiar, though now almost complete with his adult teeth. His laugh was familiar, still infectious and warm. And the way he looked at me with admiration—as though I had the secrets of the world written down somewhere just for him—was familiar, if undeserved. I felt I owed Christian an apology, but apologizing to him would be more difficult than it had been to Xavier: I had done Christian a greater harm in insisting he take the path that both provided me protection and conspired in my destruction. It would take more than a simple "I'm sorry" to remedy.

"Hey."

"..."

"Hey!"

"..."

"Jacob," Christian said, "are you still awake?"

"No."

"Oh, ok," he responded, trying to hide the urgency in his voice.

"Well, I'm awake now. What is it?"

"I can't sleep."

"That's why you woke me up?"

"No… why'd you get kicked out of school?"

"*That's* why you woke me up? I got kicked out like a year ago. Why are you just now asking?"

"I don't know. I was scared to ask. They said you killed someone."

"Go to sleep, Christian."

"Ok… wait though, remember that time when we broke the bed trying to put the stars on the ceiling?" he said, chuckling.

I rolled over onto my back and stared up at the dim luminescence of the glow-in-the-dark star stickers on the ceiling. It had taken forever for Christian and me to get them up there. Having no ladder, we took turns jumping on the bed to paste them on. I smiled at the sparse cluster, remembering we couldn't plaster the rest of them because the bed broke. My mom was angry when she found out, but we had lied about what had happened, so neither of us had gotten in trouble. Had she looked up, we would have been found out, but she never noticed the universe above her head.

"Yeah, I do. I can't believe she didn't know we were lying. We looked so guilty."

We laughed.

"Remember, you were gonna take the blame if we got caught?"

"Yeah, I do."

"I don't believe them… just so you know."

"Go to sleep, Christian."

"Ok. Mom said you're going to camp."

"Christian…"

"I wish I could go to camp too."

"I don't want to go. You're more than welcome to take my spot."

"I think it could be fun."

"Offer's still open."

"I can't. I'm leaving tomorrow to stay with my dad for the rest of the summer."

"Oh," I responded.

The light of the stars seemed to dim until they died completely, leaving tiny black holes in the ceiling that sucked up the oxygen in the room. I wanted to ask why he hadn't told me sooner, but it didn't matter. I wanted to tell him I would miss him, but the words couldn't traverse the vast space I had put between us. Instead, the heavy darkness settled into my bones, and I closed my eyes to go to sleep.

"And sorry I won't be here for your birthday."

"…"

"Jacob."

"Christian, go to sleep."

"Ok… but remember when—"

"Just go the fuck to sleep! I don't care what you remember! I don't care that you're leaving! I don't care what they're saying about me at that school! You know why? Because it's true! And if you don't shut up, I'm going to do the same to you. Now go to sleep!"

"Ok," he whispered, sniffling.

One Week Before Camp

With my days no longer busied by rigorous martial arts training or long gaming sessions, I was bored. "An idle mind is the Satan's playground," Pastor Hooks often preached, so I kept the Devil at bay by watching tv, which was where I got the idea to journal. Really, the main character wrote in her diary every night, but men didn't keep diaries. I had tried to mimic the main character, starting every entry with, "Dear Journal," but never got past those two words. I then removed the greeting—deciding that this play at formality was inhibiting my thoughts—and welcomed the deluge, yet the page remained blank, the spaces between the lines becoming emptier the more I stared at them. Ironically, I was bursting at the seams with thoughts spoken to life by the chatter of the Dead, but the volume itself was the problem—I couldn't hear my own voice through the static.

That black-and-white marble composition book meant to house my secrets became a repository of abstract doodles. Although I couldn't bring myself to write anything, I enjoyed sketching. The act allowed me to be a bystander, to examine my thoughts without having to interpret them. Drawing a line on the paper, a curved upper bound, and another, the lower bound, I would then add concentric circles and shading to give depth to the lifeless eye. I often found myself unconsciously starting my pieces with an eye—my note-book was littered with eyes staring back at me.

For one piece—the chef d'oeuvre of my short stint as an artist—I began with my nested circles enclosed by their usual boundaries. The upper bound, heavy with thoughts of Xavier, was dark and bold, drenched with desire and longing and shame; the lower bound was faint as flickers of What's-His-Name and of Herb's party flashed across my mind. Thoughts of my mom, of God, of Christian danced in the light of my conscious mind before scurrying back into oblivion as I added shading to the white of the eye. The eyeball took form, seeming to lift off the page while staring at me from the depths of the mostly blank sheet. I caught a glimpse of my tattoo, which reminded me to add light to the pupil—I drew small empty circles within the pupil and then shaded in the pupil itself. Parallel lines then erupted from the eyelids, twisting, bending, connecting, and fad-ing, until they resembled the branches of a tree. With my eyes closed, I saw my life with Xavier projected like a movie inside my eyelids; then, opening my eyes, I added leaves to the tree. The piece looked complete, but it *felt* like some-thing was missing. As this thought crossed my mind, a sense of dread gripped my insides. I drew dozens of circles that looked like they had been pinched and pulled at one end; the pinched-pulled circles clung to the branches and rolled off the leaves, landing on the eye and rolling off the sheet of paper. The rain stopped where the pencil reached the paper's edge, but persisted where my desires and reality conflicted, where my thoughts shaped themselves into art, the meaning of which eluded me, cool to the touch as the Snake Hill stream. It was done.

This is a piece of shit. Just like you. What is this supposed to mean? Shading needs work. You're not a good person. This isn't good art.

Xavier would like it.

What is this supposed to mean?? Piece of shit mirroring as art. Piece of shit mirroring as a person. SHADING NEEDS WORK! Just give up. So lonely. Pathetic.

Xavier knows art. Xavier would love it.

So lonely. So lonely. He loves you not.

He loves you.

I hate you. Everyone hates you. No one can love you. The sin is the sinner. Shading needs fucking work. What is this supposed to mean? WHAT IS THIS SUPPOSED TO MEAN???

I laid bare a piece of my soul and the core of my identity on that sheet of paper to be displayed to the world but grew weary of the invisible public's scrutiny, so I retired and again tried my hand as an author. This time, instead of journaling, I attempted to retell fictional stories I already knew: *Harry Potter* was my first work. I made it my own by changing the names and some plot points but shelved it after a few paragraphs when I decided that it was better as a movie. I then moved into critiques of movies and tv shows, but this too was short-lived, and I resigned from my self-appointed role as lead critic.

My loneliness had become stark. When reminded of it, it felt like a presence that existed solely as a foil to the Dead, filling me with a preference for their chatter versus the empty silence. I was reminded of it when prompted by the main menu of a video game asking if I wanted to play with two players. I was reminded of it on days when I was greeted by notes from my mom stating that she would be working late and that dinner was in the fridge. I was reminded of it on nights when I sat on the stoop and looked up at the starless sky. I was reminded of it when watching tv ceased to prevent the idling of my mind, when thoughts turned into landmines that were set throughout the playground for my demise.

Xavier was gone. Herb was gone. Christian was gone.

I would be leaving for camp to be surrounded by total strangers, and the thought made me anxious, like my body was filling up with sand.

Since signing me up, save for the sparse "yes" or "no," I had refused to speak to my mom. I had come to understand going to camp as another one of those things that was out of my control—some would say a fact of life or destiny, I called it an exercise of power—but my anger towards her was firmly within my grasp, and I didn't want to relinquish this last bastion of agency. Separated by my stubbornness and her ignorance of it all, my mom and I passed each other at home like two shades in Limbo who had known each other in life, but whose memory of the other was now eroded, the space occupied with an unquenchable longing for something familiar.

Given her frequent absences, holding on to this smoldering anger felt moot, and it eventually passed. My frustration was replaced with anxiety and then with nothing. Resigned to my fate, I floated through the remaining time like a ghost condemned to a torturous loop until I solved the mystery of my death or let go of the memory of a past love. I had resolved not to discover what was binding my soul to this plane and surrendered to the unrelenting nothingness that numbed my senses and dulled the sharpness of the Dead's voices to a smooth hum. Instead, I ate, slept, watched tv, ate, shat, showered, ate, and slept through the days. I greeted the day's arrival with a quietude that resembled the sky—storm clouds silently carrying rain and holding the heat close to the earth.

One Day Before Camp

It was my last starless night before leaving for church camp and my birthday. To my surprise, my mom insisted we sit at the table and have dinner together. It was Sunday, so a big meal was in order: fish, rice and peas, cabbage, and a salad that was just washed lettuce in a bowl and a few slices of tomato. She cooked just as much as she would have had Christian been there. It made me wonder if she missed him, too.

It was always hard to tell what my mom was feeling besides anger, which she often stated was not anger and I later understood to be frustration: frustration that we didn't take the chicken out to thaw, frustration that Christian wasn't understanding math concepts when she helped him with homework, frustration that she didn't understand my math concepts enough to help, frustration that she sometimes couldn't afford to pay for a school trip or buy us the things we asked for, frustration that she had to work so much, frustration that she had missed so much, frustration that she could no longer pick us up and rock us in her arms when the world knocked us down, frustration that sometimes it wasn't enough, frustration that she wasn't enough. Besides frustration, she never showed emotion. Yes, she smiled and laughed and displayed gestures that conveyed joy, but they always felt disingenuous, like she was an extraterrestrial playing at a human. I had only seen my mom cry once, and it was when she got the call that Grandma Junie had died—in that moment, I couldn't help but think that Grandma Junie would have been happy to see that.

"How was church?" My mom asked.

"It was fine."

"What was the sermon about?"

"The fruits of the Spirit," I said, responding with the topic from Sunday School because I had fallen asleep during the sermon. *Please forgive me, God.*

"I picked up a shift, so I couldn't make it."

"Yup."

"And did you talk to your brother? He said he would call today."

Christian had called earlier that day to wish me a happy birthday. I had rushed him off the phone when he began to tell me about how much he loved North Carolina and how much he wished I were there too, but before hanging up, he told me to check under my mattress. Tucked underneath was a list of cheat codes he had compiled for a video game. "Happy birthday! I miss you," he had said. "Yeah, thanks," I had responded.

"He did," I told her.

"That's good. I talked to him the other day. He's having fun over there, but he misses you. I think this will be the longest you two have been apart. You know he asked me why you got kicked out of school? He reminds me a lot of you when you were his age. You used to ask so many questions: 'why is the sky blue,' 'why do I have to go to Catholic school,' 'why is that lady nails so long,' 'why do I have to walk home, can't you pick me up,' 'why can't I hold another boy's hand?' I asked him why he doesn't ask you himself, and he said he was scared."

"What did you say to him?"

"That you wanted to go to public school…" She dug at the porcelain plate until she unearthed something else to talk about. "Do you like it?"

"It's fine."

"And how's Herb? I talked to his mom last week; she said that the basketball thing is going well, and some private schools are looking at him."

"He's good."

"And what about your other friend?"

"What friend?"

"The one you were smiling and laughing with when I came to pick you up. I saw you two when I was at the stoplight."

"Oh, that's not my friend. We have class together and were just in the same group for the trip."

"I thought you really liked him… that's the one whose house you been going to lately, right?"

"I don't *like* him." The blood in my veins crystallized and burst, turning my cheeks purple against my black skin and prickling the surface like thousands of tiny needles. "And we're not friends, we're just cool."

"Well, it's ok if you are. He seems nice, and you two seem… friendly." Her eyes met mine, and I looked away for fear she would see the Dead. "Oh! Guess who I ran into today at 69th Street…," she said, removing the bones from a piece of fish and placing them in a pile on the plate, analyzing them as if the future were written there. She talked about seeing our old babysitter and then mentioned the death of a great uncle in Jamaica I had met once when I was seven. She shared a secret about a family member and told me not to repeat it to anyone and then explained how the water bill was late, but the mortgage was coming due soon, so she would have to pay a little here, move some things there, and trust that everything would work out because what other option remained. She said all this with zero affect, as if these events had happened to someone else. Perhaps she saw the world for what it was and was demonstrating to us what it took to face it. It seemed, however, this untethered optimism, honed to perfection for survival, encased her world in a light, making her incapable of seeing the darkness that separated us: what she mistook for a rosy glow was instead the ruddy shimmer of a bond which had rusted from years of neglect. *Shading needs work!* Her mechanical smile slid into a scowl—I imagined the bones revealed Xavier's and my future.

"You excited for camp tomorrow?"

"Sure."

"I know you don't want to go, but it'll be good for you, trust me."

"Dear Journal,

What do I say here? I don't know. It's been nice having the room to myself, I guess. Every time I look at a hole in the wall it makes me laugh at how we would get into fights, and I would wish that he was never born. But now it feels like too much space. It seems too clean. Too quiet. Video games aren't as fun. And kung fu movies seem dumb. He called today to say happy birthday, and I was so mean to him. I'm always so mean to him, but I don't know why. The night before he left, I told him I would kill him if he didn't go to sleep. Wtf is wrong with me???? I wish I didn't say it. It was just a joke! He knows I was joking... He has to because he still called. He said he misses me. But I couldn't say it back. I wish he didn't. He shouldn't miss me. I'm not a good person and I wish he would see that. I keep trying to show him that. He doesn't deserve me as a brother. He deserves someone better. I haven't spoken to Herb in a while. I miss him, even though I know I shouldn't. The school trip, Eastern, the group chat...idk, he's been excluding me for some reason. I turned my phone back on today and there was a text from him saying happy birthday, I didn't respond. He was the only one from the group who remembered, but mom forgot, so they get a pass. Xavier texted too, reminding me to read his card. Of course, I remembered to read his card, it was the first thing I did this morning. Not gonna repeat everything he said, but he wished me a happy birthday, said he was glad we had become good friends, and then told a very, very, <u>very</u>, corny joke about turning 14 hahahahaha. we really hung out every day, all day. I miss him too, but not in the same way that I miss Christian and Herb. I miss Xavier like I miss fireflies. I miss him like I miss not knowing right from wrong. I miss him like I miss What's-His-Name (damn, what was his name?) ... but different. I really shouldn't even be writing this, but I miss him. I shouldn't want to listen to him play the piano in the den, the notes absorbing into the black velvet couch and ancient fireplace. I shouldn't want to watch a movie in his living room and hope a jump scare drives him into my arms. I shouldn't imagine how soft his sheets are or what posters are on his wall or whether his slender arms connect to his body in the same fashion as mine or do they connect to an ever-expanding universe contained and given form by his t-shirt...I miss him in ways I can't write here. But the endless eyes see me. They're always fucking watching. I try to keep the thoughts buried, but they keep clawing their way to the surface. God, please forgive me. Please, God. I need Your help. Please. Maybe camp will be good. Maybe this is the experience I need to get rid of these thoughts and these feelings. I don't feel anything, but I pray that that is a lead-up to hope. Only way to go is up, right? Maybe I'll find the thing I'm missing so that I can go to Herb's party. So that I can fuck Brianna."

PART II

CHAPTER 7

In first grade, I had a friend named Laila with whom I spent all my time, and she was my wife. We never had an official ceremony, but at the start of the school year, we started a game of "house" that never ended. Some would say this was precocious, but others would say we were two kids who were being raised right. Encouraged by the "awws" when we held hands while coloring or the photos of "Jacob and his little girlfriend" taken by our teacher, we embodied our parents' hope for our future—normalcy. In first grade, I broke from this normalcy, not by choice but by nature. It wasn't until third grade, though, that I gleaned what the consequences of this difference meant.

As the husband, it was my job to provide, and so I always shared my snacks with Laila at lunch. During recess, we lived in an unassuming, one-story plastic house, but to us it was a home with two driveways and a dog. As the wife, it was her job to make our house a home, so she would cook and clean while I ran around the play area. Some days I was a cop, others a racecar driver, but she was always the wife. Laila eventually became bored with having to stay home, so she hung out with the other girls who existed outside of the home but were confined to hopscotch or Double Dutch or other "girl games." Like most marriages, ours ended in divorce. It was around this time I met Andrew.

No longer occupied with the trappings of adulthood, I played with the other kids in the schoolyard. Andrew was in the other first grade class, but these boundaries didn't exist outdoors, where the walls that divided us evaporated into the open air.

It was a warm summer day when we met. The season was characterized by many thunderstorms that seemed to target our tiny piece of the world. Lightning had struck a large oak tree in the schoolyard several times that year, but it remained standing—because of this, many of us had taken to believing that the tree was at least lucky if not holy.

"I hope everyone touched the tree," Mika said. Huddled under the canopy that sheltered us from the punishing sun, we exchanged looks that confirmed we had taken the necessary precaution. "Ok. Spit, spit, spit, you are not it," Mika tapped my shoe twice to remove my foot from the circle. "Spit, spit, spit, you are not it," he tapped another foot. Those of us who were not "it" patted each other on the back and giggled as Mika sped up his cadence: "spit, spit, spit, you are not it. Spit, spit, spit, you are not it. Spit, spit, spit, you are not it." Mika removed his foot. There were two people left. "Spit... spit... spit...," he said slowly, teasing the remaining two who squealed anxiously, "you... are... not... it." Andrew covered his face in defeat and began counting. We, the lucky ones, laughed as we scattered like dandelion seeds in the wind.

We were playing freeze tag, and strategically Andrew had forced the group into two. We watched as half of us stood frozen in place on the other side of the schoolyard. One-by-one Andrew picked us off. Frozen in time, those tagged decorated the grounds like statues made of onyx and limestone.

"Nooo," Mika exclaimed as Andrew tagged him, one leg lifted in the air as if he were in the middle of jumping.

Andrew lifted his arms in celebration but quickly lowered them when he realized I hadn't been caught yet. We locked eyes and a pursuit ensued. I made a beeline to the jungle gym, and he honed in on me like a shark driven by the scent of blood. He closed the gap, but I twisted my body through the metal bars and took off again. My heart knocked against my chest with fear, and I thought I would collapse under the weight of its beating. Too tired to think, I had backed myself into a corner. With the chain-link fence behind me, Andrew descended, savoring the moment with a ravenous smile. I scanned the yard for assistance and noticed that the statues had come to life and were tossing a ball around. No one would be coming to save me.

My breath returned to me in pieces, and I slunk down into the corner and accepted imminent defeat.

"You're giving up?" he asked with his hands on his hips.

"There's nowhere for me to go! You got me!"

"I didn't tag you yet." He dropped his hands from his hips to his knees, bending over to catch his breath. "You're fast. I bet if you ran now, you'd get away."

His eyes traced a path for me to follow, and my feet inched along it. He hung his head low and swung back and forth like a pendulum. I moved cautiously out of the corner, my eyes glued to his swaying body, drenched in sweat. When I thought I was in the clear, my legs sprang into action and I took off along the fence. My heart pounded in my ears, and I smiled with relief. However, the moment was short-lived as my heartbeat was overcome by the quick patter of feet behind me. The fence to my right, I looked left and saw Andrew gaining on me. I juked to cross him over but slipped on some gravel and fell.

Andrew stood over me as I picked pebbles from my palm. "Here," he said, extending his hand to help me up.

"You can't trick me."

"I'm not tricking you. Timeout." He made a "T" with his hands, and a look of concern replaced the look of assured victory. "We can pause the game." I took his hand, and he lifted me to my feet. He held onto my hand and picked the pebbles out. "There. Are you ok?"

I nodded. My hand throbbed as mottled drops of blood clotted under the skin and rippled with every heartbeat, like pebbles were being skipped across the tiny crimson ponds. His hand, still holding mine, was sweaty and rough, covered in small cuts and calluses that I would later learn were from helping his mom weed their garden. Although my heart raced, my body was at rest, void of any adrenaline and resistance.

The bell rang, and he smiled. "You win!"

I opened my mouth to protest the unearned victory, but

Andrew had already moved on. His slender fingers inter-twined with mine and squeezed, making me focus on his touch and not the pain. Hand-in-hand, we walked towards the school, and for two years, we never let go.

By third grade, Andrew and I were inseparable: we colored and snacked together, we napped on the same mat until they told us this was wrong, we hugged until they told us this was wrong, and we held hands until they told us that this was wrong. The reasons for why were never the same, but all of them held a common underlying message: "You're boys, and boys don't do this with each other." We obliged, thinking we were doing our part to prevent the spread of germs—one of the explanations we received—and exchanged our hand-holding for high-fives and our hugs for fist-bumps. Despite the lessening of our outward affection for each other, I still felt a closeness to him I didn't under-stand. In many respects, he was like Laila, except when I went to work, he went too.

Thursday arrived, crisp and partly sunny, evoking mid-spring or early fall. And I know it was a Thursday because on that fall-spring day my best friend told me he was trans-ferring schools.

Often during recess, we drove around the schoolyard pretending to pick up trash as garbagemen or run around as firefighters or chase after each other as a cop did a rob-ber and then retire to our home where we lived together as roommates. We had no reference for two men being mar-ried; however, we understood our relationship; there was no pretense.

That day—the day before our home burned to the ground—we were firefighters battling a fire on the far side of the school. The fire raged, tearing through an imaginary two-story home with a velocity we had never seen before. But as always, we got the fire under control and with no casualties. Andrew had even saved a cat. Afterwards, we returned to our home in the middle of the yard where the large oak tree had existed. Where once the tree had provided shade in the summer and whose leaves had cushioned the frozen ground in the winter, it was now just a stump. The school had cut down our lucky tree, which had withstood lightning strikes, for fear of its integrity.

That day—the day before our home burned to the ground—Andrew and I sat at the stump, which served as our dinner table, and twirled spaghetti on our forks, laughing at the imaginary tomato sauce that covered our faces. Andrew had been in the middle of recalling how he had heard the cat meowing in the pantry when the bell rang, and he fell silent. Tears welled in his eyes and overflowed onto his cheeks. I asked if the spaghetti had been too hot or if he had been hurt in the fire, but he shook his head. As we cleared the table and walked to the line, he told me that the following day would be his last: he was moving, and his parents wanted to put him in a school closer to home. I began to cry but used my shirt to wipe the tears away, knowing that crying wasn't something "big boys" do.

The second half of the day had no respect for our predicament and ended faster than usual. At the end of class, he asked me for my notebook and then wrote his home number. I promised him that we would always be best friends.

number. I promised him that we would always be best
friends.

—

"Oh! That's my car when I grow up!" Christian yelled, pointing to a blue 2004 Kia Sorrento.

"Ok. Well, that's my car," I pointed to a black 2004 Cadillac CTS.

We started our cars and drove on the sidewalk, swerving around trees and light poles and beeping at the cars in front of us when the traffic light turned green.

"Hold my hand, Jacob," Christian said as we arrived at an intersection.

"What did I tell you last time? You're a big boy. You don't need me to hold your hand."

"Ok," he said, dejected, but then revved his car and ran across the street. "Race you home!"

"Stop cheating!" I put my car into gear and chased after him.

"I win!" Christian cheered and whooped at the top of the block.

"I let you win," I said, smiling.

Our mom was working late that night, so, as usual, I was in charge. After helping Christian finish his homework and finishing my own, I told him to go shower while I warmed up dinner. When my mom knew she would be working late, she would cook the night before so that she knew we ate, even if she wasn't there to witness it.

That night, we had spaghetti.

"Where is your shirt?" I asked Christian, who only had on his pajama bottoms.

"It's hot. I don't need one." He scooped some spaghetti onto his fork and held it high above his mouth.

"Stop playing with your food."

"I'm not." The spaghetti slid off the fork and onto his mouth. He slurped up the noodles that didn't make it inside. "See?"

He looked ridiculous, but I didn't want to laugh and encourage his behavior.

"Did you put lotion on?" It was a moot question because I knew he hadn't. His brown skin was visibly dry and scaly, as if a lizard had been dusted in powdered sugar.

"Yes."

"Christian, no, you didn't."

"Well, I'm about to go to bed. What does it matter anyway?"

"Because… shut up. Hurry up and eat. It's getting late."

"Ok, look…" He balanced a piece of spaghetti on his top lip. "I have a mustache." He looked ridiculous, but I couldn't keep myself from laughing this time.

We finished eating, and as I cleared the table, Christian approached me with his arms open. "No hugs, Christian. I told you that already."

"Why not?" He whined.

"Because you're gonna be eight soon, and it's not something big boys do."

"Ok," he said and rubbed his eyes. "I know big boys

don't cry. Sorry."

"Come here." I wrapped my arms around him and hugged him tighter than usual. "Stop crying."

"Ok."

"Come on." I walked him out of the dining room to the stairs. "Wash your face and go get in bed."

"Ok," Christian responded, tiny feet climbing up the steps. "Good night, Jacob!" he yelled from the top of the stairs.

"Night, Christian!"

Unlike most nine-year-olds, or even most people, I enjoyed washing dishes. It was a trait I'd inherited from my mom, who cleaned as a form of problem-solving, of therapy, of resting, and of necessity. For me, washing dishes helped me to turn off my brain. It was repetitive and methodical: first, put soap and water in the pots to soak and set those to the side; next, clean the cups, then the utensils and the flatware; lastly, scrub the pots, disinfect the sink, and dry the counter.

I ran the dishcloth over the counter and turned off the kitchen lights. I checked the parking spot across the street where my mom usually parked—it was empty, but it was ten-ish, so she would be home soon—and then started up the steps. I laughed at the tomato sauce all over Christian's face and the strand of spaghetti that fashioned itself a goatee wrapping around his mouth. In the same breath, my laughter turned into sobbing and tears stung my feet like acid rain. "Boys don't cry," I evoked the salve given me to soothe both sadness and pain, but the tears wouldn't stop, so I went to the living room until I calmed down.

"It's not fair," I whispered to myself like a mantra. The words repeated themselves before and after I had even spoken them, blending into a *shhh* sound that resembled a wave swallowing itself. It was soothing. Being only nine, I didn't know what "it" was, nor fully understand the concept of fairness, but these seemed the only words to express what was happening. I thought of how the day started like any other and how suddenly everything could change. I thought of who I would eat lunch and fight fires with, who would be my partner on class projects, who would be my best friend. I thought of our dinner table and our meals together—alfredo, mac and cheese, chicken fingers, fruit snacks—but spaghetti was our favorite. I thought of his face covered in sauce, and though imaginary, it was as real to me as the home we'd built together, as real as our friendship, as real as the sadness that gripped my heart with a truth that nine-year-olds shouldn't know, at least not yet. "It's not fair."

Without noticing, I had fallen asleep on the couch. In my dreams, Andrew and I tended a garden shaded by the large oak tree that had miraculously regrown. Our hands poked holes into the warm earth and dropped tomato, basil, and rosemary seeds into them; we covered the holes with dirt and watched as the plants bloomed before our eyes. Clouds blanketed the sky and pelted the ground with a warm summer rain—the dirt turned to paste beneath our feet, and we covered our heads with it. We painted our necks and shoulders, our arms, our chests, our legs, and then finally our eyes. Andrew took my hand in his. The rain stopped and the sun returned, baking the wet clay and turning our bodies into statues. In the darkness, Andrew never let go—our hands cemented together—two Black boys committed to the earth.

"Jacob," her voice called from a place I couldn't see. "Jacob," her hand gently shook the dirt off my body and brought me back to the world of the living, "why are you sleeping on the couch?" My eyes hadn't yet adjusted to the light, so I couldn't see her face, but I could hear the frustration in her voice.

"Hmm?" I responded, my mouth still filled with dirt.

"Come on, get up and go to bed. It's late." The memory of the dream quickly faded, but the image of Andrew's face stayed. I began to cry again. "Why are you crying?" she asked. Her tone was biting, but it stirred shame instead of fear. I didn't answer; I couldn't, and this made her more frustrated. I felt my cry deepen and my body stiffen as she gripped my arm. "Jacob, why are you crying?"

I choked up the dirt and the words came out with it: "An-Andrew is switching schools."

She sat on the couch next to me and pulled me in. "What? Wipe your face and stop all that crying. You said Andrew's switching schools?"

I nodded. "He's leaving and going to a different school."

"That's what you're crying for? You're a big boy, right?" I didn't know how to respond, so I mimicked her nodding. "Good. Then you shouldn't be crying like a little girl. Don't you have other friends? All this crying for nothing. You'll make new friends."

I know now that the phrase, "you're a big boy," wasn't

said to inspire resilience or bravery but rather embarrassment. It was used all at once to characterize you, endowing you with all the expectations of the title, and then to castigate you for failing to meet the newly assumed norms. It wasn't a balm, but an imposed role that insisted on you not breaking character. It was the tone in which she said it while she held me that conveyed the sincerity and commensurate disappointment in her words, or it was the forgotten dream whose sentiment still lingered, but the words hurt more than the previous times I had heard them.

She wiped the tears from my face. Her cold hands stung against my cheeks. "Come." She stood me up and hugged me. "Things don't always happen the way you want them to, but they always happen as they should. That's life." She led me into the kitchen and grabbed two spoons and a carton of ice cream. I waited for her to scoop a spoonful of the cookies and cream into her mouth and then, following her direction, did the same. She wiped off the ice cream dribbling down my chin. I smiled, and she did the same.

"See, you'll be alright. It gets better. One day you won't even remember him, and you'll wonder why you were even sad," she said. I wanted to believe that wasn't true, but I couldn't even recall Grandma Junie's face anymore. I knew once Andrew left, the same fate would await the memory of him. I could feel the tears building again, but I held my smile for both our sakes.

"What?" I asked, responding to her smile, which looked as if she longed for more moments like this one.

"You have a mustache."

Christian's spaghetti mustache came to mind, and then Andrew's spaghetti-covered face, and then the fact that tomorrow's meal would be our last and I would never see him again. I held my smile, but the tears flowed, nonetheless.

"Jacob…," she said, her voice stern.

But I couldn't hold it back: something within me had broken, and the resulting flood was out of my control. The day after the large oak tree had been cut down, we all gathered around the hallowed ground in dismay, horrified something we had believed to be immutable could be so easily destroyed. In the same way, the shame I felt was great. However, it paled compared to the hollowing grief that was reshaping my understanding of the world—boys don't cry.

"I'm sorry," I said through my sniffling. "I'm sorry. I'm sorry. I'm sorry."

She pulled me into her arms as I sobbed. "It's ok," she whispered, her voice trembling, "it's ok."

***

The next day we had a pizza party to send Andrew off. After a brief lesson, we made and decorated cards for Andrew. Well, the class made and decorated cards for Andrew—I didn't understand how words were supposed to capture the complicated and confusing emotions I was feeling or how words could relay to him what our friendship meant to me. The exercise seemed futile, so I sat alone by Mrs. Whittaker's desk while my classmates expressed how much they would miss him.

"Hey, T," Mrs. Whittaker said as Ms. LaGrange walked into the classroom, two straight lines filing in behind her. Ms. LaGrange was the teacher for the other third-grade class and Mrs. Whittaker's work best friend. Ms. LaGrange stopped in multiple times a week, often with her small army trailing behind her, to drop off treats she'd baked or to share a lesson plan, but mostly to gossip.

"Hey, girl," Ms. LaGrange placed a small, ribboned box onto the desk. "I made some macaroons."

"Thanks!"

"Did you hear about Diana?"

"No. What happened?" Mrs. Whittaker's eyebrows popped up.

"Well," Ms. LaGrange lowered her voice to a loud whisper, "I heard that her and her husband got arrested?"

"ARRESTED?!"

The class went silent.

"Shhhhhh," Ms. LaGrange laughed. "Bitch, shut up!"

The chatter resumed.

"Arrested?!" Mrs. Whitaker asked again.

"Yes, arrested. Apparently, they were runnin' some credit scam. Remember how I was tellin' you the other day some detectives came up here lookin' for her after school, but she wasn't here?" Mrs. Whitaker nodded. "Turns out, she wasn't here because they fled the city. They caught her ass at the Newark airport, tryin' to board a flight to Thailand."

"Whaaat? Wait, how you know?"

"You know I know people in high places." Ms. LaGrange winked and then laughed.

"You're a trip. I'll catch up with you later, though. One of the student's parents is bringing cupcakes, so I have to go meet them at the door soon."

"Sounds good." Ms. LaGrange did a little curtsy, to which Mrs. Whittaker shook her head and laughed, and then she spun around to leave. "Bryce, can you back up off him, please?" She asked in a tone that indicated it wasn't an actual question. "What did I tell you about personal space?" Bryce's cheeks rouged as he took a step back. Ms. LaGrange did another 360 and leaned over the desk: "That's the gay one I was telling you about."

"Teresa…"

"What! He is. He's always huggin' on the other boys. I'm constantly havin' to tell him to chill out."

"That doesn't mean he's gay."

"Maybe. But he has two moms at home, so I'm sure he doesn't know any better either. Someone gotta teach him right from wrong. I'm surprised they even let them in, knowin' about their parents. His sister in your class, right?"

Mrs. Whittaker shook her head and then looked down at the papers on her desk.

Ms. LaGrange scanned the room and saw me staring at her. "Anyway, I'll talk to you later," she said, still looking at me. She rolled her eyes, made her soldiers do an about-face, and then led them out of the room.

Gay. I thought to myself. I had heard the word on tv, but I had no context until now. I was still unsure what it meant, but I understood now why Andrew and I couldn't hug, why we couldn't hold hands, and why I couldn't cry because my best friend was leaving. He was a boy, and because of that, it was gay. "…to teach him right from wrong," Ms. LaGrange had said. I didn't need to know what the word meant to understand right from wrong.

I took the piece of paper with Andrew's number on it out of my Spiderman notebook—the one he gave to me because he knew Spiderman was my favorite superhero—and ripped it up.

The second half of the day flew by just as it had the day before, and I realized nothing lasts forever. Andrew and I were firefighters for the last time that day—our home caught fire, and I watched it burn as he tried to put it out, knowing that he couldn't save it. The roaring fire tore through the memories we had created and ignited whatever hope still lingered of us being friends. The bell rang while the fire calmed into a smolder, marking the end of recess and the end of our friendship. He swore we would stay in contact; he believed it too, yet I knew we couldn't because I had set the house on fire.

Andrew looked for me after school. I supposed to say one final goodbye, but I snuck by him in a passing crowd of students. As Christian and I started our cars, I looked back one more time to see his face. His eyes were fixed on the entrance of the school, searching, hoping the next person to exit would be me. From where I was standing, he looked like he was crying.

CHAPTER 8

Third grade ended, and I had all but forgotten about Andrew. Days passed when I hoped his dad would decide he didn't like the new job, return to his previous one, and put Andrew back in his old school. I thought about whether he had forgotten about me or wondered why I didn't call, and this made me question whether I did the right thing by ripping up his number. I missed him, even though I knew I shouldn't, yet the burning desire I had to see him was being violently stomped out by an impending manhood and the word Ms. LaGrange had said weeks earlier: gay.

Like many things, I didn't have a complete picture of what it meant to be a man, but I knew men didn't cry, especially over a boy. Still, Andrew had been a fixture in my life, and I couldn't forget him overnight. With his abrupt departure came a feeling of abandonment. I felt like an unanchored ship, set adrift at sea and subject to the capricious waves that moved me in every direction but never towards land. I cried several times in the weeks after Andrew left, but always in secret and always in fear of the person my tears implied me to be.

Tears about the situation dried up when I turned ten that summer. For my birthday, my mom threw a small party for me at our house, and with every, "you're turning into a man" or "man of the house" I was pushed to an adulthood I wasn't ready for yet barreling towards. So, when July rolled around, and it was time for our annual trip to Jamaica, I was eager for something consistent.

Every summer since I was five, my mom would take us to Jamaica to visit family for two months. It was the one time of year where Christian and I had her undivided attention—no fatigue from work, no worries of bills, and no calls from school; so, when she only stayed for one week, instead of the usual two, I was devastated. Although I longed for familiarity, the length of Christian's and my stay was the only thing that remained the same.

Everywhere I turned, harbingers of adulthood reminded me I was no longer a child. My mom leaving was just one example. Recognizing the permanence of death was another. Having only encountered death as endless respawns in a video game, it remained an amorphous concept. So, when my mom took time off to attend Grandma Junie's funeral in April of that year, the reality of what had happened didn't immediately settle in. When we landed, I expected to see her stout figure waiting for us outside the airport but remembered she was gone as we got into a taxi. "Boom Bye Bye," blasted over the car radio until my mom instructed the driver to change the station. At ten, with the advent of manhood, the effects of death became tangible and took the form of Grandma Junie.

By blood, Grandma Junie was my mom's great aunt, but in spirit, she was more like her mother. When my mom was seven years old, her actual mother passed away from pneumonia, and six years later her dad died in a car accident, so she was raised by my great grandfather and his sister, Grandma Junie, with whom my mom stayed most summers as a girl. I loved visiting Grandma Junie's house in the mountains. It wasn't extravagant—a two-bedroom, single-level house constructed of ashen cinderblocks and red-orange sheets of zinc rusted from years of exposure to the dense fog that crowned the mountain—but she always told us that her home extended beyond the walls. She had extensive knowledge of the land: growing, raising, or foraging everything she ate, and navigating the forest by the twisted trunk of a particular tree or the ubiquitous whispers of the nearby river.

The summer following her death, I would miss the hikes through the forest. I would miss the dips in the river to wash dirt, mango juices, and heat from our bodies. I would miss the smell of burning trash sweetened with food scraps, the shells of coconuts, the breadfruit skins, and whatever else Grandma Junie had gathered for us that day. I would miss the nighttime sky alight with thousands of stars that seemed to start where Grandma Junie's fingertips stopped as she traced the constellations for us to see. And, most importantly, I would miss Grandma Junie's ability to make me feel safe.

There was an instance the previous summer—the last one before she died—where I lost my footing on a muddy slope and tumbled to the foot of the hill while on a hike to the river. My mom, seeing me on the verge of tears, pulled me out of the mud and told me to keep going. Some dirt had gotten into my eyes, and in trying to get it out, I made it worse. Frustrated, I began to cry.

"Stop crying!" she barked.

"Why you so rough with him?" Grandma Junie asked.

"This is why he so soft now. He needs to grow up."

"Go along," Grandma Junie responded. "We'll catch up." My mom continued with Christian down the path, and Grandma Junie took my hand. She whispered softly, her voice reminiscent of the rushing river as though it had taught her to speak. "Tears will help to get the dirt off."

"She's so mean," I said, sniffling.

"She can be, but she's doing her best. Close your eyes." Grandma Junie took my face into her hands and wiped the mud off. I opened my eyes to see her smiling at me, not knowing that this would be one of my last times doing so. She took my hand and guided me through the forest as the trees parted for her. "Your mom has been through so much. She's lost a lot of people—her mom, my nephew, which was her dad, your dad—and she carries it all right here." Grandma Junie pointed to her heart. "When she was little, she was such a sweet girl, but each time she loss someone, a piece of her went with them. You boys are all she has. She loves you and your brother, even if sometimes she's mean, but all the sadness she carries in her heart makes her scared for you guys. You understand?"

"No."

"That's ok. You will when you get older. The world is scary, and you need to be tough to face it, but you can't let it take all the softness out of you. You can't let fear lead you. Remember that."

Grandma Junie's face slowly faded from memory after her death, but I was reminded of her every time I smelled the smoke of burning trash—a scent that watered my eyes but satisfied my desire to seek in the mountains she who was no longer there.

Instead of splitting time at Grandma Junie's that summer, we stayed at my great granddad's home in Kingston for the full two months. My granddad was a retired electrician who lived in a quiet neighborhood. In the past, he would allow Christian and me to play outside under his supervision; however, he now permitted us to play outside alone. He said it was because I was man enough to be responsible for Christian and myself, but I believed it was because he was older and preferred not to leave his daytime television— he loved his soap operas. This extension of responsibility and freedom gave me a chance to wander a little further away from home and interact with the other kids in the community.

I spent most of my time with one boy. His name was Rashawn. He was thirteen and didn't live in the neighborhood but would stop by every day to talk about tv shows or to ask what America was like. Mostly, we talked about video games, and eventually he began inviting me over to play. My granddad didn't like him and told me to stay away from him, but I believed we could be good friends. The day I met the rest of his friend group, he introduced me as "Jay." No one had ever called me that, but I liked it. It was the first time since Andrew had left that I felt like I belonged.

Not uncommon during summers in Jamaica were the heavy rains and subsequent blackouts. One night, following a day of torrential down-pour, the power went out in the neighborhood. The world became as dark as the sky above us, illuminated by the headlights of passing cars or the flickering candlelight of the neighbors navigating their homes. From the enclosed porch, I could hear my friends laughing and yelling, wanting to join them but ordered not to go outside by my grandfather.

"Whoever is in, is in, and whoever is out, better find somewhere else to sleep," my grandfather joked as he placed the locks on the door.

"Goodnight, granddad," I laughed.

"Goodnight. Don't stay out here too late." I didn't turn to look at him but could feel the faint warmth of the candle fade as he departed. The house was quiet, and the longer I lingered, staring into the darkness, the more the screams and laughs took shape.

As I sat there, I thought back to the first time I'd stayed at Grandma Junie's. It was the first time I had experienced being in complete darkness. That night, the stars were so dim the boundary between us and the sky disappeared. I confided in her it was frightening to be in such an open space, and she nodded in agreement. "Boxes are comfortable," she responded, "and existing outside of them can be scary." She then grasped my hand and told me to close my eyes, saying, "But let yourself be, and you'll find freedom." I didn't understand what she meant, but I trusted her. Eyes closed, I felt the night sky lift me into its palm to kiss the stars—dissolving into the infinite blackness, not to be reconstructed until God once again separated the light from the dark.

"Jay!" Rashawn called, "Jay!"

"You scared me," I said, holding my heart in my hand. "I was about to go to sleep."

"Come outside."

"I can't. My granddad said not to."

"Is he sleep?"

"Yeah."

"Then he won't find out." His bright smile floated in the darkness. "Hurry up, too; we're about to play manhunt."

There was a sinking feeling in my stomach, but the fear of missing out overrode whatever consequences could come from disobeying my granddad. Besides, Rashawn was right; he was asleep. How would he find out?

"Ok," I said, which made his detached smile grow wider. "Wait here. I have to go get the key." I slid into the living room, feeling my way around the space until I found the bookshelf where the keys were kept. I clenched them tightly in my hands to prevent them from jingling and then slipped into the streets.

"Sky blue, sky blue, everyone's out except... for... you," Rashawn said.

"I was just it!" one boy said. I hadn't met him before. Looking around at the others, I realized Rashawn was the only familiar face, and it made me uneasy. The house was just a few feet away. I could have gone home, but then the game started.

"Count to fifty," Rashawn responded.

The boy began counting: "One... two... three... five... ten..."

Adrenaline and familiarity directed my footsteps, so I followed Rashawn.

"You're skipping numbers!" Rashawn yelled; his echoing voice made it hard to place where we were.

"You didn't say I couldn't count by fives," the boy laughed and then continued, "fifteen... twenty."

Rashawn crouched down behind a low wall and became invisible in the shadows. I squatted down next to him, and my hand caressed his as I felt around in the darkness. He pulled his hand away and pushed me. "Why are you following me?"

"... twenty-five... thirty..."

"Stop cheating!" someone shouted.

The boy groaned, "... thirty-one... thirty-two... thirty-three..."

Embarrassed and out of time, I ran in circles until hiding behind a parked car.

Panic subsided and shame set in. Warm tears streamed down my face, but I quickly wiped them away. I wished I had just gone to bed but found comfort in the fact that the game would soon be over.

"… forty-eight… forty-nine… fifty! Ready or not, here I come!"

When the game ended, everyone regrouped at the large tree on the corner. I started home, but Rashawn begged me to stay for one more round. Another boy I didn't know was the last to be found, so he had to choose the next person to be it. "Spit, spit, spit, you are not it. Take your foot out. Spit, spit, spit, you are not it. Foot. Spit, spit, spit, you are not it. Spit, spit—"

"Wait, let's play catch-a-girl, freak-a-girl," Rashawn interrupted. The guys clamored in excitement as I looked around in bewilderment and the girls exchanged coy looks. "Come on," Rashawn pleaded. They didn't respond, only reciprocated his smile, which was answer enough.

"What's that?" I asked. The question was met with snickers from the boys.

"You're about to find out," Rashawn said. "Go hide, and we'll start counting." The girls squealed as they ran away in a clump. "When you find them, bring them back here," he instructed, looking at me.

We counted and then sought them out. The guys went together, but I ventured off alone. I had never played this game before, but I knew I didn't want to find anyone. As I wandered around in the dark, I decided not to wait until the game was over and just go home. Although I was initially happy that Rashawn had invited me out to join, his sudden dismissal of me left me reeling and feeling isolated. I thought I had found in him what I had found in Andrew, but it was clear now what I had with Andrew was special. He was more than a fixture; he was my best friend. Yet I had thrown our friendship away.

On my way home, it became apparent I had gone the wrong way as I turned into the alley where Rashawn had hidden. Tucked behind the low wall was one of the girls and seeing her made my heart drop. She emerged from the shadows, discarding the darkness like a bathrobe as she stepped into the moonlight. Before I could tell her, she could keep hiding and I wouldn't say anything, she grabbed my hand and led us back to the meeting spot.

"You found someone!" Rashawn shouted.

"I have to go now, though." I wiped my sweaty palms on my cargo shorts. The girls stood in a line to face us, shoulder-to-shoulder and rigid, as if awaiting orders from a captain.

"Hold on." Rashawn placed his hand on the back of my neck. "We're almost done. You two," he said to one of the boys, who stepped forward to claim his prize. The girl took two meandering steps toward him and then placed a kiss on his cheek. The boy grabbed her hand and told her to stop playing, to which she rolled her eyes and then gave him a kiss on the lips. Rashawn must have felt me tense up, because he gripped me tighter to prevent me from running away. "Go ahead," he said to one girl, who didn't move but gestured for the boy to come to her. Without hesitation, she kissed him and then pushed him away. Rashawn kissed a girl and said, "One person left."

"I have to get back in the house," I said as the girl I found took a step towards me. I placed my hand on Rashawn's and tried to pry it off my neck. With no success, I grabbed one of his fingers and tried to wrest them off, one-by-one, but his hold only tightened, his fingernails digging into me. "Let me go! Let me go!" I thrashed under his iron grip while the others watched in silence. The moonlight illuminated their faces to show nothing but blank stares. Rashawn's nails sunk into my skin, as if to pierce it, and I felt at any moment I would feel blood dripping down my neck. With all my strength, I gave one last tug: "LET… ME… GO!" Rashawn let go and I went tumbling to the ground.

My heart was pounding. Once again, I found myself with bloodied hands, but where before dull pebbles had pro-voked drops of blood just below the skin, sharp rocks and bits of broken glass now drew blood, and Andrew wouldn't be coming this time to check if I were ok.

"Batty bwoy," Rashawn declared.

"'Fraid of girls," one boy laughed. Then, Rashawn. Then, a girl. And then what sounded like all of them. I watched as crimson lines striped my hands and then changed form, turning into drops that pelted the ground.

There was no ambiguity this time. If I hadn't known what "gay" meant then, I knew what "batty bwoy" meant and understood the relationship between the two and the violence behind them both. *It's not fair.* The words came back to me and with clearer meaning. I knew what "it" was now. "It" was the fact that there were sharper things in life than rocks and glass. "It" was the truth that sticks and stones do break bones and the lie that words could never hurt me, when in fact they could hurt and often killed. There were sharper things in life, and "it" had carved out the people I needed most, leaving only their silhouettes for comfort.

I picked myself up off the ground and ran home.

"Leave him alone," someone said. I didn't stop to look back and would wonder whether anyone had actually spoken, whether their faces returned to blank masks and their bodies retreated into the darkness.

Placing the keys back where I found them, I sank into the couch and wiped the tears from my eyes. *I'm a big boy. I'm a big boy. Big boys don't cry. I'm… I'm a man. I'm a man. Men don't cry. I'm a man. Men don't cry.* These thoughts replaced my old mantra. Yes, "it" wasn't fair, but this mantra provided no solutions for dealing with such callous knowledge. *I'm a man.* This mantra was practical. A man was something tangible, something actionable: men didn't cry, men didn't hug, men didn't hold hands, men didn't play house with other men, men ridiculed, men kissed girls, men weren't soft, men were hard like sticks and stones, men weren't named "Jacob," men were named "Rashawn," men were named "Jay."

A hand landed on my shoulder. I looked up to see my granddad standing over me.

"Jacob, why are you still up?"

"I…" I wanted to tell him what happened. But as I started to, I thought about how I wasn't supposed to hang out with Rashawn, let alone go outside during the blackout, so I lied. Men lied to protect others from the truth. "I miss my mom." The sentence began as a lie, but after I had spoken the words, nothing in that moment was truer.

"Come on, let's go to bed." He helped me off the couch and escorted me to my room. "You can call your mom in the morning, and you'll see her in a few more days. Go to sleep now, ok?"

"Ok," I parroted.

Through the window drifted the smoky smell of burning trash, and I heard the voice of Grandma Junie whisper, "Tears will help to wash the dirt off." I picked the small bits of glass out of my hands and smeared the blood on my pillow. "Men don't cry, Grandma Junie," I responded into the implacable darkness.

CHAPTER 9

The end of summer arrived, and school would start on Monday. Some weeks had passed since the night with Rashawn and the others, and while I tried my best to bury memories of that scene, I had this feeling burrowed within me I couldn't fish out. It had been the first time I had truly felt "fear," but it was a different type of fear, one that stemmed from a lack of control. Grandma Junie had said that my mom carried a sadness in her heart that made her afraid for us. After that night, I understood what Grandma Junie meant, and I understood the helplessness my mom felt.

I had managed to push Andrew out of my mind. However, with school around the corner, his absence became notable. Andrew and I had a "first day of school" tradition, and this would be the first year since we had met it wouldn't happen. Our tradition included a fervent retelling of our summer over a spaghetti dinner at our stump, impassioned declarations of how much we missed each other, a hug when the teachers weren't looking, and a souvenir exchange. The prior year, he had given me a brown leather necklace with a silver charm that clung to the thin strap like an autumn leaf holding onto a branch. I had thrown it away during the summer when I stopped hoping for his return. Absentmindedly, I had bought a twine bracelet with the words "one love" attached to it for our exchange this year. I still missed him. But after the night with Rashawn, more than anything, I hated him. He left me by myself, and for that I had resolved never to forgive him, even if forgetting him proved to be difficult.

"Hey, Remy," I said as I entered the shop, "how many do you have?"

"Wassup, Jacob. I have one more, then you're next," he answered.

At 11:30 AM, the shop had only been open for thirty minutes but was already full. I sat in a chair close to the window. Next to me, a teenage boy, who looked to be fourteen or fifteen, slouched deep into his seat with his legs wide open. With his fingers, he twisted a tiny section of his hair into a coil, unraveled it, and then twisted it again. In small movements, I shifted in my chair to match his posture. As I slid into my seat, I could hear my mom's austere voice saying, "fix yourself in the chair and close up your legs," but she wasn't there, so I slid deeper into my seat until he and I were mirror images.

It was my first time being allowed to get a haircut on my own, and her absence was noted. Under my mom's watchful eye, everyone sat up straight with their legs together and spoke in hushed whispers like students cheating on a test—loud enough to hear each other but always softer than the silky R&B silhouettes whose melodies meshed like various shades of black. When she was around, she was everyone's teacher, caretaker, mom, aunt, sister, without ever saying anything. There was an air of decorum for she who represented the most vulnerable part of ourselves; for she whom we would willingly lay down our lives but withheld expressions of love that weren't wrapped in our willingness to enact violence on her behalf; for she who brought us into the world, however, in attempting to shelter us from it, unveiled its darkest parts.

The morning crept into afternoon, and outside, life picked up.

"Hurry the fuck up," a young woman yelled to the boy in tow as she walked past the window with a baby on her hip.

Sashaying past the trailing child, a group of girls with mango water ices passed into view and then disappeared. Muffled screams, then laughter. The girls doubled back, a group of boys in pursuit with water guns.

The transparent glass between us muted their world.

Mine muted too, but they weren't checking for me.

A vicarious moment teeming with the last breaths of summer proved just as ephemeral when a homeless man entered the scene. With supplicant hands and rheumy eyes, he approached them.

"Eww, he stank!" a girl yelled, pinching her nose.

"Wash up, old head." One boy sprayed the man with his water gun.

The man closed his eyes as the water hit his face. For a moment, I thought I saw a smile, as if he were remembering summers as a child where you had to wash the smell of "outside" off before sitting down for dinner. When he opened them, his toothless mouth formed insults that cascaded limply onto the pavement, soon to be trampled by those who would later step over him on the street.

I felt bad for him but couldn't help but wonder what he had done to deserve this. I shook my head at the thought and turned away from the window.

The bells on the door clanged, but it wasn't the sound that drew everyone's attention. I wondered again how he had gotten here. In school, they taught us there existed only good and evil, right and wrong, and one's life was an outcome of which one they chose. Was this God's punishment for having done something wrong? Or was this a test of faith, where if he passed, there existed blessings on the other side? I prayed for the latter, convinced it was the only thing I could do for him.

His sordid stench permeated the shop and everyone tried their best to ignore it, but there were signs: conversations continued but slowed and contorted as if his smell were bending time and space, faces crumpled like Spiderman paper, and Terry, who was mid-bite, put the lid back on his food; still, everyone averted their eyes, deciding that the polite thing was to not acknowledge his humanity rather than for him to see the pity or disgust on their faces. He shuffled to the far end of the shop, where his silent solicitations fell on uninterested ears, and then turned to make his way back to the door.

His head whipped around as if some built-up tension in his neck had released, and we locked eyes. I quickly turned my gaze to the black-and-white checkered tiles but real-ized it was too late when his tattered shoes came into my view. He stopped in front of me and whispered, "Foo." If my mom had been present, she would have told me not to stare. "Foo," he said again, this time holding his stomach. *Food* was the word he attempted to say. I fiddled with the ten-dollar bill in my pocket to check that it was still there. If my mom had been present, she would have gone to the papi store across the street to buy him a soft pretzel—but she would never have given him money. Standing over me, I couldn't avoid his stench, which demanded my attention. It reached out and held my face in its hands, forcing me to bear witness to the man: my eyes traced his body up from his tattered shoes, past his holey pants, past his tank top smeared with black and brown that showed evidence of once being white, past the scarring and bruises on his forearms, past the cracked lips and runny nose, until I once again was looking into his eyes. "Foo," he said, making one final plea. I crunched the bill in my hand, the ten-dollar bill that would make me into a man. I enclosed it in a fist and told him I couldn't help.

Devon turned up the volume on the radio to drown out the silence that had descended with the homeless man's departure.

"That was 'Rock the Boat' by Aaliyah. You already know what it is. It's the five-year anniversary of baby girl's passing, so we're doing an Aaliyah takeover. Let us know what you wanna hear. Call 215—"

"Turn that sweet shit off," Terry grumbled. "They been

playin' the same music all mornin'."

"Watch your mouth. There won't be any Aaliyah slander in here," Rock said.

"What's wrong with you?" AJ turned off her clippers.

"Man, that old head fucked my stomach up," Terry replied. They laughed. Remy smirked as he listened to the conversation but focused on the head he was cutting.

"Watch all that cussin' in here," Devon said, brushing hair off the chair and gesturing for a boy to come sit. "Shit, if I knew that's all it took to get you to stop that loud ass chewin', I would've walked his ass up in here a long time ago." Devon wrapped the cape around the boy, whose dad signaled for Devon to cut it all off.

"Yeah, you was fuckin' that jawn up," Rock added.

"What I just say about the cussin'?" Devon asked.

"You just said 'shit,'" Terry jumped in.

"And whose shop is it?" Devon lobbed off a chunk of hair and then turned off his clippers. "The only mother-fucker that's gon' be cussin' is me." He turned his clippers back on.

Terry and Rock looked at each other. "Mannnn, shut your old ass up," Terry said.

"Just be talkin'." Rock said, laughing.

Terry took the lid off his food and took a bite out of his cheesesteak. The barbershop was a sacred place, and these were the gatekeepers of its teachings.

Devon was the owner of the shop and the oldest. He rarely cut hair anymore—preferring to handle the day-to-day management of the shop—but refused to rent his chair because for holidays and the back-to-school weekend, he offered free haircuts to kids under ten. Terry, his son, was an aspiring comedian and could be found eating a cheesesteak platter regardless of the time of day. He wasn't a barber but helped Devon with the shop some Saturdays. Rock, whose real name was "Antoine," had received the nickname from his older brothers because of a) the shape of his head or b) his stubbornness. He refused to confirm which was true, so two camps had developed around the theories. On slow days, heated debates sometimes erupted between the two sides.

"Rocks don't have any particular shape, so how does that even make sense?"

"Have you ever met a stubborn rock, dickhead?"

"Are you dumb?! It's a figure of speech!"

I had once asked Rock which was correct, and he told me neither. "Rock" was short for his middle name, "Raquel," which was his grandma's name. He told me to keep it a secret. Then there was AJ. She was the youngest and the only female barber. Her hair, cut short and dyed red, always had an intricate pattern cut into it, and her nails were long except on her middle and index fingers. She wore baggy clothes that made her look like a backup dancer, but you could tell that she was small underneath. Last, there was Remington, known as just "Remy."

Remy was the most popular with the neighborhood kids because they found him relatable. He had grown up a few blocks from the barbershop, so he knew the hood and how it worked. He had done some time in prison—for what, no one knew—but Remy always summarized the reason as, "I was just in the wrong place at the wrong time." If uttered by anyone else, this would have seemed as if they were holding themselves blameless. But coming from Remy, his autonomy was amplified. "You don't need to know what I did to get there, just know that I did it. It was my choice. They were my choices." According to Remy, life was just a series of options—to which he would admit he had not always chosen the best one—and all it took was solid intuition to discern which was the right one, an intuition that many of the neighborhood boys sought from him.

In one fluid movement, Remy removed the black cape from his customer with a fluttering sound like a flock of pigeons taking off. He dapped up the young man, sending him back into the world with a, "be safe, stay out of trouble," and gestured for me to get in the chair, while he stepped out outside to smoke a cigarette.

As I waited for him to return, I scanned the shop, taking care not to linger on anyone for too long, until my focus anchored on the haircut guide posted on the wall. Number fifteen on the guide was a haircut a shade above being bald and included a shape-up. It also was the style my mom always picked for me. Her reasoning was less upkeep, while preventing her from having to worry about how I looked if I didn't brush my hair, given I was still an age where my actions and outward appearance reflected on her.

I studied the haircut guide to no end, having already decided on my haircut weeks ago. It was exciting to know what happened next would be my choice. This was my first sense of autonomy, and it was bittersweet with the taste of adulthood. This moment, I had decided, would be *my* rite of passage into manhood. I was ten, and I was ready to accept that I was now a man.

Remy came back inside and carried the smell of smoke with him. He picked up the clippers to clean them and asked, "What we doin' today?"

Cool spritzes of clippercide landed on my neck as I recited the haircut once more in my head, checking the cadence and reminding myself to deepen my voice. I took a deep breath.

"Hi—."

"Yo!" Remy exclaimed, putting the clippers down to greet the group of teenagers that entered the shop. "Is that who I think it is?!"

"What's good, Remy?"

"Man, it's been a minute since I saw you! Gotta be like a year or two. How you been, 'Mir? I thought y'all moved out to Sharon Hill. What you doin' back around here?"

"I been busy, man, tryin' to stay out the way for real. That's why I don't be down here too often. But you know Trey just came home, right?" Remy nodded. "Yeah, I came down to say wassup." He surveyed the shop and then continued, "How many you got? I'm tryin' get a shape-up right quick."

"I'm about to cut young boul, then I got two more."

"Damn, you can't hook me up?" He side-stepped Remy and stood over me. "Young boul, you good if he cut me first?" His friends watched with blank faces, making his sneer feel more intense like a singular black dot pressed against white paper, and I remembered that night in Jamaica.

"Uhm… sure." I shifted to get out of the seat, but Remy placed his hand on my shoulder.

"Amir, leave him alone," Remy said, laughing.

"He said I can go next," he grinned, and then he looked at me, "I'm fuckin' with you, young boul." He took my hand in his and gave it a firm shake. My fear melted into something else that fluttered in my stomach—he was handsome.

"So, how's your mom doin'?" Remy asked, wrapping the cape around me in a rote manner.

"She's good. She be trippin,' though. Why the other day she asked me how come I ain't bring no jawns home to meet her yet and then asked if I was gay? I had to tell her to stop fuckin' playin' with me. Had to pull my phone out to show her all the bitches I'm talkin' to."

"Toya don't play with that gay shit," Remy said, "I don't really play that shit either, though. For real." He got silent, then, as if compelled, he put down the clippers and continued, "like I'm cool with everybody and mind my business, but that faggot shit not natural."

The word rang out like a gunshot, but no one flinched. When I was younger, having a flurry of shots wake me from my sleep would send my heart racing, and once the panic dissipated, dread would set in as I thought about who was on the other side of the barrel. As I got older, however, I became accustomed to both the sound and the action. I thought of the shots as things that existed in and of themselves like thunder, no flash, just the rumbling afterwards that let you know the sky was breaking. My face didn't show it, but the fluttering—which erupted in my stomach when Amir took my hand into his—twisted itself into the dread that I would feel when I was younger.

"Am I lyin'?" he asked no one specifically. Amir and his friends shook their heads in agreement. A few others in the shop did as well, but most everyone remained still. He turned the clippers on again, and the sound poured into my ears; it was incessant and seemed to intensify inversely to the silence that had overtaken the laughter. Were the clippers always this loud? He turned them off and then continued, "I just don't understand, man, it's so many women out here." He walked over to Amir and dapped him up. "It's so many bitches out here, you feel me?" He walked back to his chair. "It's so much pussy out here, right, AJ?" She looked at him and smirked, but I recognized it wasn't genuine: this was the smile you made when being teased; the smile you made to show that you belonged, even if existing only as a joke.

"That's enough," Devon said.

"I'm joking, right, AJ?" Remy smiled. The mood in the shop elevated a bit, but just like in the moments after thunder, everyone was still on edge, waiting to see if the sky would crumble again.

She didn't look at him, only smiled through her clenched jaw as she continued to cut her customer and replied, "Right." Soft chatter returned as the storm passed.

Right.

"I'll be back, Remy," Amir announced. He reached out for a handshake and his hand lingered for a moment. Remy studied him as though he would never see him again and needed a few seconds to preserve his memory.

"Ard, be safe out there, man," Remy pulled him in for a hug and patted him on the back, "and tell your mom I said 'hi.'"

Amir nodded and then left with his friends.

"Alright." Remy spun my chair around to face the mirror. "What we doin' today?"

"High fade on the sides and back, don't touch the top."

"No mom today?"

"Nope, she said I was old enough to come by myself."

"Ok, big man!" he said, going over the back of my neck again and again with the trimmers. The words sounded different coming from him, like they were true as opposed to something to be conjured as when my mom uttered them. "You excited for the first day of school?"

"I am…" I wondered whether to tell him the truth. I suddenly felt like I didn't know who he was.

"You don't sound like it. Shoot, when I was younger, I couldn't sleep the whole weekend leadin' up to the first day back to school. Would have my 'fit laid out on the bed from Friday. And with a fresh haircut like you're gettin'? Man." He laughed that familiar laugh, and I laughed too.

"I am excited. But my best friend, Andrew, switched schools, so I'll have to figure out who I'm going to hang out with."

"I know how that goes. When I was a little bit older than you, my best friend from around the way moved to New York to live with family after his dad got killed." He turned off the clippers and spoke to my reflection in the mirror. "Man, we used to do everything together. He was like my brother. And when he moved, we lost touch. It messed me up a little bit, to tell you the truth. Like I said, we did everything together, so when he left, it was like, ard, cool, where does that leave me? Felt a little lost." He turned the clippers back on and resumed cutting.

"So, what did you do?"

"I got some new friends. They were a lot different from my homie, but they were cool. Started hangin' around them more, and eventually I just stopped thinkin' about boul. This the first time I've talked about him in years. Can't even remember his name right now."

"Are you still friends with them?"

"One or two. But the rest moved away, got locked up, I lost touch, or they dead."

"You ever thought about moving?"

"Of course." He pulled out the straight razor and started on my hairline. "Me and boul used to talk about moving to Boston to play for the Celtics." Remy laughed. "That's back when they were on a decent championship run. We were good too. Couldn't nobody touch us on the court. Anyway, when I started hangin' out with the other guys, I stopped playin' and practicin' as much. Got wrapped up in dumb stuff. They sat me down for a few years, learned how to cut while I was locked up, then came back here."

"Do you wish you left before all that happened?"

"I used to. But it's no point in thinkin' like that; you can't turn back time. I could have left when I got out. I could still leave now—that's actually why I started cuttin' hair. Because you can be a barber anywhere—but this my hood. Some of these cats around here are just so miserable that they take it out on other people. That's why the city like this. They right and wrong is fucked up, and they friends gassin' 'em up. The blind leadin' the blind. The blind killin' the blind. The blind killin' themselves. So, nah, no regrets for comin' or stayin'. Here, I can give you young bouls game, keep y'all out of trouble."

"Not me," I smiled.

"I know. You one of the smart ones," he spun the chair around to face the mirror, "plus your mom don't play." He gave me a handheld mirror to check the back. "What we think?" I nodded in approval. "Jeremiah! That was his name!"

"Huh?"

"My homie's name… it just came back to me. Damn." His eyes became sad. He stared at nothing as he removed the cape from around me—it was the same absent stare my mom had while she did the dishes, right before the forced smile that came when she caught me watching. "You're all set, Jacob," he said, smiling. "The girls are gonna be all over you on Monday!"

I observed the new me once more in the mirror and then handed him my ten bucks. "Thanks. And it's just 'Jay.'"

CHAPTER 10

The usually black-and-white checkered floor was a uniform black. As I looked around, I realized the entire shop was engulfed in darkness: the paint on the walls peeled, revealing deeper hues of black; while the mirrors, even with the absence of light, reflected my face. Seated in Remy's chair and as hard as I tried, I couldn't get up. The shop was full of people, but in my panic, I hadn't noticed that everyone was frozen. Devon, with his left hand outstretched, was calling for a crying boy to let go of his mother and get in the chair. Terry, to the right of him, was lifting the last bite of his cheesesteak to his bearded mouth. Rock and Remy were nowhere to be found, but AJ seemed to be in the process of clawing her way out of the wall that had swallowed her.

The mood of the dream shifted. I smiled at the outcome of the haircut. "Looks good," I heard myself say to Remy, who appeared out of nowhere and in a frozen state like everyone else. My curls cascaded upwards like smoke from a chimney until they touched the ceiling. A breeze from the door wafted my hair back to its original height, and I turned to see Amir enter. The light from outside couldn't penetrate the darkness, so I couldn't see his face, but I knew it was him. He stood in front of me and then stretched out his right hand. "I'm just fuckin' with you, young boul," he said, taking my hand. His touch injected summer directly into my arm and chest, setting fire to my lungs. "I'm fuckin' with you, young boul," he repeated as our faces got closer. I couldn't tell whether he was pulling me in, or I him, but there was no resistance on either part. My heart pumped inflamed blood through my body—pulsating into my budding erection until I was fully hard—and then stopped altogether. With my left hand, I grabbed his belt buckle. And then, like a symphony restarting after a movement, life was put in motion. The barbershop came alive with a crescendo of chatter. My heart began to pump again. Amir was gone. Sunlight poured through the thin lace curtains and woke me up. I changed my underwear, pushing the stained pair to the bottom of the hamper and tried to get some more sleep before the alarm went off.

I flipped the pillow over every few minutes for the brief moments of coolness and prayed for a breeze to find its way through the window. It was hot, but the heat wasn't the cause of my restlessness. I was always anxious about the first day of school. But now, unable to make sense of what had happened, I tossed and turned—feeling shameful for the cause of the sticky mess and even more so because it felt good. I closed my eyes and hoped Amir would be there waiting.

I didn't notice I had fallen asleep until I woke up to the blaring alarm clock. Amir wasn't in my dreams, but thinking of his previous appearance, I decided I should get rid of the evidence before my mom saw it. I pulled the underwear from the bottom of the hamper, rinsed them in the bathroom sink and hung them to dry on the shower rod, and then hopped in the shower.

The warm water hit my head with a soft patter. I listened to the "thumps" that were only audible when I shut my eyes as though shutting them trapped the sounds inside. I closed my eyes and kept them shut, allowing the echoing thumps to drown out thoughts of him, but then the echoes turned into whispers of his name—Amir. The thumps became rhythmic like drumming and sent a tingling sensation down my spine that traced the water trickling down my body. My mind anchored on his smile, his voice, his touch, so much so it was like he was there with me. I felt myself getting hard, so I squeezed my eyes tighter to push him away, but the drumbeat only propelled him closer. In harmony with my heartbeat, the drums intensified and pulsed thoughts of him to my throbbing erection. Every thought devolved into him, so I turned up the temperature of the water to focus my attention elsewhere. Steam enveloped the bathroom as the hot water clawed at my skin—I winced at the pain, but it was working.

"GET OUT OF THE BATHROOM!" Christian yelled from the other side of the door.

"I'M GETTING OUT NOW!"

Blood raced from my erection to the areas of my body that felt like they would blister at any moment.

"GET OUT!"

Despite the initial anxiety, I was looking forward to the first day of school and what it represented. For one, it returned structure to my life. Summer was fun—marked by boundless days that blended one into the other, making weekends insignificant and leaving nothing to be longed for—but got old fast. That summer especially had brought a wave of new experiences, so the first day of school would also be a much-needed break from the confusion and wayward thoughts. The first day of school meant a chance to start fresh—a renaissance.

Since kindergarten, I had been attending St. Luke's Catholic School and always defined myself by my relationship to someone else. Before he left, people knew me as Andrew's best friend, and before that, I was Laila's husband. Now I was returning to school with neither of them and subject to the direction of the wind like a kite with no string. I was excited to define myself, to be my own person. Though having been in a fantasy world with Andrew, I was unsure of how I would relate to the other students, who organized themselves by whose parents drove the latest Lexus or by how far they were in their journey through Catholicism.

Although there was a public school around the corner, my mom insisted that Christian and I go to private school—no matter the cost, no matter the religious denomination—because she wanted us to get a "good education." While I never looked forward to mass each month, I liked St. Luke's: the campus, the teachers, the food, and even the uniforms; but mass bored me. It was so structured and precise that it made me believe God was only accessible through measured practice. And the music was so mono-tone, as though God could only hear one or two notes, that the droning often lulled me to sleep. I often got into trouble for falling asleep during mass until Andrew came along, and we would take turns waking each other up. It would be an adjustment without Andrew, but I hoped that, like Remy and his friend, he would slip from memory.

That year, three new students enrolled. Alex, Travis, and Malcolm had transferred to St. Luke's from another Catholic school in the diocese, which closed because of lack of enrollment. It was unclear what had precipitated the drop in enrollment. Some speculated it was the rising cost of tuition; others in hushed tones spoke of a scandal; either way, St. Luke's readily accepted any new students if they could pay tuition. Any other considerations were secondary and reviewed less rigorously. Mrs. Graves asked them to introduce themselves, so they lined up at the front of the room. Two of them stood shoulder-to-shoulder and laughed about which one of them should go first, while the third leaned on Mrs. Graves' desk, an action that was rep-rimanded by Mrs. Graves with throat clearing and adjust-ment of her glasses.

"Ok, gentlemen, please tell us your first and last names, your age, and a fun fact or hobby that you enjoy," she enun-ciated every syllable and held the volume of her voice steady somewhere between speaking and yelling. The effect was her voice carried but did not undulate. There were no curvatures to her words, as if shaped with a straightedge before leaving her mouth.

The one off to the side cleared his throat and spoke. "Hi, everyone, I'm Malcolm Brixton." His voice was soft and had a lilt that gave his words a rhythmic cadence. "I'm nine years old, and I like video games, comic books, and singing."

The boy in the middle snickered, eliciting a response from Mrs. Graves, who had a disdain for rudeness.

"Young man, you clearly have something to say. Why don't you go next? Thank you, Malcolm."

"No problem." He stepped forward and cleared his throat playfully, hacking and coughing to clear the fake blockage, which made the class laugh, me included, but not Mrs. Graves, who looked displeased.

"Wassup, my name Alex Smalls. I turned ten a few weeks ago… um, what else was I supposed to say?" The class laughed. "Oh, I remember," he said as he flashed a smile at Mrs. Graves, "I like to play basketball and football, and I like telling jokes."

"Oh, can you tell us one?" a girl next to me blurted out. Alex looked to Mrs. Graves, who simply responded, "You may." Alex smiled at the girl, who blushed. He glanced briefly at me, and I felt the same fluttering that I'd felt with Amir.

"Ok." He cleared his throat again and then slipped his hand into his armpit. He flapped his arm like a bird taking flight, and the result was a farting sound. The class broke into boisterous laughter.

"Alright, that's enough. Thank you, Mr. Smalls. Young man, you're next," she said to the last boy, "please be brief."

The third boy stepped forward. "I'm Travis Collins, and I'm ten. Uhhh, what do I like to do?" he asked himself, looking up at the ceiling and tapping his foot to a rhythm that lived inside his head. The class laughed, and having earned that laughter, he continued. "I like to play basketball and football too. I also like telling jokes, but unlike Alex, I'm actually funny." Alex gave him a light push as he laughed along with the class. Without waiting for permission from Mrs. Graves, Travis told his joke: "Yo momma so dumb, she thought a quarterback was a refund."

Mrs. Graves, who was not amused, took two strides to the front of the room. "Thank you, gentlemen, you may take your seats." Malcolm found a seat by Mrs. Graves's desk. Travis and Alex attempted to sit next to each other in the back of the room, but Mrs. Graves ordered them to separate. So Travis remained in the back corner, while Alex took a vacant seat next to me. Many of the girls turned around to look at him and quickly turned away, giggling, when he glanced at them. They had only been here an hour and were already the funniest and most popular kids in class—I wanted that too.

"Your attention, class, please take out your religion textbooks and turn to page five. Please take out your religion workbooks and turn to page three." Inevitably, someone's hand shot up to ask her to repeat the instructions, but she turned her back to the room and wrote the directions on the chalkboard. The hand lowered. "Read pages five to twelve of the textbook and then complete the exercises on pages three and four in the workbook. Is that understood?"

"Yes, Mrs. Graves," the class responded in unison.

The lesson was a review of the Seven Sacraments of the Catholic Church, starting with baptism. The text started with the story of Adam and Eve eating the forbidden fruit and being kicked out of Eden. It went on to explain that all people, as descendants of Adam and Eve, were born with "original sin," which could only be washed away by the Sacrament of Baptism. While some viewed parts of the Bible allegorically, people treated baptism literally; the priest either sprinkled water on the participant's forehead or fully submerged them, making them a new person.

There was something appealing about being reborn as a new person. While I had elevated myself to the status of "man" and was now "Jay," it was harder than I thought to shed the skin of "Jacob." His memories were still mine. His feelings were still mine. His thoughts were still mine. But here was a solution: through baptism, the old me would be dead to the world. I reached the end of the reading, which revealed that many Christians were publicly baptized as babies and that it was an induction into the Church and, by proxy, God's grace.

"Yo, what's your name?" Alex leaned over and whispered into my ear.

"I'm Jac—, Jay. I'm Jay."

"Did you finish the exercises?"

"Yeah, I just finished the last question." The question read: "Were you baptized as a child? Ask your family, and, if 'yes,' ask them to describe the experience." I was unsure of whether I had been, so I answered, "yes," and gave a description of what I thought the event was like. I would later ask my mom that day had I been baptized, to which she responded that I had been "christened," which was a sort of "dry" baptism, a soft initiation into the Church.

"Lemme see that jawn." His breath made the hair on my neck stand up and excited the flutters in my stomach.

"Mrs. Graves, can I go to the bathroom?" My right arm shot up while the other pushed my workbook closer to Alex.

"I don't know, *can* you?" she responded, peering over her glasses in a way that assured me she was seriously asking.

"*May* I go to the bathroom?" I rolled my eyes but made sure she didn't see.

"You may."

In the bathroom, I ran my hands under scalding hot water to distract myself from my growing erection.

"Alex Smalls and Travis Collins, please report to the front office," the school secretary said over the PA.

Malcolm walked in as I resigned my efforts to cleanse myself in the sink. He was short up close, much shorter than the average fourth grader. And his movements were sharp and jittery, like those of a squirrel.

"Malcolm, right?" He nodded. "I'm Jay. I like your watch."

"Thanks." He rolled up his sleeve to reveal the Wolverine band. "Do you like superheroes?"

"I used to," I said and thought of the Spiderman note-book and the shreds of paper with Andrew's number, "but not anymore. You like video games, right?"

"I do. Have you played—"

"Oh! Look who it is," Travis said, he and Alex stopping in the bathroom on their way back to class. "How was your summer, Malcolm?"

"Uhm, it was good."

"That's good! Alex, how was yours?"

"It could've been better. But I spent most of it on punishment because of this snitch."

"Funny, so did I." Travis smiled. "What're we talking about?"

"Video games and superheroes," I responded.

"I love superheroes," Alex added, pushing Malcolm into the corner next to a urinal. Malcolm's eyes darted around the room as fear quieted his movements and cemented his back to the wall. "You like superheroes too, right, Travis?"

"What're you doing?" I asked, questioning out of confusion more so than worry.

"Just make sure no one is coming," Travis responded, turning on the faucets.

Malcolm's flight instinct kicked in, and he peeled himself off the wall, but they pushed him back. Alex covered Malcolm's mouth just as a small cry for help escaped his lips, the plea washed away by the sound of rushing water. Alex was whispering something in Malcolm's ear. I didn't know what, but it made him thrash. Everything was happening so fast that I debated whether it was real. I still had to be dreaming. That was the only explanation for why I couldn't move or speak.

"Who's your favorite superhero, Travis?" Alex asked.

Travis shot a look at me to see if anyone was coming,

to which I unconsciously shook my head, and then he answered, "Bat-man." With each syllable, he punched Malcolm in his stomach. Malcolm crumpled to the floor with a high-pitched squeal that sounded like a teakettle. It made me flinch, but as quickly as it came, it went. Tears flowed down his face. Alex and Travis switched places. Travis knelt on Malcolm and covered his mouth.

"Who's yours?"

"Cap-tain A-mer-i-ca," Alex said, as he pelted Malcolm's body with punches. The thud of every blow was followed by a sharp exhale through Malcolm's nose—each one pierced me like nails, holding me in place while Alex punished him.

Alex paused and walked towards me while Travis held Malcolm in place and spoke into his ear. His body trembled with Travis' words, which shook Malcolm from the inside and echoed off the cavernous walls of his chest until finally escaping. "Faggot."

"What about you, Jay? Who's your favorite superhero?" Alex pulled my arm.

"I—"

"Hurry up before someone comes!" Travis yelled in a hushed voice. If Malcolm had any fight left, I didn't see it as I stood over him. He looked so small. His eyes found mine, and I saw the boy gazing up from the gravel road, hoping for someone to intervene.

"Get off of him," I said, finally finding my voice, "leave him alone!"

"What," Travis responded. I pushed Travis, and he sprang to his feet. "What're you doing?" Travis pushed me and sent me stumbling backwards. I had never gotten into a fight before, but I clenched my fists and prepared for whatever was coming next.

"Someone's coming!" Alex shouted.

"Stay with your boyfriend," Travis sneered and ran out of the bathroom.

"Are you ok?" I asked Malcolm, helping him to his feet. He nodded and then splashed water on his face. Maybe he thought this was a dream too, but his rote movements showed this wasn't the first time. "Should we tell Mrs. Graves?"

"No!" he responded to my reflection in the mirror. "It's fine. I'm ok. It was just a joke." He lifted his shirt to inspect the damage; plum-colored blotches covered his body where he'd begun to bruise.

"You don't look fine. I'm gonna go get the nurse."

He grimaced as he lowered his shirt. "Don't! I'm fine, and I don't need your help." He looked in the mirror and took a deep breath. As he exhaled, a smile masked the pain he was in. I thought of responding, but considering the punishment I had allowed before interceding, I watched Malcolm hobble back to class.

***

"No talking, young man," Mrs. Graves said to Travis, who was whispering to Alex from the other side of the room. He rolled his eyes and shifted in his seat. "Sit still," she ordered.

"I can't. These chairs are so uncomfortable." He stood

up and slapped the plastic chair to demonstrate its hardness. "Can't I just stand, Mrs. G?"

"*Graves*," she said, the "g" so harsh it could've gotten stuck in her throat, "and it's quite evident that you *can* stand, but you *may* not." Before he could respond, Mrs. Graves returned to grading papers, signaling the conversation was over.

Travis grumbled and slid back into his seat. Smuggled in a fake cough, he uttered, "bitch."

"Excuse me?"

"Nothing, Mrs. G." She looked up at him. "Mrs. *Graves*."

I watched the scene play out from the back of the classroom. It was about half-past three, and in another thirty minutes, we would be freed from detention. Despite sitting in the back, I could smell the stale stench of cigarettes radiating from Mrs. Graves every time she exhaled. She tapped her foot and chewed on the cap of her pen while brushing the same strand of hair off her forehead over and over. It was obvious she itched for a smoke break, but with each passing minute, it became clearer she wouldn't make it to four to take it.

Standing up, she swiped the wrinkles from her suede skirt, the color of which reminded me of my rusted bike chain. "I will return promptly," she said, glancing over at Travis. "Remain seated and no talking." Before the last word left her mouth, she was out the door.

"I fucking hate her," Alex said, lifting his head from the desk.

"BITCH!" Travis yelled as loud as he could when he was sure she was gone.

"Chill," Alex said. "You got it?"

"Yeah," Travis reached into his backpack with his eyes glued to the door, "I took it from my brother. He got a couple of these jawns hidden in the back of his closet."

"Won't he notice it's gone?"

Travis continued to fish around his backpack.

"Shit… where is it… nah, he got a bunch of DVDs under his mattress he doesn't know I know about." A big grin teeming with success appeared on his face. I craned my neck to see the cause of his elation. "Here," Travis flung the magazine across the room like a frisbee—the pages flapped in the air as it landed in front of the door.

"Learn to throw," Alex said, leisurely coming out from his desk to get the magazine.

"Hurry up and get it!"

"Chill out," he said as he picked up the magazine and peeked through the window in the door. "I don't think she's coming." He returned to his seat and flipped through the pages in his lap. Alex was too far away for me to see, so I broke the point of my pencil and walked to the front of the room to sharpen it.

"Damn, you nosey as shit," Travis blurted out as I looked over Alex's shoulder.

Alex looked up. "This what you trying to see?" He put the magazine on the desk: in it, there was a woman in a swimsuit eating a fudge pop on the hood of a sports car. He flipped the page, and the same woman was holding the popsicle on her neck, the melted fudge bisecting her bare breasts like a river carving through a canyon. The liquid dripped down her light brown skin and pooled in her belly button, overflowing and collecting in her vagina.

I looked away.

"Why are you showing him? He's gay," Travis said.

"No, I'm not!"

"Yes, you are. You and Malcolm are boyfriends."

"No, we're not!"

"Ho-mo. Fag-got," Travis said in a singsong way, "ho-mo, fag-got, ho-mo, fag-got."

"Ho-mo, fag-got," Alex joined in.

"No, I'm not. Stop. Stop!" Their chorus drowned out my protests until their words consumed my thoughts. The accusations coursed through my body, and I felt my body stiffen as they hardened in my veins. "No, I'm not," I said, clenching my fists so tight that my knuckles could have ripped through the skin.

Travis repeated the refrain but stopped when he saw Alex fall out of his seat. Alex held his stomach and cursed at me, while Travis scrambled across the desks towards me. Without forethought, I hit him. I was unsure of what had come over me, but somehow I knew it was what a man would do. Still trying to process what had happened, I felt Travis' arms wrap around me like a boa constrictor and squeeze. He lifted me as high as he could, about an inch or two off the floor, and then threw me to the ground. Alex continued to groan and cough while Travis and I rolled on the floor, exchanging blows. All at once, we jumped to our feet, straightened the desks, and returned to our seats.

"I will be leaving shortly," Mrs. Graves could be heard saying down the hall. The smell of cigarettes entered the room before she did. "Ok, gentlemen, I am dismissing you early." The clock read 3:55. "Let us not repeat this, shall we?"

"Yes, Mrs. Graves," we replied in unison, breathing deeply to hide our panting.

When we were finally dismissed, Travis' mom was outside waiting for both him and Alex. I exhaled a sigh of relief as they got into the car. Whatever vengeance they wished to enact on me would have to wait until tomorrow. Inhaling, however, my breath caught in my chest, and I took off, sprinting home. Although my mom would be working late again, she always called at 4:00 PM during her break to check in on us. I got halfway home before my lungs felt like they were on fire, and I had to stop to catch my breath. "It's fry time," the Checkers billboard said, the clock reading 4:10. I took my time walking the rest of the way home. If I were already going to be in trouble for getting detention and letting Christian walk home alone, there was no need to rush back. I found a quarter in my pocket, so I stopped into the papi store to get a bag of hot cheese curls.

With punishment from my mom imminent, my mind drifted to the events that had transpired. It was the first day of school, and not only did I not make any new friends, but I had alienated one potential friend and made two new enemies. The whole thing felt like a blur: from watching Malcolm get jumped and hesitating to step in to getting detention because Mrs. Graves thought I was playing paper football with Alex and Travis when the "football" landed on my desk to having to fight them both, it all felt very out of character for me. "Ho-mo, fag-got." They had repeated in the same monotonous notes as the organ at mass. *Faggot.* It was the same word Travis had been whispering to Malcolm as Alex hit him; the same word that racked his body from the inside out. I wasn't sure whether Malcolm was gay or not, but he had seemed normal to me, and this made me feel even worse for how long it had taken me to help—yet now I had a subtle, unfounded disdain for him. Having intervened, Alex and Travis thought I was just like him, but I wasn't. Alex and Travis had shown themselves to be bullies, so why did I still want to be their friend?

A few hours of sunlight remained—still, it was a day where you could tell that even sunset wouldn't bring relief from the heat. Sweat dripped down my neck and pooled where my bookbag met my back. I was a few blocks away from home and was eager for the coolness of indoors. However, the fear of the belt overrode any desire to walk faster. Never mind that my mom wouldn't be home until later. The anticipation was sometimes as painful as the act itself. The front of my shirt clung to chest as sweat ran down my abdomen to the top of my underwear. I wondered if this was what the woman from the magazine had been feeling: so hot and uncomfortable that the only solution was to strip naked and hold a popsicle against her skin. I thought of the melted ice cream sticky against her body, the resulting coolness stiffening her nipples and sweetening her lips.

When Alex had lifted the magazine from his lap to the desk, I glimpsed a bulge, a burgeoning hard-on, and the fluttering I felt in that moment before the name-calling wasn't because of the picture. *Should I have gotten hard from looking at the picture? Why didn't I? Am I normal?* The house came into view, forcing the questions into my subconscious before I could understand what answers to them meant.

"Hi, Jacob," Christian said when I walked into the house, smiling ear-to-ear.

"It's *Jay*," I responded with a straight face and a biting tone. He recoiled. "Did Mom call?"

"Yes."

"And?"

"She asked where you were, but I didn't tell her you got detention. I said that you were in the bathroom… are you mad at me? I didn't tell her."

What a stupid question, I thought to myself, but something prevented me from just answering "no."

"Did you eat?" He nodded. "Did you finish your homework?"

"A lot of it. But I need your help with math."

"You're so dumb. It's the first day of school. How do you need help already?" His eyes teared until they overflowed. I didn't know why I was being so mean. I felt bad, but I also wanted him to fear me like Malcolm feared Alex and Travis. "Stop crying like a little girl. Man up!"

In a small voice, he responded, "Ok, I'm sorry," and wiped his face on his shirt.

I wanted to apologize but doing so would have been an

admission that I had done something wrong. A cold, hard, dense thing burrowed in my stomach, stifling my apology; rather, I blamed Christian for his neediness. Still, I pulled him in for a hug. "Stop crying." I rubbed his back like I used to when the power went out during blackouts. "Go get your homework."

———

"Why did God create Adam and Eve?" Monsignor Pax read the slip of paper aloud and then crumpled it in his hand. "If you take the Bible literally, God created Adam to rule over the land and the animals and created Eve to keep Adam company. However, the leading interpretation is that the story of Adam and Eve is an allegory for the exercise of free will. See, even in the beginning, man wasn't perfect. Given all that he would ever need, man still wanted more. The question is simple, but the answer is layered—God created Adam and Eve and gave them free will to test if they would choose Him."

"But if God knows everything, then didn't He know they wouldn't?" Gabrielle asked with her hand still in the air, only lowering it when Monsignor Pax responded.

"Well," he said, glancing over at Mrs. Graves, "what you have to understand is—"

"Sorry to interrupt, Monsignor, but that's all the time we have for today. Class, what do we say?"

"Thank you, Monsignor Pax."

"Thank you, Monsignor blah blah blah," Alex said to

himself, yet loud enough for me to hear. I looked at him and chuckled. He looked at me with disdain—the look had downgraded from one of murderous rage, so I counted it as a win.

In the weeks following the first day of school, I hoped for his revenge so that we would be even and possibly move forward as friends. Instead, he and Travis pretended I didn't exist, which somehow hurt more than a punch would have. Malcolm also ignored me following the incident in the bathroom. And Christian, after walking home alone for the first time, stopped waiting for me after school. I sometimes trailed behind him as he walked, prohibited from catching up by that cold, hard thing that convinced me it was best he walked alone. When the dreams of Amir also disappeared, it was clear I had been abandoned. Yet I was still haunted by their meaning, which manifested in errant erections whenever I saw a shirtless man on tv, in a more dismissive demeanor towards Christian, and in an increasing desire for control.

"Before Monsignor leaves, can someone tell me which sacrament we just learned about?"

"Oh! Confirmation!" Gabrielle blurted out as if she were a toy and her string had been pulled.

"Correct, thank you, Ms. Grey. And can someone tell me what the sacrament of Confirmation is? Let's let another student have a chance," she said, ignoring Gabrielle's raised hand. "How about you, Mr. Brixton?"

"Uhm," he flipped through his workbook, "uhm."

"Today, please, Mr. Brixton."

"Uhh."

The class laughed.

"Enough."

"It's another rite of initiation into the Church. A public declaration of the understanding between right and wrong and the commitment to do what's right on one's own."

"Thank you, Jacob, but let's give Malcolm a chance next time." I stared at the back of Malcolm's head, waiting for him to turn around to acknowledge that I had saved him this time, but he kept forward. "That is correct. Confirmation is not just a rite, though; it is an acceptance of responsibility for your own spiritual life. Having declared that you understand what is right and what is wrong, you therefore accept the consequences of the choices you make. That said, Monsignor Pax has been impressed with the maturity shown in this class and has decided that, for those who are interested, he will serve as your sponsor, given you attend all the biweekly preparation sessions."

"Thank you, Mrs. Graves. By show of hands, who here is interested in being confirmed?" Half of the class's hands went up, including mine and Malcolm's. "I'm glad to see the enthusiasm. I want to reiterate the serious commitment that this is before God and the Church." Two hands went down. "And also note that, in order to start the Confirmation process, you must already be baptized." Three others went down, including Malcolm's. I looked around at the other hands still in the air; five of us remained. "Ah-men. Given we're heading into the holiday season, sessions will begin in January. We usually do seven or eight sessions, and then the

Confirmation ceremony takes place at a special Mass at the end of the school year. But no need to think about that now. I will relay details to Mrs. Graves when finalized." He closed his eyes and bowed his head, and, without direction, we did the same. He uttered a short prayer and then concluded, "Ah-men. The Lord be with you."

"And also, with you."

CHAPTER 11

The first half of the school year ended how it had begun, with me alone and confused. The Confirmation sessions, though, had started, and I looked forward to each one. Like many of my behavior changes, I couldn't pinpoint what was driving my sudden desire to be confirmed:

Maybe it was just something a Catholic school student did at a certain point;

Maybe it was me grasping for anything that could define who "Jay" was;

Maybe it was because the line between right and wrong was blurring. I had lied about being baptized so I could join the sessions, yet I didn't feel guilty about it; and infrequent dreams of Amir had been replaced by pages of Calvin Klein underwear ads which I stashed under my mattress, inspiring both curiosity and shame.

Maybe it was a mix of these or none at all.

In the sessions, Monsignor Pax encouraged us to ask questions about things we didn't understand. A significant portion focused on the text we were reading that month. In the remaining time, we explored subjects we were often told we were too young to talk about.

"Last one, and then we'll move on to the teaching for this month." Monsignor Pax sat straight up to make himself more visible in the circle. "Yes, Gabrielle?"

Satisfied, her hand lowered. "Can two women or two men get married? My cousin said that they can't, but I don't believe her."

"No." Silence lingered, punctuating the sharpness of his response.

"Why," Teo chimed in.

"To clarify, in some countries, like Canada, where it's recently become legal to do so, they *can*—but they *shouldn't*. The Church does not recognize this type of union. *Holy* Matrimony is a sacrament reserved for a man and a woman. Any relationship outside of this is unnatural and unholy in the eyes of God. As discussed last month, family and marriage are important parts of the community and Church, so we must uphold the standards given us by the Lord."

The thought of two women or two men being married made me uncomfortable. I tried to imagine what this would look like, but the only images I could see were of Andrew and me seated at our stump, which made my discomfort more acute. The lights became brighter, and the colors of the stained glass became more vibrant and intense. The chair became awkward to sit on as every wood molecule became palpable, vibrating beneath me to keep their form. Andrew came to mind for the first time in months, and it made me feel ashamed, like how Adam and Eve must have felt when they realized they were naked. Yet even in my discomfort, I attempted to imagine what life would be like in Canada.

Monsignor Pax read us the story of Cain and Abel and then asked if we had questions. We had none.

"Since there are no questions, we can go right into the social principle for this month, solidarity. As God searched for Abel, he asked Cain where his brother was. What was Cain's response?"

"'Am I my brother's keeper'," Thomas answered.

"That's right. And why did he answer that way?"

"Denial," Teo said.

"Good. What else?"

"Guilt," Renee added.

"He felt guilty. Good. Any other reasons?"

"Fear," I said.

"Good, he feared God's wrath. Now—"

"No," I interjected, "not fear of God's wrath. I think when he killed his brother, he figured he would be caught. Aren't his brother and parents the only other people in the world at this point? So, he already accepted he would be punished. I think he feared the responsibility that was in God's question, like being asked where's your homework, but not knowing you were assigned any in the first place."

"That's an interesting observation, Jay. It's also a good segue into the theme of this principle. God calls us to take care of each other, to love each other, to be *responsible* for each other. All these things are important for a healthy community and, thus, a healthy Church. And, as Jay pointed out, being responsible for another person can be scary, but it's what we're called to do, and we pray for God's strength to do so.

"When asked if we are our brother's keeper, the teaching of the Church tells us that the answer is 'yes.' Close your eyes and think about a time when you were not your brother's keeper. What could you have done differently? Is it possible to be that for the person going forward?"

I closed my eyes.

In the distance, I could see Christian walking. His hands were up in front of him, and he was pretending to steer a car, which made me smile. He didn't appear to be moving fast, so I started running to catch up to him. A voice spoke: "idiot," "stupid," "you're so dumb," and the words fed the cold, hard thing forming in my stomach. With each step, the voice grew louder. "Stop crying like a little girl," "man up!" It was me. The cold, hard thing grew denser, and I felt heavy, like my legs were two marble columns. Still, I kept going, anxious to hear his "beeps" and "vrooms" in this place void of any sound except my voice. "No hugs!" "I don't care if you need help. I don't care about YOU." The cold, hard thing spread throughout my body until, within an inch of pulling Christian into my arms, I was consumed entirely. "I wish you weren't born." My body froze in space. Christian continued to drive, moving further and further away until he was out of view. A strong wind blew, and I fell over, shattering into millions of tiny pieces.

When I had been put back together, I was back in Mrs. Whittaker's class, alone. Glimmers of red and blue caught my eye, and I noticed the shredded paper with Andrew's number on it. I put the pieces back together, painstakingly matching a crumpled edge to a squiggled corner, until the red and blue pieces once again resembled Spiderman. It was almost complete, but the piece with the last four digits of his phone number was missing. I searched the room, but there was nothing. Out of instinct, I gathered the pieces and brought them out to the schoolyard. The ground felt cold and hard, as if frozen solid, although the outside air was warm, like midsummer. I scraped at the frozen earth until I'd made a hole. With bloodied hands, I buried the scraps of paper. Storm clouds blanketed the sky. Lightening flashed. The air filled with the sound of glass shattering, and then the screams started. From the hole I dug, the scraps of paper were crying out—like Abel's blood. It began to rain, and the water turned to ice as it touched my skin.

I was dry when I reentered the school, but my hands were still bloody. All the doors in the hallway had disappeared, except for one, so I made my way towards it. The sounds of grunting and laughter drifted under the door and out into the hallway. The familiar fluttering began in my stomach and spread throughout my lower body as I got closer to the door. Entering the bathroom, I saw Travis and Alex, who were throwing baseball-sized rocks at Malcolm. Travis and Alex looked at me as I entered, and a lust for blood came over me as the fluttering intensified.

Travis grunted as the rock left his hand, and it hit Malcolm in the stomach. Alex threw his, and the stone pelted Malcolm in the middle of his chest. A hollow thud followed, punctuated by a sharp exhale. They handed me a rock—it was dense and cold and now covered with the blood from my hands. I threw it. The sound of porcelain filled the room, and they laughed. I grabbed another and threw it. They laughed again and began chanting, "Ho-mo, ho-mo, ho-mo." I picked up another rock with "faggot" written on it and threw it. A squelching sound filled the room as blood gushed from Malcolm's head and cascaded across the tile. Blood dripped from my hands and pooled around my feet. Alex and Travis started laughing again. I laughed too.

"Take one and pass it back." Mrs. Graves placed a stack of papers at the top of the row and moved to the next. She licked her finger and counted how many packets were needed. "Take one and pass it back." Her jaw clenched and her hands shook. "Take one and pass it back. Take one and—"

"Mrs. Graves," someone said, "extra one."

"Thank you." She collected the extra, wiped a strand of hair from her forehead, and tried to steady her hands to count papers for the last row. "Ok, does everyone have an exam?"

"Yes, Mrs. Graves," we responded.

"You will have one hour to complete the exam. Calculators are not allowed, and all work must be shown to get credit. When finished, turn your paper over and sit quietly until everyone has finished. You may begin."

A chorus of fluttering paper filled the air as we flipped through the packet to see how many questions were on the test—there were thirty—a mix of fractions, long division, and word problems. Mrs. Graves had an advanced degree in calculus, and her exams were notoriously difficult, as though to prove to us she could be a professor at a university but decided to be an elementary school teacher for our benefit. Still, besides English, math was my strongest subject, so I felt confident going into the test. The feeling, however, wasn't universal.

"Can—may I sharpen my pencil, Mrs. Graves?" Alex asked.

"You may."

I glanced over at Alex's paper when he got up. We were twenty-five minutes into the test, and he had only completed five or six problems—at this pace, he wouldn't finish on time. On his way back to his seat, he stole glances at others' tests, including mine, which I covered with my arm. I had expected him to scowl at me or whisper something vulgar under his breath, but he just mouthed, "Please."

With twenty minutes left, I had been finished for about five and was waiting for the hour to be up so we could go to lunch. Mrs. Graves stood up and pulled her bag over her shoulder. "Class, I will be right back. When you finish, turn your test over and sit quietly. I will have Ms. LaGrange check in, so be on your best behavior."

"Let me see your test," Alex whispered immediately when she left.

"No."

"Please," he begged with his hands together like he was praying, "pretty please."

"No."

He dug into his bag and pulled out a bag of Skittles and some gum. "Here. You can have it. I have some more candy and a bag of chips in here, too. Please." He reached into his pocket, pulled out two dollars and placed them on my desk.

"Stop. I don't want your stuff."

"Please. If I fail this test, I'm going to get into so much trouble. I'll have to go to summer school… please, Jay." I shook my head. He buried his face in his hands and cursed. He then lifted his head and stared at the exam as though waiting for the answers to materialize.

I didn't feel sorry for him. He and Travis had been ignoring me for months, and my existence was only convenient because he needed something. In fact, I found the idea of him going to summer school amusing. It felt like justice was being served for both me and Malcolm, like the universe had struck a karmic balance. This was God. Still, every time I looked at him, I would get butterflies, and the resulting wings filled my insides before I sprung an erection. Monsignor had said that the true tests of our faith would come once we get confirmed, and that in those moments we would either apply our teachings to uphold the Church's standards or we would crumble—but the choice, and thus the consequences, was ours.

There were a few weeks remaining until Confirmation, but I felt like the tests of my faith were already beginning. Our sessions had posited black and white decisions, as if an explicit line existed between the dichotomy of right and wrong. Although Confirmation meant becoming adults spiritually, we would still be children, so a non-nuanced morality was necessary until eroded over time through experience, resulting in wisdom. Sure, there was a hard line—what complexity could Monsignor have foreseen children having to endure—but it was drawn in sand, continuously washed away by waves of cognitive dissonance and redrawn with capricious justifications.

"Hurry up," I said, handing my test to him. His hand brushed mine as he took it from me, and I started to get hard.

"Thank you."

He handed the test back just as Mrs. Graves returned to the room. She had said Ms. LaGrange would check-in on us, but I doubted she had even spoken to her. The stale stench of smoke permeated the room, as did the smell of freshly cut grass that passed through the window.

"Ok, class, time is up. Please pass your papers to the front."

***

"Jay," Alex waved to me in the cafeteria as I passed by on my way to sit with the other Confirmation kids, "come sit with us."

"Why are you calling him over here?" Travis asked, he and I sharing the same look of perplexity.

"Because he hits hard."

It was the last Mass of the school year, and it was extended another half hour for the ceremony. In the first pew, I sat with the other Confirmation kids, and behind us were our families. The first half of Mass preceded as usual with some songs, some prayer, and the Eucharist. In the latter half, we were called up one-by-one to briefly say why we had chosen to get confirmed and to acknowledge the commitment of this rite before being blessed by the Monsignor. Most of the Confirmation kids had gone. Gabrielle was next, then me.

Monsignor asked her parents to stand. "Gabrielle, please tell us why you are being confirmed today."

Gabrielle pulled a piece of paper out of her pocket and unfolded it. Scattered chuckles filled the room. "1) I have met the requirements to be confirmed, including being baptized and adequately mature," everyone laughed. "2) I have a clear understanding of right and wrong and the tools to detangle the two when not obvious. 3) I'm ready for the next step in my spiritual journey. And 4) I want to make my parents proud."

"All amazing reasons, Gabrielle. You've been an excellent student, and I look forward to seeing you grow in your relationship with the Lord." He placed his hand on her shoulder and prayed. "Ah-men."

I was next.

It was hot up on the altar. I couldn't tell whether it was the bright lights or the heat from all the eyes on me, but I was sweating. Monsignor asked my parents to stand, but my mom wasn't there. I hadn't told her I was getting confirmed. I had even gone as far as forging her signature on the permission slip to start the Confirmation process so that she wouldn't find out and had made Christian swear not to tell her. I had told myself it wasn't important enough for her to miss work, but seeing that she wasn't there for this vulnerable moment made me happy to have it to myself. He then asked for someone to stand as a witness. I had expected Christian to stand up but wasn't surprised when he didn't. I spotted him in the audience looking down, trying to avoid my stare. Just as Monsignor appeared to move on and not prolong this awkward moment, Alex and Travis stood up and cheered. I could see Mrs. Graves scolding them. I smiled.

"Thank you, gentlemen. Jay, please explain to us why you have decided to be confirmed."

In our last Confirmation session, we had been told to prepare an explanation for why we were being confirmed as it showed we were indeed aware of its implications. For weeks following that session, I struggled to identify my reasons. At the same time, I had become friends with Alex and Travis, which was unearthing the questions about myself I had buried. Travis had continued to bring his brother's magazines to school, and during recess, we would find a secluded spot to look at them. "I wanna fuck her so bad," Travis would sometimes say, or Alex would grab himself and announce, "I'm so hard right now." *Is something wrong with me? Am I normal? Am I gay?* were the questions that clouded my mind before I would add, "me too."

"I chose to be confirmed because I wanted to belong," I answered, feeling more alienated than ever standing up there.

"The Body of Christ welcomes you," he said after praying for me. He then gave the benediction and closed the ceremony: "The Lord be with you."

After Mass, the other Confirmation kids lined up to take pictures with their parents at the altar. They asked if I wanted to join, but I declined. Instead, I grabbed my things and went to find Alex and Travis.

CHAPTER 12

I spent the summer hanging out with Alex and Travis and found what I had been looking for since Andrew left—belonging—which looked different with them than it had with Andrew. For them, it meant coalescing into a single body. It reminded me of the sessions to be confirmed; so, I took the steps to join the church. I memorized the rap lyrics and pounded out the beat of "Grindin'" on the roof of a stranger's car; I slap boxed Alex and Travis, sometimes simultaneously; and I looked at the magazines filled with naked women and voiced my desire to be with them, burying the intrusive questions that didn't merit an answer. For the start of the school year, I had even gotten a new haircut, trading in my curly top for a low cut and brushing incessantly to get waves like Alex and Travis' to complete my initiation into the "Peaks and Troughs." I was still unsure of who Jay was—an uncertainty that increased, yet whose significance decreased as I dissolved into this homogenous solution—but I knew who he wasn't, and I felt that was good enough.

"Ok, last one."

"Diamond," I said.

"Really? Over her?!" Travis held up Hilary, who was in contention for first place.

"She's not as cute."

"Who cares what she looks like? Look at her ass." Travis snatched the page out of my hand and gave them both to Alex. "What do you think?"

"I gotta go with Jay on this one. Diamond wins."

Travis snatched the Jet Beauties from Alex and placed them in the lineup. "Y'all only chose her because y'all wouldn't know what to do with Hilary."

Alex and I looked at each other and rolled our eyes. "And you would?" I asked.

"Of course." He held his hands in front of him and then thrust his hips back and forth. We laughed. "Oh, yeah!" Travis added in a high-pitched, girly voice, which made us laugh harder. A gust of wind fluttered the Jet Beauties that were meticulously laid out from one to ten based on their level of desirability to three fifth graders. Hilary, having had enough, took flight and floated across the schoolyard. "Fuck," Travis said as he gathered the pages.

"I'll get it," I responded, springing to my feet and jogging across the gray pavement adorned with chalk landscapes and elaborate hopscotch grids. The page landed in the brown patch where the tree stump used to be. Nothing grew there anymore. As I bent down to pick it up, Hilary took flight again, landing at his feet just as he was running past.

"Here." Malcolm glanced at the page and then handed it to me.

"Thanks."

He ran off to catch up with his friends, and I walked back to Alex and Travis.

"What did he want?" Travis asked.

I glanced back at Malcolm leading the pack as he raced across the schoolyard. "Nothing." I gave Hilary back to Travis.

Slivers of sunlight slipped through the pale clouds that rolled across the sky. Small drops of rain touched down just as the bell rang.

"I fuckin' hate him," Travis said, stuffing the page into his bag with the rest.

"Why?"

"Because he's a faggot," Alex responded bluntly, as if that was answer enough. The word made me grit my teeth.

"So?"

"What do you mean 'so?' What else is there to say?" Travis asked.

"I mean, why is him being… you know, a reason to hate him?"

"A faggot," Alex corrected.

"Why is being *that* a reason to hate him?"

"Say it," Alex said.

"What?"

"Say it," Travis joined in. "He's a faggot. Say it."

The rain picked up and turned into a light shower. It was the tail end of summer, but the rain felt like ice on my skin.

"I'm not saying it."

Alex pushed me. "Say it."

"Fuck you," I said, balling my fists.

Travis looked at Alex, and they started laughing. "We're messin' with you," Alex said. "You always so serious."

I smiled and laughed. "I knew that."

"He is a faggot, though," Travis said.

"Is that why you jumped him in the bathroom?"

"Did you help him because you're a faggot too?" Alex asked. Lightning bisected the sky, and thunder followed soon after. I shook my head. The light shower turned into a downpour, and the freezing rain held me together even as my insides melted into a puddle.

"Plus, we don't know what you're talkin' about," Travis said, holding his backpack over his head.

"LET'S GO!" Mr. Jadell yelled from the door.

It was a year to the day since Monsignor Pax had come to ask about Confirmation when he returned to discuss another sacrament. Since then, some other students had been confirmed, so when he asked about prep sessions for Penance, half the class raised their hands, and they stayed up. I felt the eyes of the original Confirmation kids on me, but the same pull that had driven me to be confirmed wasn't there, so I kept my hand lowered. Monsignor Pax counted the raised hands. Seeing mine wasn't up, he inquired with a slight raise of his eyebrows. I responded with a shake of the head that only he could see and interpret, and with a knowing smile, he ended the conversation between us. Monsignor prayed, exchanged hushed words with Mr. Jadell, and then left, his too-long cassock trailing behind him like a ruffled shadow.

"Why didn't you raise your hand?" Travis asked, folding a piece of paper over itself several times.

"Why didn't *you*?" Alex responded. Travis shrugged. "You should ask Jay. He's the church boy." They laughed.

Travis and Alex's desks flanked mine. What was supposed to be a way for us all to sit together—and for them to copy my assignments without being caught—had become a manifestation of how I had been feeling lately. Surrounded and outgunned. Although we were supposed to be friends, the Peaks and Troughs, they had a way of reminding me that my membership in the group was new and thus not as valuable as theirs.

"Why didn't you raise your hand, church boy?" Travis asked, intently tucking the last corner of the paper into place until he had a perfect triangle.

"That's not my name."

"*Jacob*," he corrected himself. They knew I hated being called that. Even as I looked forward, my periphery becoming cloudy with anger, I could feel them both smiling. "You not gonna answer me?"

Alex held his fingers together to make a goalpost, and Travis plucked the football. It flew in front of my face and landed on the floor.

"You suck," Alex said, sliding the piece of paper closer to him with his foot. "Jacob. Jacob. *Jaaacob,*" he whispered loudly.

"Shhhh," Mr. Jadell's eyes barely cleared the stack of books on his desk as he addressed no one in particular.

Alex lined up his shot and aimed for Travis, whose turn

it was to hold up the goal post. The paper football flew across my face again. This time, it was so close that I could almost read the math problem Travis left unfinished. It missed the goal but landed on the desk.

"Stop," I said to Travis, who was gearing up for his turn.

"What you say, church boy?"

"That's not his name," Alex chimed in, "it's Jacob."

"I said that, but he didn't respond. It must be somethin' else." Travis plucked the football and scored. "You see that, Jacob? I got one… see, he's not respondin'."

"Faggot," Alex called out in a breathy whisper. My head snapped to face him. "He responded!" Alex plucked the paper, and it flew over my head.

"You missed," Travis said. Alex and I stared at each other, but he was looking through me, holding up his fingers, waiting for Travis to take his turn. "Faggot, look at this."

"Stop." The letters poured through the gaps of my clenched teeth to form the word. I was still looking at Alex, who was turning red as he laughed. My bones, deep below the trembling surface, felt like they had turned to magma. The resulting heat set my blood to boil, and I could feel the crimson bubbles bursting just below my skin.

"What you say, faggot?" Travis asked. And just as I turned to face him, he plucked the paper, and it hit me in the face. They laughed, and in an instant, I was on my feet.

"Can I go to the bathroom?"

Scalding water poured over my hands, turning them into glowing red embers. Unlike before, this wasn't an attempt at salvation. I knew that water, no matter how hot, couldn't burn away that word. I had tried to use the pain to distract from how angry I was, but it was indistinguishable from what I was already feeling, so I turned off the faucet. Looking in the mirror, I saw Jacob staring back; dirt, gravel, and blood covered his hands, and tears filled his eyes. I wiped away the tears streaming down my face and told him to "man up."

"Are you talking to me?" The stall door opened, and Malcolm stepped out.

"Shut up, faggot!" I pushed him and left the bathroom.

It didn't start with physical punishment, but what effigy could be complete without it? He died on a crisp and partly sunny day like the beginning of fall, but it was the tail end of spring. I don't remember the day of the week, but it was the day I killed him.

It didn't start with physical punishment. Pieces of me that still clung to Jacob prevented it. First, we stripped away his dignity. We spread rumors about him around school, memorializing them on bathroom walls and lunch tables until our classmates stopped associating with him. We threw his things in the toilet and forced him to fish them out, and stole items from his backpack and laughed when he couldn't find them. Then, we took away his humanity: he wasn't Malcolm anymore, he was "Faggot." He was an embodiment of the word, a pyre on which to burn our fears, our insecurities, our feelings of loneliness, of confusion, of longing, our hidden selves, our unacknowledged selves, our softness, our vulnerability, our innocence. There had been a sense of guilt, but this faded like a flame without oxygen. What we didn't realize was that as we stripped away his humanity, ours too was uprooted, leaving a misshapen hole where our sense of self no longer fit, a patch of dirt where nothing no longer grew—he became an object of our derision, and we became monsters.

It was a half day at school—professional development—so the Peaks and Troughs took to the streets. After grabbing a slice of pizza, we wandered around, taking turns rapping verses and crafting some of our own.

"Damn, ma, that ass too fat. You got a two-for-one, but you should give one back," Alex rapped into his invisible mic.

"Hol' up," Travis said. "Is that Faggot?"

"Where?" I held my hand over my brow to shield my eyes from the sun.

"Right there," Travis pointed down the block.

It was him. This was a rare opportunity. Normally his mom would pick him up from school, but it seemed because of the early dismissal, he had to walk home. It was obvious he didn't do this often because his face was buried in a comic book.

"Oh shit," Alex said, "let's jump him."

My heart raced with excitement at the thought.

"If he sees us, though, he's gonna run. Alex and I will stay over here. Travis, cross the street and then come back and get behind him. That way, if he runs, you can catch him."

Travis nodded and crossed the street. Alex and I walked towards Malcolm, obscuring our faces as much as we could in the chance he looked up and saw us. We were about four cars away when he glanced up as he flipped the page. He turned heel and was in full sprint when he ran into Travis. Alex and I jogged over to him. The three of us looked down at him as he cowered on the ground. "Where you goin', Faggot?" Alex asked with a sardonic smile so wide that he resembled a cartoon character.

Travis delivered the first blow, punching him in his leg and yelling, "Charley horse!" Malcolm grunted and reached for his leg, but quickly brought his hands back up to protect his head and face. Alex went next. He danced around him like a pagan around a fire and then stepped on him, lingering for a minute to impress his full body weight and then stepping off. He repeated this several times as if it were a ritual that needed to be completed, and then he kicked him in his head.

"Not in his face, dickhead!" Travis pushed Alex, who laughed.

I looked down at Malcolm. His hands were covering his face, but peeking through them, I could see his tearful eyes. They plead. In them was Jacob, fully realized. This was the ultimate step to join the church—a baptism by blood. As hard as I could, I kicked Malcolm in the side, and he yelled out in pain. He placed his hands on the ground and tried to scramble to his feet, but I kicked him again. "STOP!" He yelled out, tears streaming down his face. Gravel covered his hands. Jacob looked up at me. I kicked him again. His whimpering died down, and with each kick, he let out a sharp exhale.

I kicked him again.

And again.

And again.

"Ard, chill," Travis said. His voice was shaking a bit.

But I couldn't stop, not until he was gone. I kicked him again. A sharp exhale followed. Then, again. And another. Then, again. And again, until no breaths were left. Malcolm's eyes were closed, and his body was limp.

"HEY!" a man yelled from his stoop, "what y'all doing over there?!"

———

Weeks had passed since Malcolm had been in school. I dismissed it, but only because I had forced thoughts of him out of my mind. I had become adept at burying unwanted thoughts and feelings; however, it wasn't a skill that Alex and Travis possessed. After the incident, things changed between us. We still ate lunch together, but we didn't hang out after school anymore. During recess, the three of us didn't play alone and were always in a group setting—Travis had even stopped bringing in his brother's magazines. In class, Alex and Travis still sat next to me, but they no longer played paper football, and neither one copied my work. Instead, they stared at Malcolm's empty desk. It was like that misshapen hole had regained form, and they had found themselves. I felt betrayed. They had molded me in their image, and now, disgusted with their creation, they hid their clay-covered hands and dismissed me from Eden.

The end of sixth grade arrived and still no sign of Malcolm. Alex and Travis's slow departure had culminated with them avoiding me altogether, and the Peaks and Troughs had come to rest.

The phone rang, and Mr. Jadell hobbled across the classroom to answer it.

"You three," Mr. Jadell pointed to me, Alex, and Travis, "to the office."

We went to the front desk, and the secretary directed us to Dr. Simon's office. Travis's dad and Alex's mom, who sat next to each other, looked at us as we entered the room. My mom, with her carefully pressed uniform and taut bun, held her legs together as she faced forward. Two other people were in the room, but I didn't recognize them. Seated behind her desk was Dr. Simon; on the wall were her degrees from the University of Pennsylvania and Temple University.

"Good morning, gentlemen," Dr. Simon greeted us. Her face indicated this was out of habit rather than respect. "Do you know why you're here?" We shook our heads, but Alex's near-white face turned a bright red, while Travis blinked rapidly to hold back tears. My face was blank—I had buried the day of the incident so deep in my mind that the realization of what was happening was not immediate. Instead, I focused on the two strangers in the back, racking my brain to figure out who they could be. "Since you don't know, I'll tell you. This is Mr. and Mrs. Brixton, Malcolm's parents. You may have noticed that Malcolm has not been in school for the past two months. Do you know why?" Alex and Travis tried to hold their composure, while I studied Malcolm's parents, who looked like statues had replaced them. I thought of Malcolm's jittery movements and questioned whether these were his actual parents. "Weeks ago, they asked to remove Malcolm from school. Given his stellar academic performance and his interest in the track team, I was surprised by this request. It wasn't until today that I found out that Malcolm was being bullied and by whom."

"We were just playing with him; they were jokes," Alex said, cracking immediately while Travis sobbed.

"After the beating you gave him, Malcolm was taken to the hospital to be treated for a concussion, three cracked ribs, and internal bleeding. Please show me the humor in that, Mr. Smalls."

"We weren't trying to kill him," he said. "We weren't trying—" Alex's mom told him to stop talking, and he fell silent.

My mom didn't move, her expression sharp as if it had been drawn with only straight lines. I wondered if someone had replaced her with a statue too. Although there was a somatic reaction, my heart having slipped into my stomach, my mind skipped what Dr. Simon had said and latched onto Alex's statement:

"We weren't trying to kill him." I thought of Jacob looking up at me and wondered if he still existed there in Malcolm's eyes.

"In any case, today will be your last day here. Though well within their rights, Mr. and Mrs. Brixton have decided not to press charges." Alex's mom and Travis' dad sighed with relief. My mom wiped a wrinkle from her skirt and continued to study the degrees on the wall. Movement. At least I knew she was real now. "After a lengthy discussion with Mr. and Mrs. Brixton and your parents, I've also decided not to put an expulsion on your record. However, you will not return to this school nor be permitted to attend any other in the archdiocese. Please return to your classroom and gather your things."

Travis's dad glared at him with contempt and rested a hand on his belt buckle. Alex's mom mouthed the words, "Wait until I tell your dad." My mom continued to stare at the wall.

Dr. Simon stood, halting our recession. "One final thing, gentlemen. While not requested, I would like each of you to apologize to Mr. and Mrs. Brixton."

Alex went first. "I'm sorry, Mr. and Mrs. Brixton. We were just joking… I'm sorry."

Then Travis. "Mr. Brixton, I'm sorry. Mrs. Brixton, I'm sorry."

Then me. I opened my mouth to speak, but the words weren't there. I scanned my mind for the appropriate morphemes to put together, but I kept getting stuck on the pieces of the Spiderman paper on the corner of my desk, wondering what things would be like had I not ripped up What's-His-Name's number. "Mr. Hayles, today, please." Dr. Simon said. My mother suddenly stood and turned to face me. I considered her sullen, red eyes like melancholic rubies and thought of how her response to me telling her my best friend, What's-His-Name, was moving was "man up." I wanted to tell her to look at the man she raised, but my mind kept getting stuck on the pieces of the Spiderman paper on the corner of my desk.

"I—I." I had located the words, but that cold, hard thing shielded them. I looked for some warmth within me to tear down the wall and thought of his smiling face as we shared spaghetti at our stump. The stump that had been our home once but was cut down and uprooted, leaving behind a barren space. I tried to fill the gap, but nothing fit. I tried to till the soil, but nothing grew. I could see his face, but I couldn't remember his name. Suddenly, I was overcome with sorrow and guilt ripped through me. I wept.

"That'll be all, gentlemen," Dr. Simon said, dismissing us.

I gathered my things and met my mom in the car. With the same statuesque posture, she drove with no ostentatious movements. At first I thought she was just too angry to speak, but I never knew my mom to be at a loss for words when she was angry. It was as if she were shrinking herself to hide from me, like she was afraid.

The engine droned. It was sweet and calming and reminded me of the hymns my mom used to hum on Saturday mornings as she cleaned. I would catch her staring at me in the rearview mirror, only for her to look away. I imagined she didn't recognize me—at times I didn't recognize myself. Maybe it was her first time seeing me, and she was trying to relate to this new being in front of her. Maybe. I watched the parked cars fly by as we passed through the city. "That's my car when I grow up," he would say to Christian as they walked home together. It was in this silence, buttressed by the car's steady tenor, that I first realized they were there.

What was his name? The voice was clear and distinct. I looked into the rearview mirror, waiting for my mom to speak again, but then they spoke: **What was his name! He's gone now. You killed him! What was his name? What was his name? It's ok.**

I watched the house come into view and thought about how he used to race Christian the last few blocks. I had killed him.

What was his name?

Am I my brother's keeper?

It's ok.

PART III

CHAPTER 13

Me: How was Chicago?

Xavier: It was good :))

Xavier: I'll tell you about it when you get back

Me: I can't believe I'm gonna be here for two weeks :D!

Xavier: XD. How far away are you?

Me: Close, I think. There aren't any signs but we've been driving on the same dirt road for like 10 minutes

Xavier: You know that's how all the horror movies start, right? lol

Me: ROFL! Based on the people on the bus, you can guess who's dying first!

Xavier: XD

Me: What do you think is gonna do me in? Ghosts? Ooooo maybe the camp is built on an ancient Native American burial ground

Me: Or, plot twist, the camp is actually some kind of cult and they're gonna sacrifice me

Xavier: XD

Xavier: It'll be a Jason type thing for sure lol. If you see fog drifting off a lake, RUN!

Me: LOL

Xavier: I'm sure you're gonna have a great time

Me: It's two weeks of church camp with strangers from all over the state, and from what I can see, none of them look like me. It's gonna be a great time!

Xavier: Haha Fair. Could still be fun though

Me: Yeah…I wish you were coming too though. We could get murdered together =D

Xavier: Lol won't be crossing that off my summer to-do list I guess :(

Me: XD. But seriously, it's gonna be a long two weeks. I wanna hear all about Chicago when I get back

Xavier: Of course!

Me: I'll text you when I get settled to confirm which horror theory is right :)

Xavier: haha ok!

Xavier: It's definitely gonna be a long two weeks. Can't believe you just missed me :/

Me: Just? I still miss you! :'(

…

[Text could not be delivered.]

I tried to resend the text, but the same error message appeared. After several more failed attempts, I gave up and was grateful it hadn't gone through. It was the Dead's influence that had convinced me to send such a message. Men didn't tell other men that they missed them—that was a lesson that I had already learned.

The bus slowed to a stop in front of the cabins that

would be my home for the next two weeks. With a long *hiss*, the bus exhaled and lowered, and we filed out into the muggy evening. The other buses emptied their contents, and we waited en masse to check in. I had hoped that there would be Black kids on the other buses; however, I found myself in a sea of white faces. Outside of the two or three teachers at Blanche Creek, I had never interacted with a white person, let alone one my age. I wondered whether they faced the same pressures to grow up as we did or whether invisible hands also guided their actions and shaped their personalities. From what tv had depicted, society worked together to ensure their childhood was protected. "Boys will be boys," they would say before absolving the main character of any wrongdoing as though the world were his sandbox—and creation and destruction his birthright. I wasn't sure, but I knew that if a door opened on its own or if I were to glimpse a shadowy figure moving through the trees, I wouldn't be going to investigate.

If you see fog drifting off a lake, RUN!

After standing around for some time, we were assigned to our cabins and given a packet of papers—the itinerary for the next thirteen days—and then introduced to the youth pastors who would also serve as the cabin leaders. Each of the cabins was named after a biblical reference, and I, along with fourteen other boys, was assigned to Damascus. From there, we were further divided into four pods and then left to choose our bunkmates. Everyone quickly paired up, choosing prior-year bunkmates or familiar church members, but due to the odd number of people in our cabin, I was left without one. Pastor Gabe assured me this was a good thing; that I wouldn't have to fight for the top bunk. Beneath my smile, which echoed agreement with his sentiment, though, I wanted the fight—like having the room to myself with Christian being gone. It felt like too much space. I lugged my duffle bag over my shoulder and trailed behind as we followed him on the road to Damascus.

Our room was a 300 sq. ft box with a pair of dark-stained wooden bunk beds and dressers to match. A window looked out onto the campground and an adjacent metal door led outside. I looked at the door that led back into the common area and smiled with relief—if a masked murderer came slashing through here, at least I had an escape.

"Hey, Jay. Gresh' and I are going to hang out in the lounge. You wanna come?" Michael Sandro, one of two of my podmates, asked.

"I think I'm gonna get some sleep—I'm exhausted. But next time."

They nodded and then left.

I checked my phone again for service, but the singular connection to the outside world, I was told, was the landline in the admin building. I wanted to let Xavier know I had made it safely; that we did a tour of the campgrounds, and it was actually pretty cool; that there was a lake, so his theory was likely right; and that I missed him.

I'll tell you about it when you get back...

I sat by the window and studied the subtle tide of the forest that moved with the wind while I dreamed of home. It made me feel good that Xavier anticipated my return.

Although it would have been better if he were there with me, it was nice to think he was back in Philly rehearsing all the details of his story—structuring events sequentially but also noting where to jump in time to enhance the story, contemplating where and which gestures to insert for comedic effect, and practicing his inflections in the mirror—and our loneliness shared, only to be quelled by embracing each other again.

Just? I still miss you!

Across the courtyard, a dark figure meandered in a way that made me uneasy. The text made me cringe. The more I thought about it, the more I wanted to curl up into the smallest ball possible, to walk out into the sea of black and disappear. I looked at the text saying that the message couldn't be delivered and thought it possible he wouldn't have responded well. "Haha, that's so gay," he might have said before he told everyone. *Nah...he wouldn't say that.* I was happy the text had failed, but there was a part of me that wished it had gone through—the same part of me that despised the Dead's desires yet harbored them in my heart until they turned to sadness. Still, men didn't say they missed other men. The dark figure swayed back and forth, giving itself over to the wind, and then receded into the brush. I resolved that, in the chance some masked serial killer stalked the camp, I would not be the first to die.

I unpacked my things into the dresser and put a sheet on the bottom bunk, leaving the top one open in case Xavier changed his mind about joining me. On the underside of the top bunk, I etched a tally mark into the wood. It was going to be a long two weeks.

Camp staff meticulously ordered our days. Each one began at 9 AM with breakfast. Then, a short morning devotional followed, featuring scriptures related to the year's theme, "Youth on Fire." Next, we broke into teams based on our cabins and earned points through physical challenges, puzzles, and competitions against the other cabins. Afterwards, lunch, free time, fireside chats led by the cabin leader, dinner, and a longer evening devotional all before lights out at 9:30 PM. Through regimen or will, I had come to enjoy most of the camp activities and even come to like my podmates. I was fit enough to excel at the physical obstacles and mental ones alike; and after a few late-night talks with Gresham and Michael, I realized the same invisible forces shaped their experiences and personalities. Gresham, goofy and charming, reminded me of Meat, while Michael's popularity with the girls reminded me of Herb. I missed Herb just as much as I did Xavier, although differently—and while voicing either as a man was unacceptable, one form was more acceptable than the other.

A week passed, and the vigor with which I marked the passage of the days faded. Staunch engravings that cut deeply into the splintered wood were replaced with hastily strewn scratches I made before joining Gresh' and Mikey in the lounge. I even slept on the top bunk, accepting Xavier wouldn't be joining me, but I would see him soon. The idea to stop counting the days dawned on me—to my surprise, I was enjoying camp—yet there was one principal aspect that demanded I hold on to the reality that stopped where the asphalt met the tempered dirt road.

Although there had been a glimmer of optimism that camp could provide the deliverance I needed to attend Herb's party, this line of thinking revealed itself as a search for a silver lining in an inescapable situation. A justification of the inevitable, not a manifestation of hope. This aspiration for deliverance proved futile as we drove deeper into the woods, where the Dead's longing for Xavier accelerated my heartbeat with every "lol" or smiley face from him. The level of spirituality I needed to change–I already knew—was inaccessible to me; a fact made clearer every night.

"Youth on Fire" signified an intentional burning away of fleshly desires—a dedication of mind and body to God—brought on through rigorous prayer and worship. I had found comfort in my similarities with my podmates, yet watching them sing songs and wave their hands in praise at every evening service was where we diverged. Each night, I was forced to bear witness to their ability to hold contradictory existences in mind. It frustrated me that their spiritual self-immolation didn't necessitate a negation of their identity, that their "Dead" staying buried wasn't consequential to their belonging or salvation. I had killed Jacob, but to my dismay, it didn't result in a grand metamorphosis restoring in me what was natural. Instead, it put me in a Sisyphean struggle of digging a hole deep enough to keep him buried, yet still shallow enough from which I could escape.

In the presence of all the overt religiosity, I would often leave evening devotionals feeling like I was bare and covered in grime. So, after lights out when Gresh' and Mikey were sound asleep, I would sneak out into the courtyard. Under the cloak of the night sky lit up with stars, I remembered the summers spent in the mountains at Grandma Junie's and her lasting words: "Tears will help to wash the dirt off." Tears never came, but floating in the sea of black, protected from God's eyes, often did the trick.

***

"It's called 'Mischief Night.'"

"Isn't that a Halloween thing?" I asked.

"It is, but it has a different meaning here. Every year, some of the teenagers sneak out and meet up at the old gazebo by the lake." Mikey pulled a tan canvas bag from the bottom of his drawer and gave it a little shake, double-checking its volume before stuffing it into his backpack. "I took a bottle of whiskey from my parent's bar," he said, answering the question written on my face, "we tried to join last year, but some of the older guys were being dicks, so this is to make sure we get in."

"So, you just drink by the lake?"

"More than that," Gresh' added, standing guard by the door. "Some of the girls sneak out, too." He had an eager smile that pushed his cheeks up towards his eyes and made him look younger than he was. "And we... you know."

"You...?"

"You *know*..."

"Don't tell me you're a virgin." Mikey slipped his

backpack on and then pulled his hoodie on over it.

The Dead shifted in their graves.

"Of course not. I've fucked more girls than both of you combined." The words didn't sound believable, but I felt myself get a little angry when Mikey responded with, "Riiight."

"You should come and see for yourself. It'll be fun," Gresh' said. He looked at Mikey, who gave him a nod, and Mikey took watch at the door while Gresh' got ready. "Mikey's being a dick." I watched Mikey from the top bunk, his large backpack "inconspicuously" hidden under his hoodie, and shook my head. "Just come. From what I heard, there's not much that happens. But, you know, things *can* happen." Gresh' pulled his suitcase out from under his bunk and began rifling through it.

"He knows I'm joking." Mikey looked at me for confirmation. I nodded, and he smiled. "But things *do* happen. That girl, Leann, gave some guy a blowjob last year."

"Oh, right! And some other girl, I forget her name, fucked Bradley Hersh the year before."

"Wait, what?!" Mikey yelled.

"Shhh!" Gresh' said, throwing a pair of balled up socks at him.

"What?" he repeated, whispering. "Dude, why didn't you tell me that?"

"I thought you knew. Besides, my mom is friends with his mom, and she asked us not to say anything. Apparently, the girl got pregnant or something."

"Dude, no fucking way!"

I watched the exchange between the two and couldn't help but laugh. Gresh' pulled several small bottles out of his suitcase and stuffed them into his pants and crotch.

"What'd you rob an airplane?" I asked.

"Ha-ha-ha, no. My mom is a flight attendant and takes home some of the leftover shooters to fill up this old-timey glass decanter she got from my grandpa. White people, dude."

We laughed.

"Would you know her if you saw her again? You think she'll be there tonight?" Mikey left his post to interrogate Gresh'.

"No, I don't think she's coming. I've been scouring the place since last year looking for her."

Tap. Tap. Tap. Hollow thuds echoed through the wooden door as they scurried into their beds and under the covers.

"Lights out, fellas," Pastor Gabe said, switching the lights off.

"Good night," I said.

"Good night, Pastor Gabe," Mikey added.

"Night, PG," Gresh' said, rounding out the chorus.

"Good night, guys. See you bright and early." He shut the door and walked to the next room. Light knocking could be heard down the hall.

"Shit, that was close," Gresh' said, laughing in the dark.

"Oh, oh, remember the time when we did that obstacle course last year, and the rope snapped while you were swinging?" Mikey asked.

"Of course I remember. It was so embarrassing. I fell in the mud pit, and they had to hose me off before I could go take a shower."

They laughed, and then their voices dropped to a whisper—a few seconds went by, and then they erupted in laughter again. About a half an hour had passed since Pastor Gabe checked on us, and Mikey and Gresh' had filled the time by reminiscing on their experiences from the previous year. I occasionally contributed with a question or by laughing too but mainly remained silent, feeling locked out of the world they were crafting from their shared memories.

"Shh," Mikey said, "haha, you're such an asshole."

"Dude, imagine if that spot hadn't opened up or if your bunkmate had shown, we probably wouldn't have met." Gresh's voice was soft and filled with gratitude.

"I know. That would've been a bummer. Must mean it was meant to happen."

"That's… kinda gay, dude." Gresh' laughed.

"I'm so gay for you, man," Mikey hopped down from the top bunk and jumped into Gresh's bed, playfully trying to give him a kiss. The two wrestled, and then Mikey went to check the lounge.

"Are we good?" Gresh' asked.

"Yeah," he replied, doing a final scan of the lounge before closing the door, "we're good. Are you ready?"

Gresh' turned on his flashlight and shone it on his face. "Mwahahaha! Ready."

"You're such a weirdo," Mikey said, chuckling. "You

coming, Jay?" he asked, holding the door open to the courtyard.

"Yeah, I just have to get ready."

"Do you want us to wait?"

"Nah, I'll be right behind you."

"Cool. Just cut straight through the courtyard and follow the trail. When you get to the end, make a left, walk for a little bit then you'll see a side path that'll take you right to the lake. The gazebo is kinda hidden, but I'm sure you'll be able to hear us."

"Bet, I'll see you soon."

"I'm hoping to at least get a hand job," Gresh' was saying as Michael closed the door behind him.

"You think he'll come?"

"Probably not anymore, since you made fun of him."

"Shit. You think he's mad at me? Should I go apologize?"

"Do it later. We're already late and I wanted to..." Gresh's voice trailed off as they kicked up the dirt road.

I put on some jeans and a hoodie and sat on the edge of the bed. I just needed to put on my shoes, and then I could go. The moonlight pouring in through the blinds striped the room with luminescent prison bars, as I concentrated on the depth of the darkness between the lines. The necessary neurons fired, telling my body to put on some shoes, but I couldn't move—I just kept focusing on the darkness. It felt like it was alive, growing and breathing and responding to something that pulsed deep within me, although my heart was still.

You can't go. His voice was as clear as if it were mine.

You don't want to go, so you shouldn't go. If Xavier were here, you wouldn't even consider going.

Stop.

I wish Xavier were here. If he were here, this wouldn't be happening. Imagine: him sleeping a few feet away from us, him lying next to us.

Stop. STOP!

Imagine: his smile, his eyes...

STOP! STOP! STOP!

Imagine: his lips...

Stop... please.

The fight had gone out of me.

There was this one time, when I was about nine or ten, my mom worked a late-night shift on a Saturday. It wasn't unusual for her to work weekends—she often worked mornings and finished by the early afternoon. However, when Grandma Junie had died, she switched shifts with coworkers to get the time off, so now she had to repay the favor. Like all the other times when my mom worked late, she had prepared dinner beforehand. After dinner that night—a hearty serving of leftover curry chicken and white rice—I put on a horror movie and told Christian to head to bed. Christian was as stubborn as he was brave and, against all my warnings, insisted that I let him stay up to watch; so, I did. To my surprise, he had handled the movie well, but when it was time for bed, he refused to turn out the lights, believing that some supernatural evil would whisk him away in the darkness. I had tried logic, telling him it was all just make-believe and that he would be fine, but that didn't work. I had tried putting on cartoons to "cleanse his palette" in a sense, but it had the opposite effect of energizing him. After an hour of trying to get him to fall asleep, I told him if he clenched his eyes tight and counted to 100, it would make a force field that would protect him from the darkness and the monsters. "Trust me," I said and turned off the light. Christian clenched his eyes as tight as he could and then began to count: one… two… three… four… five… six… seven… eight…I called to him softly to ask why he stopped, but he had fallen asleep. After that night, electrical work on our block caused several blackouts, and each time Christian clenched his eyes to keep out the darkness, opening them only when he felt safe from whatever lurked within.

In the same fashion, I closed my eyes as tight as I could to keep out the encroaching darkness and counted. At the end, I whispered, "Please." I didn't know with whom I was pleading, whether with the Dead or with God, but I begged for it to stop. When I opened my eyes, I saw the darkness retreat and confine itself to the space between the bars of moonlight. Regaining control of my body, I slipped on my shoes and left the room.

Ok. He said follow this trail and then make a left.

I could still feel the Dead rapping against their coffins, but with all the mental fortitude I could gather, I ordered my steps—*left, right, left, right, left*—and treaded the dirt road to meet up with my podmates. As instructed, I cut across the courtyard and was on the trail that would split into two. In truth, I had run through the courtyard, which, although unobscured by trees, was more shadowed than the trail whose boundaries blurred the deeper I walked into the woods. The courtyard, devoid of life, felt haunted, as if the chatter and laughter that had permeated the area earlier that day had evaporated into dust and scattered into echoes that could faintly be heard on the wind. I thought I could hear laughter in the brush, so I walked faster.

The trail ended at the crossroads. There was a wooden sign with two arrows nailed to it: one pointing left, the other to the right. Below each arrow was written what awaited in that direction: to the left, an elusive identity that will forever be just at your fingertips as you drown in a sea of your own self-denial—you'll reach for it, and maybe sometimes grab on, but it'll always break and send you careening back into the depths of your shame—to the right, life. Salvation. Truth. I clenched my eyes shut, waiting for the darkness to retreat, and when I reopened them, I read the words that were written: the arrow pointing to the left led to the lake, and the one pointing to the right only said "construction." I turned left at the crossroad and continued down the path that was familiar.

Walking along, enveloped by the night, I felt as if I had dissolved, weightless and scattered to the moon's pale fingers. The day's shower had pressed the heat into the soft, muddy ground—leaving the air light and cool—but I could feel the earth's warm exhalations released with each step, reminding me of the infinite density of my being. The path was unlit, illuminated only by stray rays of moonlight passing through the forest canopy. I studied the brush to find the opening that would lead to the gazebo and in navigating the tides of the black sea, I saw it—the same shadowy figure I had seen in the courtyard. It moved like a person, but I could feel it was not of this world. I kept hearing Xavier's voice saying, "If you see fog… run!" But there was no fog, and I couldn't explain why, but the figure felt familiar, so I followed it. We trod along the narrow path, passing a small opening I was sure branched off to the gazebo. I thought I could hear my podmates laughing in the distance. However, the invisible thread connecting me to the figure tugged at me until we reached a clearing in the middle of the forest.

Tall grass glowing in the moonlight covered the field; brown patches connected by tread marks dotted it. On the perimeter of the clearing, I saw yellow bulldozers caked in mud and concluded that the camp was expanding. I took a seat on the stump of a tree that hadn't been uprooted yet and traced the treads as they passed from one brown dot to the other. Constellations formed among the glowing grass, and I thought of Xavier. The shadowy figure had disappeared, but I could still feel its pull. Striated clouds rolled through the sky like waves at high tide and obscured stars and portions of the naked moon as though hiding its shame. I looked up at the stars and what I saw was a sky stretched like canvas on a boundless easel, aching for a masterpiece to be painted, yet one that didn't contain Xavier. Here, light pollution was absent. Outside the context of the sickly glow of the city, the alternate life with Xavier—stitched together by a patch in the sky—crumbled into pieces and scattered across infinite timelines, never intersecting to create a full picture. I thought of Romeo and Juliet and the conditions that made their meeting inevitable, yet their love impossible. So much sky existed outside the patch, but I desired nothing more than our small window above Snake Hill.

It scared me.

The Dead often whispered of freedom, of life, of happiness, but the closer I got to understanding what they meant, the greater the desire grew to bury them. *For the wages of sin is death, but the gift of God is eternal life.* "For the wages of sin is death, but the gift of God is eternal life," I said, repeating the thought out loud to confirm I still had a voice. Romans 6:23 was the motto chosen in line with that year's theme and repeated after every prayer, service, and fireside chat. Although I had shut out the spiritual aspects of camp, I couldn't blame the retention of these words on passive absorption. Looking up at the stars and seeking to piece together a mosaic future with Xavier, I finally acknowledged what I knew to be true but was afraid to admit: I was holding on to the Dead.

The clouds passed and left the sky bare in all its glory. As I began to grieve the Dead, who longed for the future with Xavier that was now scattered into pieces across the universe, I thought of stars that had exploded eons ago and lived on in the enduring light that was now reaching Earth. What history did these rays carry with them? What stories, what time, what mystery? And what did it matter if all I could perceive were these tiny shimmers whose light died in my eyes? I considered whether in a million years, the sky would be empty, and what cosmic event would have to occur for this to happen. What supernatural event would have to occur to change the composition of the sky?

I closed my eyes. "For the wages of sin is death, but the gift of God is eternal life," I said, sparking the kindling. Vibrations echoed throughout my body as the Dead pounded on their coffins. I chanted the words into the wind, praying that it carried them to God's ears, praying for fire. The vibrations intensified, and I felt my lungs swell as my chest heaved. I was crying—the first time since the incident with Malcolm. The Dead's resistance became violent, and I convulsed. Fire shut up in my bones. I raised my hands to the sky, as I had seen them do in church, and continued to pray. The Dead pleaded. Flames ripped through their coffins, burning away the pieces of me that held on to the unnatural, that held on to the Dead, that held on to Jacob. The vibrations stopped. The pleas stopped. The flames subsided, leaving nothing but ashes strewn in the wind and feelings of relief and gratitude.

———

Dark clouds drifted off the gray silhouette of the mountains and billowed upwards like smoke from a chimney. I said goodbye to Gresh' and Mikey and to Pastor Gabe and climbed onto the yellow school bus. My desire to leave camp had fluxed since arriving, yet as I stared out the window and watched the campground fall away, I felt sadness with what I was leaving behind. Neither Gresh' or Mikey had asked why I didn't make it to the gazebo. Maybe because they had stumbled into our room at 2 AM drunk or the invitation itself was just a formality, but I was going to miss them. The bus kicked up dirt as it chugged down the road. In time, memories of the events here would become covered in dust, and Damascus would fade into a general recollection that I slept somewhere for the duration of camp.

Outside this wooded dream, the gritty concrete of reality awaited. I had turned my phone off because there was no service, but watching the patchwork of trees and brush change into turnpike signs, I decided that there was no rush to turn it back on. Heavy drops of rain pounded the metal roof of the school bus. It sounded like I was inside a steel drum. I closed my eyes and let the rhythm carry me. Herb could wait. Xavier could wait. The future could wait. The faint smell of smoke lingered between the drops of rain.

Tears will help to wash the dirt off.

CHAPTER 14

"Ok, I told you about Chicago. Now it's your turn. How was church camp?"

"*Youth* camp," I responded.

"How was *youth* camp?" Xavier corrected, rolling his eyes. "Must not have been all bad. You're still alive."

"Unfortunately, there was no masked killer to put me out of my misery sooner. It actually wasn't all bad, though."

"What was your favorite part?"

"Uhm… oh, my podmates were fun. Two white bouls, Michael and Gresham, kind of weird, but also cool. And I don't know… I think I'm an outdoors person now?"

We laughed.

"See, I knew you would like it," Xavier said, smiling. "You feel any different after *church* camp?"

I chuckled and gave him the finger. After the spiritual experience in the clearing, I did feel different, but not in a way that I could articulate. I felt lighter. I felt clean. I felt new. However, I couldn't share this without explaining what I had been cleansed of, so I responded, "No."

"Cool, glad you had fun." Xavier returned to sketching.

"Hey, can I call you 'X'?"

"Huh?" Xavier looked up from his sketchbook. "Why?"

"I don't know. 'Xavier' is such a mouthful: X-say-vee-err. See?" I pulled one of my curls straight. "Look at this gray hair. I've aged so much."

"You're annoying," he laughed.

"You can call me 'Jay' too. Everyone does."

"Why?"

"Why what?"

"Do they call you 'Jay'?"

"It's a nickname that just kinda stuck. The only people who call me 'Jacob' are my mom, my brother, a few family members, and you."

"You can call me 'X,' but I'm not calling you 'Jay.'"

"Deal. I'm gonna save sooo much time. Maybe I'll pick up a hobby or a part-time job with all the time I'll save."

"I like Jacob." He smiled, and the freckles around his mouth scurried up to his eyes. I felt myself blushing, so I looked away. "He has an interesting story in the Bible."

"Another one of your fun facts?"

"No, ass," he chuckled, "I got bored one day while you were gone and randomly looked it up."

"Ahhh, so he doesn't know everything."

"Shut up. Do you want to know the story or not?"

"School me, oh wise one."

"It's pretty long, but I'll give you the highlights. Jacob, in the beginning, is this super ambitious guy who'll do anything to achieve social and material gains. In the story, he tricks his dad and steals his brother's inheritance and then runs away to work for his uncle. There's some other stuff that happens, but after like a decade, he heads home to make things right with his brother. On the way back—and this is where it gets interesting—he gets into a wrestling match with God. Like physically fights God! But the website I was on said that the fight was a metaphor for his struggle with his identity and past or something."

"And that's how it ends?"

"After the fight, God blesses him. Jacob becomes a new person and changes his name."

The library was mostly empty, as it tended to be in the middle of the day. There were one or two boys whom I recognized in passing from Blanche Creek and a group of children and their parents who were there for a book reading. Also present were a handful of adult regulars who came to use the computers or to escape the heat or both. X and I sat in the history section, which no one ever visited, so we had the space to ourselves.

"Why are you practicing Chinese calligraphy again?" I asked as X dipped his fountain pen in ink.

"When I was in Chicago, my uncle let me shadow him during an operation."

"Right, right. He does lap-, laparous-something surgery?"

"Laparoscopic surgery," he said proudly. "Minimally invasive. And you do the whole thing while watching a screen. It's like a video game. My uncle said calligraphy helped him with dexterity and hand-eye coordination, which are great qualities in a surgeon."

"I thought you wanted to be a history professor?"

"Keeping my options open."

We laughed.

"Shhhh," the librarian said from the other side of the stacks, which made us laugh even more, although quietly.

X flipped the page and started to carefully craft another character: the strokes were heavy in some areas and light at others, with a flourish that tapered off at the end. Satisfied with the outcome, he punctuated it with four dots on the inside.

"Maybe next year I'll come with you," I said jokingly, curious to see how he would respond.

His face lit up and then soured as he remembered something. "That would be fun. I don't know if I'll be able to go next year, though. Every summer after the first year at Harbor Park, the new cohort takes a trip. The last cohort went to Nashville, and I heard that next year we're supposed to go to D.C."

We're I thought to myself. "You decided to go?"

"Not yet," he said, "but there's nothing keeping me here. Harbor Park has been my dream for a while. I don't want to leave my dad by himself, but he would be disappointed if I didn't go."

"Oh," I responded, trying to find something else to add, but all I could think about was the empty feeling growing inside me.

"Yeah, but I still have time before I have to give an answer," he added to reassure me of some hope that he might stay. He twirled the fountain pen and searched me for a sign that acknowledged it wasn't an easy choice for him. A smile grew in equal measure to the grief that I was feeling, and I told X that I was proud of him, declaring that if nothing was keeping him here, he should go. He responded with a "thank you" and a fleeting look that showed his regret at saying that.

The shelves locked us into the space and blocked the airflow. Trapped in the past, we shared a desire to escape. X drew beautiful stray lines that looked like silky black ribbons on the page, while I thumbed aimlessly through an atlas. In the moments when we would catch each other's eyes, we would look away as if we had caught a stranger staring. It felt like we couldn't relate to each other anymore, like we both wanted to say something, but every topic seemed foreign and there were no questions left to be asked. Even the silence between us felt different, amplifying the outside world vs. dampening it. His pen strokes, once delicate, now sounded like they were ripping the sky apart; and the clock, with each distinct *tick* and rebutting *tock,* plotted as though its internal machinations were responsible for the passage of time. Yet even with the awkwardness, neither of us wanted to leave, so we lingered in the history section.

"Are you leaving?" X asked, shooting up in his seat.

"Just stretching."

"Oh." His body relaxed, and he sank back down into his chair. "What're you reading?"

"Nothing. Looking at some maps."

"Cool."

"Yeah, can't handle reading a full-blown textbook right now."

"There are other things over here besides maps and textbooks," he laughed. I shrugged, and he walked over to me. "I told you that my dad lived in South Africa during Apartheid, right?" He picked up the atlas, flipped through the pages until he found South Africa, and then told me how his father lived through most of it before moving to the States. "He played jazz piano in a quartet at this nightclub. He said it was like the speakeasies back in the '20s." At some point during his monologue, he switched to discussing the lasting effects of colonialism on a global scale and then dovetailed into his reason for being a history professor: "My dad told me that you can't heal without acknowledging and dealing with the past, otherwise, it just changes form and comes back to bite you in the ass."

"So, what? You're trying to heal the world?" I asked as a joke.

"Something like that," he said, packing up his notebook and pencils. His eyes caught mine, but neither of us looked away—strangers no longer. He then rushed over and hugged me. "I'm glad you're back. I missed you."

Unable to say it back, I squeezed X and hoped he felt the sentiment in the gesture.

Don't leave. Please.

I wanted to just come out and say it, but I couldn't. I had felt reborn after that experience in the field; however, I was still subject to the norms that governed my status as a man. What were the rules for telling another man that you loved him and didn't want to lose him? All answers pointed to this not being allowed.

When I was with X, I felt engulfed in the moment and filled with an elation that was familiar and foreign. Familiar in what I felt for X, I had felt for What's-His-Name. I knew I loved X, even if I hadn't realized it until this moment. Foreign in when we were apart, I yearned to be near him—as if a portion of my soul lived in his body and vice versa, and we were in a perpetual struggle to rejoin them. At Snake Hill, when X had asked me had I ever been in love, I almost answered by telling him about What's-His-Name, but I could see now this would have been in error. What I felt for X, I hadn't felt for What's-His-Name. In fact, I didn't know what I was feeling for X—but when I tried to identify it, my mind kept coming back to the passion shared by Romeo and Juliet: their fatal love.

"Do you want to hear the new piece I've been practicing?"

"Always," I answered.

"What did that character mean? The one with the four dots that you kept practicing over and over?" I asked. We threw open the doors of the library and squinted while our eyes adjusted to the sunlight.

"Rain."

CHAPTER 15

"Yo," I called to him, standing at the base of the steps. Herb sat in a shaded area of the stoop and spat sunflower seed shells into the black plastic bag at his feet.

"Yo." He glanced at me and then turned his attention to the end of the street as if he were expecting someone to turn the corner.

I loitered on the sidewalk and scanned the street to find what or whom he was looking for. *Go.* I said to myself, attempting to compel my steps. *Just go. Go! Ok, go on three: one…two…three. Three. Three!* My legs felt like they were filled with wet sand, and I labored to lift them up the steps as I climbed closer to him. Like a subject seeking audience from a king or a child trying to catch a butterfly, I took careful steps, unsure whether he would behead me or take flight. I got to the landing and stopped out of fear he would hear my heart beating inside my chest. Leaning on the railing, I waited for the words I needed to turn the corner.

"Nacho cheese. I love that flavor."

"What?"

"The sunflower seeds. That's a good flavor."

His right cheek was packed with empty shells, which he volleyed into the black plastic bag. He poured the remainder of the seeds from the bag directly into his mouth, packing his left cheek, and then repeated the process, cracking one shell at a time, eating the seed, and then maneuvering the empty shell to his right cheek. His eyes were still fixed on the corner. I imagined he was considering whether to buy more sunflower seeds from the papi store.

"I got your birthday text, by the way. Thanks."

"Yup."

"I would've texted back, but my mom took my phone. And then gave it back as I was goin' to camp—oh, did I mention that I was goin' to camp? My mom signed me up for this bullshit church camp that was two weeks long! They had me in the middle of the sticks in cabins and shit with all these White… anyway, I didn't have service out there. I just got back last night."

"Yup."

"So… what you been up to?"

"What you mean?"

"Like what you been doin' all summer?"

"Just chillin'."

"Cool," I responded.

For a moment, the entire world had paused—no cars passed, no kids ran by, no birds chirped. The air didn't move, and my breath grew stagnant in my lungs in hopes of the king's mercy. The only sound was that of the cracking shells of the sunflower seeds. In the silence, I cracked my knuckles, doing one finger at a time, hoping that he would say something before I got to ten.

"How about you?"

I got to nine, and the world raced back in a beautiful cacophony.

"Chillin'," I said.

"True."

It didn't seem like much, but in this short exchange of words, I had extended an apology, and in his response he had accepted. That cold, hard thing—that I was sure existed in Herb too—prevented us from saying what we really felt, but we spoke in gestures that recognized the wound we had dealt to each other without acknowledging what the injury was. Our reconciliation didn't need to be voiced. We held it for each other in our hearts.

He emptied the shells in his mouth into the black plastic bag, tied it off, and then tossed it into the air as he yelled, "Kobe!" I put my hand up in a faux effort to block his shot and then told him he got lucky when it went into the trashcan. "Yeah, whatever," he said, smiling. "I'm goin' to the courts. You comin'?"

Herb's hand shot up in the air, signaling for the ball while darting back and forth to evade his defender. His teammate went to pass the ball, but someone from the other team stole it and scored. "Oh my fuckin' God, bro. What are you doin'? Pass the fuckin' ball!"

Herb inbounded the ball to one of his teammates, who immediately passed it back, and then walked the ball down the court. Herb's defender tracked him closely, but Herb dribbled around him and raced down center court. Herb crossed to the left and drove towards the basket for a layup. He leaped into the air and out of thin air, his defender attempted to block it. The ball rolled off his fingers onto the backboard, circling the rim before falling into the net. "AND FUCKIN' ONE, dickhead!" Herb cheered, walking to the free throw line. He dribbled twice and released the ball: "That's game."

Herb dapped up one of his teammates and then walked over to the other, who was hanging his head. "Lift your head up. You good," Herb said, placing a hand on his shoulder and lowering his voice to a whisper. He patted his teammate on the back and then shook the hands of the players on the other team. "Good game."

"Nah, run that shit back," one of them said, grinning and wiping the sweat off his forehead with his t-shirt.

"I got you on the next one."

"Bet."

Herb came and sat next to me on the bench. He was dripping with sweat and his chest was heaving, but he sat upright. It was important for him not to show he was tired.

"You wanna get in this next game?" I shook my head. I didn't play basketball and only came to the courts to hang out with Herb, even if that meant watching from the sideline. But I appreciated that he would always ask. "Why don't you ever play?"

"Eh, I like watchin' better."

"How come?"

"Because I'm not any good," I laughed.

"Won't get any better if all you do is watch."

"True."

"I could help you," his voice went up in excitement, which he immediately dispersed by clearing his throat, "if you want."

"Nah, basketball isn't really my thing, but good lookin' out."

"Bet… what is your thing?" He asked after a brief silence.

"I don't know. Readin', movies, other shit."

"Right," he smiled, "I be forgettin' you into smart-nigga shit." Unsure of how to respond to his comment, I forced a laugh but stopped when I noticed he wasn't laughing too. He just sat there with the same vacant smile on his face while his eyes followed the game up and down the court.

"I think you could get into it. You're smart enough."

"Eh, not really my *thing*," he replied in a mocking tone.

"Uhm, ok," I said, chuckling awkwardly.

"King Jacob thinks I'm smart enough to share his interests—how lucky I am."

"You know that's not how I meant it."

"It is, though," he said, turning to face me. "I see your face whenever we makin' jokes or we just bullshittin' around, like you can't be bothered to listen to what any of us have to say because it's not interestin' to you. Who wants to be around that all the time? Just because we don't want to talk about fuckin' space and jazz all day, doesn't mean we're dumb."

"That's not true."

"Yeah, ard," he said and turned his attention back to the game. "Why are you even here?"

"What… I haven't seen you all summer. I wanted to hang out."

"Nah, nigga, I meant why are you *here*. You don't like any of the shit we like. You clearly too smart for us. So, why the fuck are you here?"

"I don't know anymore… so, I guess I'll head out."

"Yup."

"Is that why you switched me out the group for the trip?"

He glanced at me and then returned to the game. "No."

When the game ended, they once again called on Herb to see if he was playing, and he replied he was heading home. He dapped up his friends, exchanged barbs with some of the other guys, promising to take their money next time, and then began walking away. I didn't know why I hadn't left, but now I felt like I couldn't. Herb lingered at the entrance, stopping to tie his laces and checking his duffle bag for something, and then walked over to me. "You comin'?"

We walked in silence as Herb communicated turns with a nudge or a careful tug on the arm. The streetlights came on, even though the sun hadn't fully set, and the wind picked up as the air became heavier—it would rain soon. My fingernails dug curved lines into my palm while I struggled to swallow the words that sat in my throat—words like, "fuck you," or "why," now seemed inappropriate for use with a stranger. After about twenty minutes, we crossed the footbridge over the trickling stream and climbed to the top of the hill. The grass was still wet from the night before, so he took a hoodie from his bag and laid it on the ground, sitting on the edge to leave room for me to join him. We huddled together on the hoodie—both of us equally half-wet and half-dry—and looked up at the storm clouds chasing the wispy stretch of clouds strung across the sky like tinsel on a Christmas tree. The sun sank below the horizon, and I searched the sky for the patch but couldn't see beyond the clouds.

"I used to come here all the time when I was younger. It used to be my favorite spot in the city."

"Why are we here?" I asked.

He lifted his arm and drew circles in the sky where the patch would have been. "You're not the only one who's interested in the stars and space."

"Herb, why the fuck—"

"Did you know the universe is still expandin'?" He let his arm fall to his side with a thump. "Trillions of years later, and a universe that's already large beyond comprehension is growing larger. Oh! And did you know it's expandin' at an accelerating rate? I don't know… that shit bugs me out."

"What'd you just Google some astronomy facts to spout at me?"

"Fuck you," he said.

"Fuck you, too."

Herb fell over, laughing. I looked at him and smiled.

"Damn, I thought you said I was 'smart enough.'"

"You know I didn't mean it like that," I said, exasperated. A feeble attempt at an apology, but it was the only version of, "I'm sorry," that the cold, hard thing inside me would permit. I didn't want to fight with Herb anymore, so I hoped it was sufficient.

"I know."

"So then what was all of this for?"

He stretched out on the wet grass and stared up at the sky, "because we're friends and you needed to hear it. The truth hurts sometimes."

The air condensed and enveloped us in a fine mist. Under the cover of the mist, I found courage enough to lie next to him and watch the clouds pass. There was no patch, no escape into another dimension, only the uncomfortable, partially wet reality beneath us. I wondered whether he was seeing the same sky I was, whether the stars ceased to exist if neither of us could witness them. His breathing quieted. I slowed mine to match. Pressed against each other, I could feel his heartbeat–possibly through his skin—but I believed it was radiating through the ground and into my body. Like a magnet, it pulled me deeper into the earth while repelling me towards the sky, creating a feeling of weightlessness as I navigated its rhythm. At one point, it raced, communicating the disquietude moving through his body like electricity. Maybe he was thinking about the universe again. As it reached rest, thumping with the subtle shifts of the Earth's crust and the violent gyrations of its core, it sent out pangs that felt like an ice pick chipping away at my insides.

I couldn't name what he was feeling but regretted my responsibility in causing it. The longer we lay there, the more intense the pangs became, as well as my desire to quell them. I could feel the bile in the back of my throat. My insides contorted. I was going to be sick. And then it happened—the cold, hard thing in me crumbled. The resulting commotion could have deafened the world and sent the birds scrambling to the sky, but in its silent wake I said, "I'm sorry." Herb's skin grew warm against mine, and his heartbeat picked up. "I do sometimes look at the guys like what they have to say is stupid, and you gotta admit they say some stupid shit, but I never thought about any of you that way. Honestly. You are 'smart enough.' I meant that, even though it came out in a shitty way. What I meant was that my interests can be your interests if you want them to be. And even if we don't share all the same interests, that doesn't mean that there aren't other things that we can do together."

He sat up and scanned the horizon for the skyline. Gravity overcame the magnetic force of his heartbeat, turning my feeling of weightlessness into one of sinking. A sense of dread filled me as I anticipated the ground opening to swallow me whole.

"They do say some stupid shit," he laughed in a manner that invited me to do the same.

I exhaled, and the earth released its grip on me. Herb motioned for me to stand and then picked up the hoodie. He shook off the stray blades of grass and then held it over our heads as we sat on the ground.

"Thanks," I said, running my index finger through my

eyebrows to press the water out. The drizzle turned into a light shower, but neither of us budged, finding shelter enough under his hoodie. "So… the universe is still expandin', huh?"

"You didn't know that?"

"I did, but I still want to hear you talk about it."

"I don't know how much more I could tell you that you don't already know," he stopped for a second and then said, "when we first became friends, you mentioned some beginner's guide to understandin' the universe—you were so excited about it. So, I ordered the book and read it. I never told anyone that. But I guess you know now. From what I could understand, and it wasn't a lot, it was interestin'. It took me forever to actually get through it, though, to be honest. I had to reread pages to understand what was happenin' and still didn't know what the fuck was goin' on," he chuckled. "Galaxies light years away. Explodin' stars. I don't know. Made me realize how much I don't know. So, yeah, the universe is expandin'. I don't know why, but neither does anyone else. You ever think about what the universe is expandin' into?"

"Huh, no, I haven't. See, that's somethin' we have in common," I said.

"What?"

"Curiosity… and bein' confused as fuck." We laughed. "It also took me a long time to read. And I also didn't understand everything. I don't know. For me it's a good kind of confusion, though. With space stuff, the more you study it, the more you'll understand it. That's a problem I can solve.

I wish more stuff was like that."

"What else are you confused about?"

"The person I'm supposed to be."

"Definitely was expectin' a harder problem."

"Is that so?" I chuckled. "School me, then, oh wise one."

"Simple, King Jacob. Just be the person you wanna be."

"And if I don't know who that person is?"

"Then be one you can be proud of."

"How was your first year at Creek?"

The rain had stopped, so once again we sat on the hoodie. By this point, the hoodie was soaked, probably wetter than the ground itself, but we found a certain comfort that came with having something beneath us.

"It was good. An adjustment for sure," I answered.

"What do you mean?"

"I don't know. It's just really different from my old school."

"In a good way?"

It was a difficult question to answer, more difficult than I thought it would be. I hadn't thought much about my time at Blanche Creek Middle School, but outside of hanging out with the guys and with X, what else was there to consider? The teachers were good, more dedicated than those at my previous school, so that was a plus. The school-yard here was bare, though, hard, gray concrete encased by a chain-link fence. The difference was stark compared to St.

Luke's, which boasted lush lawns meticulously cared for by the groundskeeper. Breakfast and lunch were free at Blanche Creek, another plus, although most of the meals were hit or miss. I rattled off several other pros and cons, and after tallying the score, Blanche Creek came out as the loser. It was impossible, however, to quantify the intangibles—the new friends, the laughter, the feeling of belonging. Each had its own complex composition of good and bad, so I replied with, "In a good way."

"Cool," he said, sounding pleased with his role in my experience at the school. "I remember you saying that you really liked your old one."

I smiled at the idea of my saying I really liked St. Luke's when for years I had begged my mom to transfer. Nostalgia was peculiar in that way—it was great at distorting history.

"What made you leave?"

"Damn, you nosey as shit," I said, laughing to soften the statement. I thought about telling him I got kicked out, but then I would have to recount what had happened to Malcolm. It felt like it had happened so long ago; so much so I didn't feel it worth bringing up.

"Shit, never mind then," he laughed.

"Just needed a change. I got bored."

"I feel that… is that why you started hangin' out with Xavier?"

"Oh," I said, unsure if I was more surprised by the question or how direct he was in asking it. "I wouldn't say we've been hangin' out. We have classes together, but that's it."

Herb made a sound that expressed some doubt in my

response but left it at that.

"You said you used to come here all the time, right?" I asked, changing the subject.

"Yeah."

"Why'd you stop comin'?"

"Did you know that—"

"Herb…"

"It's not about space shit." He chuckled and then became solemn. "Did you know that we used to be friends?"

"Who?"

"Me and Xavier."

"Is that why you stopped comin' here?"

"You grow outta certain things, you know? There are a lot of things I used to do that I don't anymore. Do you still pee the bed?" I laughed and told him to "shut the fuck up." "But, yeah…," he continued, "had to grow up. We started going to Creek at the same time, since kindergarten, and were best friends from the jump. I taught him how to play basketball, and he made me fall in love with books. I used to be a bookworm, believe it or not. We would to go to the library to read Goosebumps books and then come here if it wasn't rainin'. Shit, sometimes even when it was rainin'. We got in trouble so many times for staying out late," his voice trembled, but not as if he were about to cry, it was as though he had stuffed his nostalgia into a box, and it was now beating against the sides, reshaping his memories and perception of X. His voice trembled, but in the same way that thunder shakes the sky—it was indifferent.

"Why'd you stop being friends?"

"Up until about a year and a half or so ago, we did everything together. We basically lived at each other's houses. If we were late getting' home, all we had to do was say that we were at the other's place and everything would be fine. That's how close we had become. One day we were at mine playin' video games." Herb's voice went up a little bit, so he coughed to clear his throat and then continued, "And he says he has to pee. He's gone for about ten minutes, and I'm thinkin', 'what the fuck is he doin'?' All of a sudden, he comes back into the room, and he has on one of my mom's wigs, her bra, lipstick, and a pair of heels. I start crackin' the fuck up. He always did some dumb shit to make me laugh, and he knew this would make me laugh. He looked stupid as hell, but it was funny. Anyway, after a few minutes, he sat down and picked up the controller to finish the game, but I told him he should go take that stuff off. As soon as he steps out of my room, my dad walks up the steps to see him like that. He was pissed.

"I've only seen my dad that angry one other time, and it was when my grandma, his mom, died. Mind you, my dad is a pretty chill boul—always laughin', always smilin'. But that night when he got the call, his eyes—I swear to God— went black. Leadin' up to the funeral, every word that came out of his mouth was shouted. And at the funeral, his jaw was clenched so tight I thought the vein in his temple would burst. Once the service ended and everyone left, my dad went up to the casket. It was the first time he had gotten up to look at her. My older brother and mom had gone off somewhere. I don't know why I stuck around, but I watched him up there from the back of the room. After a few minutes, I see his body start to quake. I'm thinkin', 'oh shit, is he cryin'?' so I move closer to try and see his face. I'm two rows away but still can't see because he's bent over the coffin, so I just say, 'fuck it,' and go up next to him. I had never seen my dad cry before. There was like an excitement and nervousness as I got closer—like I felt like my view of him was going to change forever but wasn't sure if that meant in a good or bad way. It took a minute for him to realize I was standin' there, but when he finally looked up, there were no tears. Just the same black spaces that had replaced his eyes. But the way he was lookin' at me… bro, swear to God, if his hands weren't grippin' the handles on the coffin, I feel like he would've choked me.

"That's how angry he was when he called me out of my room. So badly I wanted Xavier to explain to him that it was just a joke or to do somethin' so that he would calm down—or at the very least, not leave me by myself. But he took all that stuff off and rushed home. He was shakin' and lookin' at me through those same black eyes, like how he looked at her coffin, and his hands were clenched into fists. Honestly… I wanted him to just hit me so that it could be over… I couldn't take him lookin' at me like that anymore, like I was dead. We stood there for like a good five minutes not sayin' anything. And then very suddenly and very calmly, he said, 'If I ever find out you on some faggot shit, I'll fuckin' kill you.'"

The words made me shudder, but Herb spoke them matter-of-factly as though he were just repeating something he had overheard. He laughed to dispel any pity that may had formed for him, a reassurance that it wasn't a big deal, and he was good; in fact, he was a better person for the experience.

"But, yeah, after that, I couldn't fuck with him anymore."

"Did your dad say you couldn't be friends with him?"

"No, he didn't say anything other than that, and we never spoke about it again."

"Then why?"

"Like I said, you grow out of certain shit. After doing some dumb shit like that and then leavin' me to deal with the fallout, I just couldn't rock with boul anymore. He turned out not to be the person I thought he was."

"Why did you bring me here?"

"I'm sorry for what I said. But you're not the only one who likes to look up at the stars… I know the guys sometimes say and do some dumb shit, but we're your friends. *I'm* your friend, no matter what; don't forget that."

I wanted to ask him why he switched me from the group if we were friends but felt that I didn't really want the answer—at least not right then when everything felt so fragile—so, I just nodded. The clouds rolled away, revealing a pale crescent moon. The faint moonlight washed over us and reminded me of the pallid streetlights and violence that awaited us just over the footbridge. We sat in silence until we could no longer ignore the calls to come home and then descended the hill.

Me: I forgot to ask, when is your party?
Herb: Didn't think you'd want to come so didn't bring it up
Me: I do. When is it?
Herb: Last Saturday of the month. It's the day after my birthday
Me: Bet. I'll be there
Herb: It's all good if you can't make it. I know your mom might still say no. Not tryna get you in trouble
Me: I think it'll be fine. If she needs convincing, I'll just have her call your mom. But she likes you, I think she'll be chill
Herb: Cool... you know you don't have to come tho, right?
Me: Do you not want me to come? lol
Me: ?

CHAPTER 16

Being with X and Herb, my days were no longer marked by day and night, but rather measured by the hours spent with one or the other. The effect of this was a continuous stream of time that carried me from one experience to the next, a stream that would eventually set me down when X left for school. But in the meantime, I was enjoying summer.

With Herb, we passed the time at the basketball court—if it weren't too busy, Herb would teach me how to dribble and shoot—or we played video games at his house. I had even introduced him to some of my favorite horror movies, so we would watch those together, but he wasn't a fan of the gore, although he would never admit it. We never went back to Snake Hill and never spoke about that night but not from lack of trying. Sometime after that night, while we sat on the sidelines waiting for Herb to get into the next game, I asked him if he wished he had handled the situation with X differently. He answered, asking, "When did you start callin' him 'X'?" which suddenly made me feel embarrassed, so I changed the subject.

Things were good between us, but a tension simmered

below the surface. Even though he didn't ask, Herb knew I was hanging out with X, and he made it known through these conspicuous declarations of what a true friendship was worth—as if he were trying to convince me of the value of his—or through snide comments about X, which he knew I wouldn't refute for fear of exposing our relationship. The tension was most acute when we talked about his party. I would text him to confirm certain details.

"Is there a theme? Do I need to bring anything? What time should I show up? Is that a hard 9 PM or a Black 9 PM? Is Brianna still going? What time is she getting there?" But he would sidestep the questions with vague answers or would simply not respond. When I posed the questions in person, his responses were even more frustrating:

"What time should I show up?"

"Doesn't matter."

"Do I need to bring anything?"

"If you want."

"Is there a theme?"

"Nigga, what…"

"Is Brianna still goin'?"

"My mom drawlin' party might not even happen anymore."

Still, he always shied away from saying he didn't want me to come, but rather implied and sometimes explicitly stated, I didn't have to. I didn't know what to make of his caprice, but when we spoke about his party, he had that flicker of disdain in his eyes I'd seen on the day of the trip. What did he see? The possible answers to that question made me anxious yet resolute in attending.

When I wasn't with Herb, I was, of course, with X. We spent our time doing the things we normally did—going to the library, stargazing at Snake Hill, listening to him play the piano. However, amid routine, he would introduce some cherished item or memory as though he were giving me small pieces of him so I wouldn't forget him.

Once, after a productive piano session, X pulled a record off the shelf and put it on. It wasn't one I had heard before, but I recognized her voice immediately. Without prompting, he said the song was titled "These Foolish Things (Remind Me of You)" and that his mom had given his dad the album on their third date. Like it was a prerecorded response, he stopped speaking and became pensive, as if lulled into a trance or a shattered memory put back together by the wistfulness in Ella Fitzgerald's voice—snapping back to life once the needle scratched off the record.

X maintained he hadn't decided whether he was going to accept the scholarship; however, his decision was becoming increasingly clear. But I chose not to let his pending departure affect the rest of our time together. I had heard somewhere "happiness is a choice," and you could trick yourself into being happy by just smiling, so I smiled, laughed, and received the subtle messages that he was leaving while I buried my grief for him next to the Dead.

X's leaving wasn't the only loss I would be dealing with. Since returning from camp, the interaction with my mom remained sparse and became even more so when I had learned Christian would stay to live with his dad. Christian had told her he liked being there more, so he wanted to stay. Although she had never admitted it, I knew she blamed me for his decision. I wanted to call and tell Christian I loved and missed him and I was sorry. But instead, I trailed behind him as he drove away, too scared to confront the cold, hard thing weighing me down and opting instead to carry the sadness of his departure in my heart. I had wanted him to see I wasn't a good person and finally he had. And so, he did what I expected all people would do once they found out who I really was, he left.

Those melded days, which blended like colorful chalk drawings washed away from the pavement, became disentangled—colored in black and white and bookended by thick, leather covers—when "Revival" began. Five days of church programming, Revival targeted the younger members of the congregation, so I was being forced to attend. Out of an unspoken obligation for the church sponsoring my trip to camp, I had to help with setup, clean up, and whatever else they needed for the week. I also would have to stand in front of the congregation and tell eager listeners what I had gained from the experience there.

Like youth camp, Revival tried to emphasize that Christianity could be fun. They organized field days, BBQs, and other activities to soften the fact that you were still in church. However, despite these plays at the secular, the full fervor of Christian spirituality came roaring back each night.

Regardless of the time at camp, I hadn't grown accustomed to devotionals, and in having to endure them for Revival, I recognized the time there had intensified my discomfort. Unlike living in a cool climate where your body would eventually adapt by making you sweat less, my body wrung out like a sponge each time I saw their tears or the convulsions preceding their collapse. Enthralled by the supernatural they would yell, "hallelujah," or babble in a language that if spoken outside of this building would have been labeled nonsense, all the while church elders stood over them with raised hands and closed eyes as they spoke in tongues to entreat the "Spirit" to show itself.

With one day of Revival left, this would be the last devotional. I watched the ceremony transpire from the back of the church as I did every night and chuckled at the stark change in behavior from some guys my age. Just earlier that day, I had overheard them talking about the girls in their school that they had fucked or wanted to fuck, and now they were on the floor shaking or doing laps around the sanctuary or bawling with their hands lifted to the sky. Often the youth pastors encouraged us to bring friends along, and as the guy doing laps zipped past me, I wondered how this scene would look to Herb or X. If the world were muted and an ominous score added, I knew it would inspire fear. Even without a soundtrack, it was chilling. Yet, I felt their curiosity would make them want to come back—the spectacle was intriguing and seductive.

It occurred to me it was all a performance, and these boys were paid actors, but I dismissed this hypothesis. Usually after the ceremony ended and their wits returned, the afflicted would look like they had "worshiper's remorse," like "buyer's remorse," except there was no level of rational justification to explain away the purchase. I doubted money was enough to suffer the cognitive dissonance I knew they were feeling—so why did they do it? I thought of my own experience of being filled with the Holy Ghost in the clearing and considered whether it was a true encounter with God or if, in a moment of extreme desperation and hopelessness, I had just been overwhelmed by my emotions. Were their actions a result of some violent spiritual revolution or simply a culmination of frustration from being told they would never be good enough? At the end of the third act, which lasted about twenty-five minutes, the boys and a few of the girls were prostrate at the altar while one of the youth pastors gave the benediction. And with that, the service ended.

Later that night, I stared up at the dim stars on the ceiling and thought about what I would say for my testimonial. I had thought it would be simple to come up with something. However, I had been so absorbed in my relationships with X and Herb, I had never truly reflected on my time at camp. I was anxious to revisit those two weeks for reasons I wasn't sure of but somehow knew precluded me from talking to X or Herb about them.

With no one to talk to, I dug my journal out from underneath my mattress. It was an interesting experience flipping through the pages and revisiting who I was just some weeks before. The pages were riddled with several half-started tv shows and movie reviews, one failed rewrite of *Harry Potter and the Chamber of Secrets*—*Henry Spencer and the Chest of Mysteries*—and dozens of detailed sketches of eyes. I examined the pages with some whimsy, oscillating between jocular embarrassment and genuine disdain, but paused when I arrived at my last entry. I skimmed over the section depicting my loneliness—afraid that reading too closely would color my current state of being—and scanned the lines describing my desire for X: "I shouldn't imagine how soft his sheets are… whether his slender arms connect to his body in the same fashion as mine or… to an ever-expanding universe… I miss him in ways I can't write here… God, please forgive me," the section ended. The last few sentences of the entry mentioned Herb's party and then concluded with, "… *to fuck Brianna.*"

When I left for camp, I did so with the hope of the Dead being silenced for good and of curing what was wrong in me. With how loud they once were, one would have thought I would have noticed the silence sooner, but since returning from camp it was quiet. Whatever desires I had once held for X—those that I couldn't memorialize on paper—had seemed to vanish. I couldn't get in front of the congregation tomorrow and tell them that camp had restored in me what was natural or that it had turned the Dead to ash, so now I could fuck Brianna. It had revived my faith in God, however, and this seemed like an appropriate middle ground.

Me: Hey, sorry again I've been MIA all week, been busy
with this church stuff.
Me: But happy birthday! Looking forward to the party
tomorrow,
it's gonna be a good time!
Herb: Thanks, bro. Appreciate it.
Me: Is Brianna still coming? ;)

———

It was hot in the sanctuary. The A/C system was old and
took a few hours to get going, and someone had forgotten
to turn it on earlier. I was sweltering under the white lights,
but it wasn't just the lights or the heavy air being moved
around by the ceiling fans, I was excited. Or at least that
was what I told myself. I'm sure nerves caused it, but soon
it would end, and my life could resume. Funny how the
nature of anxiety presumed the anticipation of the future,
yet in this moment I felt wholly present. Anxiety made the
clock on the wall stop, but I marked the passage of time by
where we were in the program. Anxiety numbed my senses,
but I clapped in time with the music I couldn't hear but
could feel. I mimicked the smiling faces around me and told
myself I was happy—it wasn't nerves, it was excitement.

After a few songs, the "Praise and Worship" section
ended, and Sister Lani made her way to the podium.
Contrary to her usual Sunday best, she donned a long denim
skirt and white blouse with modest heels that lifted her just
so off the ground.

"Good evening, brothers and sisters," she said with a wide smile that seemed genuine. "Good evening, brothers and sisters!" she repeated after only receiving a few sparse responses.

"Good evening!" The church responded.

"That's better," she said, her wide smile unchanged. "What a week it's been, yes? The Bible says, 'Blessed are they which do hunger and thirst after righteousness: for they shall be filled.' To see all these young people here hungry and thirsty for the Lord, it's a blessing, isn't it? Amen, amen. Tonight, some of our young people will be taking that next step and will be baptized. Hallelujah! Will those being baptized please stand?" The choir benches were filled with kids around my age, who stood to their feet. Applause filled the sanctuary. "Please make your way to the back to change into your gowns."

Sister Lani squeezed in an abridged version of the announcements and then asked for first-time guests to stand. She squinted over her glasses at the sheet in her hand and rattled off some names. "… and last but not least, Mr. Malcom Brixton, Sister Tally's nephew, who ran in the Penn Relays earlier this year, welcome." The church applauded.

It can't be him, I thought to myself. *It must be a different Malcolm.*

"And" she waved him up to the front of the church, "and his team won *second* place in the Middle School 4 x 100m Relays. Let's give this young man another hand." The church broke into applause again as he stood next to Sister Lani. I examined this person up there and tried to determine if he was in fact *my* Malcolm. He was taller than my Malcolm, my height, but half an inch shorter. And instead of cornrows, he had a short, clean cut. Moreover, he was muscular. All things to be expected with age and time and this person's apparently successful track career. Yet, I still doubted.

Sister Lani placed an arm on his back and nudged him back to his seat. I buried my face in a Bible until he walked past. "Thank you. If you're sitting next to our first-timers, please be sure to say 'hi' and make them feel welcome. Alright," she shuffled some papers as if trying to shake loose her next words, "recently one of our young people attended the statewide Church of God Youth Camp, and he's going to share his experience with us. Who knows, maybe I'll go next year. I'm still young …? In spirit! Amen?"

The congregation laughed and responded, "Amen."

"Amen," she said, smiling her same wide smile. She gathered her things and then stepped down from the podium.

"Good evening, everyone," I said, scanning the faces in the audience to find his. From my seat, I could register the cheerful expression of each person, but up at the podium, what I found was that the individual smiling faces had turned into a collective stony gaze—their personalities flattened, and their names carved into a cold, blank surface like a headstone—and a solemnity moved through the room like a wispy fog crawling along the floor of a cemetery. The weight of the moment settled in my legs, so I held onto the podium to steady myself.

"Good evening," the congregation replied.

"Uhm... it was good," I began. Sister Lani, whose

expression remained unchanged, brought her index fingers to the corners of her mouth and in an upward motion signaled for me to smile. I pulled my lips into a smile and began again. "It was good. Um, the campground was a few hours from here, past Harrisburg and a little to the north in the mountains. There was no service, so we couldn't use our phones, and that was hard at first because I couldn't talk to my friends. But then I started to make new friends, which made it easier. There were a lot of activities for us to do, from fishing to hiking to swimming. I don't know… I think I'm an outdoors person now," I said, repeating the same joke I had told X, which was received with modest chuckles from the audience. "Uhm, and I had two roommates who kept me entertained. We also had competitions between the cabins where we competed to earn points. My cabin finished in third and got these Bibles that highlight verses and chapters for navigating being a teenager." I held up the Bible for an awkward amount of time as I tried to find my train of thought.

"Besides the camp stuff, we also had devotionals every morning and night. The theme for this year was 'Youth on Fire,' so devotionals focused on teaching us how to pray for the Holy Spirit, like this past week's Revival. To be honest… I wasn't excited to go to camp. If you had asked me before I went, I would have told you I can't think of a worse way to spend your summer. But I'm glad I went because it restored my faith in God's power to restore what's broken."

My eyes continued to scan the cemetery for signs of life; however, there appeared to be none. But then I saw him. He was sitting at the back of the church near the door, so I couldn't see him clearly, but his sharp and mechanical movements were unmistakable. My stomach dropped, and for the first time since returning from camp, I felt them. It was subtle but undeniable—the Dead had returned. Or they had never left in the first place. A part of me was angry, but more than anything, I had an overwhelming desire to laugh.

You got me again, good one.

From the podium, where blank faces stared back at me, I'm sure his would be the only one strewn with tears. Standing over Malcolm's limp body, I thought I had seen Jacob die in Malcolm's eyes, but he was still alive—with a soft heart and bloody hands, he was there begging for me not to let him go, to remember him.

"When they asked me to speak about my experience, I was hesitant because I wasn't sure what I had learned. We read the Bible every day, but something in me prevented the Word from sinking in. But over the past week, I've recognized what stopped me from getting closer to God: it was fear. Fear of how others would see me. Fear of how I saw myself. Fear of surrendering. Fear of letting go." The cemetery regained life in this moment and amens rang out. "It's hard to surrender to God's will. It's hard because it takes realizing that we don't have control over every aspect of our lives, and that's scary. It's hard because to surrender you'll be asked to let go of certain things, to face that what you've been praying to be taken away has been something you've been holding on to. But camp taught me that the only way to truly experience the full weight of God's power is through surrender." Applause echoed through the room. "And so," I said, cutting through the chorus of amens, "and so that's what I'm going to do right now." In the sea of faces, I ensured I locked eyes with him. I wanted him to know that this was his end. For good this time.

———

Pastor Hooks stepped into the pulpit wearing a thick white robe with blue trim around the sleeves and hemline. The deacon, who stood a few feet behind him, wore something similar, but it was a plain white gown that looked like it was sewn together from bedsheets. As Pastor Hooks spoke about the commitment we were about to make in front of the congregation, the ushers rolled up the rug at the altar to reveal the baptismal pool underneath the hardwood.

"The journey is sweet …," Pastor Hooks said, descending the steps slowly down to the altar, the deacon trailing behind him. "It's sweet, but it's not easy." The truism was met with a resounding amen from the church. "It's not easy! But with this public declaration, with this sacred ceremony done by our Lord and Savior, you enter a community that understands you, that supports you, that believes in you and loves you with the love of Jesus Christ. Amen?"

"Amen!" the congregation responded.

"Amen," Pastor Hooks said. He gave his mic to an usher and then stepped into the baptismal pool.

As an old hymn about washing sins away scored the

scene, one-by-one the ushers escorted us to the pool to be baptized and then to the back where we toweled off. The process was systematic and efficient like an assembly line, which lessened the gravity of the ceremony and the "excitement" I was feeling.

This is it, I began to pray, *this is Your last chance to prove Yourself.* An usher placed his hand on my shoulder, waking me from my meditative state, and led me out of the pew.

Standing on the top step of the baptismal pool, the water was cool on my feet. White porcelain tiles, resembling glossy pearls, lined the pool, giving it a glowing effect, as if the water were made of light. The most ornate part, however, was the red tiles on the bottom of the pool that formed a cross: they were like rubies and reflected the light in a way that bloodied the water. Hands outstretched, Pastor Hooks and the deacon helped me down the steps and into the water, which was ice cold and stopped just above my belly button. The tile was smooth under my bare feet, like the polished stones in the river by Snake Hill.

"Are you ready?" Pastor Hooks asked, one hand on my back and the other on my crossed arms. I nodded. "Alright, take a breath." I inhaled deeply and said one final prayer. *I surrender.* "I baptize you in the name of the Father, the Son, and the Holy Ghost." He plunged me under the bloody water, and the shock of it forced the air out of my lungs. The sensation of drowning set in, but just as soon as it had started, it ended when they pulled me out: "Rejoice in the Lord for you were lost but now are found."

At the end of the service, a crowd formed around Malcolm to congratulate him on running the Penn Relays. I managed to get close enough to Malcolm to investigate–if I hadn't been sure before, I was sure then it was him. Standing there, he was in his element. He was charming; he made jokes, and at one point he even got down on the floor and demonstrated his starting position; yet the longer I watched him, the more I saw only the Malcolm I had known. He was taller, faster, and stronger, sure, but all I could see was the small, weak boy who wasn't quick enough to get away when we jumped him. I inched closer, and as I did, the crowd parted, and we made eye contact. He stopped mid-sentence and became still—lifeless like the day I had last seen him. Then, he smiled as though I were another stranger in the crowd. It was brief, but I had gotten my confirmation. In his eyes, there was no plea, there were no tears, there was no Jacob.

I had surrendered, and God had delivered.

CHAPTER 17

"Haven't heard this one in a while," I said, picking up the record sleeve. There were wrinkles in the cover, and the corners were weathered, but Nancy Wilson's dress remained the same vibrant orange as if no time had passed between now and the recording of the song. "Why'd you put it on?"

"Yeah, it's been a minute. I think the last time I listened to it was for our project. Uhm, I don't know. This is another one my mom gave my dad as a gift. Feeling sentimental, I guess." X began to fold a shirt but then stopped to make his bed. "I actually just found it." He fixed the fitted sheet onto one corner of the bed and then stepped into the closet.

"You should put that one on."

"Which one?" X asked.

"In A Sentimental Mooood...," I said, singing the song title.

X laughed. "Got you. I'll put it on next."

"If you can find it." I grabbed a stack of books off his desk and organized them on his bookcase. "I'm surprised your room is this messy."

This was my first time in X's bedroom, and it wasn't

what I had imagined. The floor of his room was covered with half-packed boxes, textbooks, art supplies, and several vinyl records he had borrowed from his father's collection. Where the walls weren't concealed by posters of vintage horror movies, history documentaries, and, surprisingly, cars, a peaceful, deep-green paint underlay the anxiety manifested in the clutter. Watching him race around his room, claustrophobic and chaotic, I had opportunity to peer behind the veneer X presented to everyone and realized he was just a normal kid. To the outside world, X had it all figured out and was too mature to concern himself with others' opinions of him, but I wondered if it all bothered him. The thought made me sad.

"You can't see it, but I'm giving you the finger," he yelled from the back of the closet. "It's not usually like this. I've been slowly packing things up since I won the scholarship. And I've been frantically un—" A sudden crash shut out his voice.

"You good?"

"I couldn't find the record because I had packed it into one of the boxes. I'm fine," he came out of the closet with some sheets and pillowcases and threw them onto the bed, "I only just found it today." He took a stack of canvases out of a box by the door, leaned them up against his desk, which was covered with stray pages of sheet music and a cup filled with paintbrushes, and then went back to making his bed. "Also, thanks again for coming over to help. I know it was last minute."

"I got you," I replied, picking up a painting that was

plastered in green and blue and examining it. "Snake Hill?"

"Painting isn't my ministry."

"Church joke. I like it."

He chuckled. "So, what were you saying? You got baptized?! How long were you underwater?"

"I don't know. Maybe a second or two? Felt like longer, though."

"Do you feel any different? Any superpowers?"

"I have to apply for the powers I want. If I'm approved, they kick in at the end of the year."

He smiled and patted the space next to him on the bed. "You never mentioned anything about getting baptized. What made you do it?"

"It's hard to explain… also, what have we been doing?"

"What do you mean?"

"It looks almost the same as when we started."

"No, I meant, why is it so hard to explain?"

I navigated the minefield of boxes, labeled "clothes," or "shoes," or "notebooks," or "memories," and sat next to him. From the safety of the bed, I surveyed the result of an hour of cleaning and wondered why I had agreed to help him. I had told Herb I would help him set up for his party, but when X texted me, I couldn't think of anything else I'd rather do. Yet, with him leaving, which was all but confirmed by the state of his room, I knew I needed to distance myself to prepare for his departure. Slowly I would take longer to respond to his texts until I stopped texting back altogether. Slowly I would become too busy to hang out with him until I stopped seeing him altogether. Slowly X would understand that it's over until we both let go. Funny, the same song that had marked the beginning of our friendship was now its death knell.

"Do geese see God?"

"What?"

"It's a palindrome. The question is the same if you read it forward or backward, circular in a sense: do geese see God?"

"Well?" X asked.

"'Well,' what? I told you, it's hard to explain," I responded, a bit annoyed, "there's no logical reason why, it just felt like something I needed to do."

"*Well*, 'do geese see God?' is what I was asking."

"Oh," I chuckled awkwardly to alleviate my embarrassment, "I never thought about it… but if you can fly above the clouds, I'm sure you can see everything."

Nancy's words cut through, which prompted me to ask, "What made you pick this song?"

"I told you already. I don't know, I just felt like listening to it," he responded.

"I meant for our project. I'm sure there are tons of songs about romance and losing a lover. Why this one?"

"It just…felt right."

X closed his eyes and listened.

"I think the first thing that drew me to the song was the bass. And I know you're probably thinking it was the piano, which, y'know, fair guess, the song does start with a great flourish. But once she starts singing, the bass comes through and you almost immediately forget that a piano is playing, at least I do. I can feel the strings being plucked right here," X circled his heart with his finger. "It's funny, though, because I think the piano and bass are being played in equal measure and volume, perfectly balanced, but somehow it feels like the bass is more subtle. It's like this undercurrent that carries the song's true emotions.

"I have this thing I do when I listen to jazz where I close my eyes and see what image comes to mind. It's hard to picture something different from what is being sung… but when I listen to this song, I see myself walking in this green pasture. The grass is wild and comes up to my knee, and there are sprinkles of flowers throughout. The sky is bluer than I've ever seen, bluer than it could ever be in real life. There are no clouds. The painting you picked up was my failed attempt to capture this scene," he said, chuckling. "Anyway, the sun flickers like a lantern overheard, but it's not hot. The weather is perfect actually—the heat balanced by the cool wind like the piano by the bass. It feels good.

"The wind then picks up, throwing off the balance. It becomes chilly as the wind blows clouds onto the scene. The sun cools, the lantern flickers, until it blows out. Total darkness. The emotions carried on the bass become more apparent because what once was isn't anymore—and that's what Nancy is saying. When my parents split, they said it was no one's fault. That they still loved each other, but over time, they had just become different people. There was this one time I overheard them arguing, though, before the divorce, and my mom said that he had become this hard man she didn't recognize anymore. Ever since she left, he's been the most affectionate and caring as he's ever been. I think in the beginning he was trying to show her he had changed, but now he just seems happier, like he found something he'd lost. In the same way, in the darkness, I *can't* see what's in front of me, but it's the same pasture, even if it feels foreign. And unlike Nancy, who just accepts that it's over, I can't help but hope the sun will return. And I'll feel its warmth on my face. And I'll see the blooming flowers. The nostalgia—even though she sings about the complete opposite—felt like the right fit for the project."

The record scratched off.

X hopped off the bed and went to his desk.

"I want to show you something. But, ugh," he touched his shirt, which was drenched in sweat, "let me change first."

He took off his shirt, and my heart leaped as he raised it above his abdomen, revealing shadows of a six-pack and a birthmark on his side that looked like a rectangle. He lifted the shirt over his head, exposing his bare chest. His arms did indeed connect to his body like mine. There was no ever-expanding universe, but still I felt myself getting swept up in his gravitational waves. He walked towards me on the bed, and blood flowed into my growing erection. As he got closer, I placed my hands in my lap to hide it while I prepared for what was coming next.

Please forgive me, God.

He grabbed a shirt from the box next to the bed labeled "clothes" and then put it on.

Please forgive me, God. Please forgive me.

X picked up an envelope from his desk and handed it to me. "I wanted you to be the first to know."

"What is it?" I opened the envelope and removed its contents. It was X's scholarship letter. It read that the pre-semester program would start in two weeks—his way of letting me know he'd accepted the scholarship. I smiled. It was all I could do. It was confirmation of what I had been suspected to be true over the past few weeks. Our time was coming to an end, so I smiled and committed myself to remembering the pieces of summer that would linger long after he was gone.

"You're taking the scholarship?" I grinned as wide as I could to hold back the tears that were forming. *Men don't cry. Men don't cry.* "I'm happy for you. I think you'll enjoy it, watch."

A confused look flashed across his face, and then he chuckled. "Flip it over."

I flipped it over, and it read:

"Please indicate a decision by the requested date:

❏ I accept the scholarship and will report to campus by the initiation date.

☑ I decline the scholarship."

"Are you serious?" I asked, leaping off the bed and rushing towards him.

"I'm serious," he laughed, "so… Central?"

I hugged X and he hugged me back.

I squeezed him and he squeezed me back.

X pulled us apart and smiled.

I looked into his brown eyes and he into mine. They sparkled like the stars only we could see—the future I had envisioned for us, the future I had believed could only exist through the patch in the sky, but there it was within my reach.

So, I grabbed it.

Without thinking, I leaned in and kissed him.

His lips were delicate and tender and faintly sweet like diluted caramel. There were no sparks like tv shows had said there would be. Instead, I felt altogether weightless like I would float into space if the walls weren't there to contain us and simultaneously like my knees would buckle. There were no fireworks like tv had said there would be. Instead, I went deaf, but I could hear the stars falling from the sky. The kiss felt infinite as if at any moment when I opened my eyes, we would be in our old age, reborn with memories of the life we had spent together.

But it didn't last that long.

Almost immediately after it started, it ended.

With a firm push, Xavier separated us. He studied me with frenzied eyes, like I had broken into his home. And undeniably, I was a thief. I had stolen a kiss and was unsure what had driven me to do it. This was the moment that the Dead had hoped for. Beneath their lurid desires, they whispered of the freedom and happiness that I would find in this moment, but the Dead were gone—no whispers, no vibrations, no mask for me to hide behind. There was no Jacob, only Jay.

It took some time to recognize what I was feeling, but it wasn't happiness or freedom. The longer Xavier stared at me, the more I recognized the anger that was building. I had indeed heard the stars falling because the sky had shattered and scorched the earth; the sound accompanied by the Pale Horse's whinny and the smell of smoke. I was convinced that if I went to Snake Hill, there would be shards of our patch scattered in the grass—pieces of a broken future that would no longer be accessible nor imaginable going forward.

Xavier and I had once gotten into a heated discussion about reality. Where he usually posited himself to be rational, his perception of reality was a great divergence from this. From his point of view, since reality only existed in a shared understanding of our senses, truth was just an unconscious, yet collective, decision to acknowledge the world in a certain way. For this reason, he ignored what others said about him around school; he avoided talking about the condition of the neighborhood in which we were becoming men; he chose to focus on his future and interests; and he mourned his friendship with Herb in silence. From his point of view, talking about where we were and what was happening around us would condemn us to it.

I had disagreed, arguing that truth existed whether you believed it or not, but as his look of confusion slid into worry, I considered whether he was right. Maybe acknowledging reality was binding oneself to it. I kissed Xavier. This errant kiss had acknowledged what I had masqueraded in the Dead. This was reality, and I was now bound to it.

"Jacob. Jacob," he muttered. He was within arm's length, yet he sounded far away, like an undefined space had come between us and his words were suspended in the vacuum. I had read that outer space was silent because there were no particles for sound waves to travel on, but I could hear the universe crowding out his voice and expanding, crashing in on itself while beating back against its edges. "Jay."

"DON'T…don't call me that. I mean—"

"I'm not—" he said, stopping short of acknowledging reality. "Hey, it's ok, it's ok," he repeated as if this were the key to turning back time, "it's ok." I grew angrier trying to figure out why he was saying this, and then I felt the warm tears streaming down my face. I heard Grandma Junie's words—"tears will help to get the dirt off"—and recognized that tears would never cleanse what stained me. I wiped my face and buried my resentment as I further confirmed that the dead were liars.

"Fuck," I said, wiping my face and trying to stem the irreverent flow. I had broken a cardinal rule.

"It's ok." He took a step towards me and placed a hand on my shoulder. "Hey, it was just an accident, right? You got swept up in the excitement. We can just forget it… it's ok."

The smile on his face was contrived, a familiar gesture to make me feel safe. But I believed that for him it was real. "The Masquerade Is Over," as Nancy had sung, but Xavier couldn't accept that reality. He looked at me and tried to claw back the image of a blooming pasture warmed by the steadfast sun and sheltered overhead by blue skies, refusing to recognize the darkness that was engulfing us.

Xavier pulled me in and hugged me. "It's ok, it's ok, it's ok," he repeated.

My head rested on his shoulder while my arms hung limply at my side. And from either comfort or exhaustion, the tears finally stopped. I stared blankly at the painting on his floor and whispered, "How do you know we're not asleep?"

"What'd you say?"

I pulled us apart and wiped my face again. He ran his hand along my arm and smiled.

"How you know when you're not sleeping? Have you ever thought about it?" He shook his head. "And why would you? When things are normal or happy, you probably wouldn't notice. And you probably wouldn't want to question it so it continues. But when things go wrong, do you ever hope that it's a dream? Do you keep blinking and hope that the next one wakes you up? Or wait anxiously for your alarm to go off? Do you pinch yourself only to realize that you're numb all over? Then what? How do you get the bad parts to end?"

"I—"

"Do you remember the first time we went to Snake Hill together?"

"Of course."

"You brought your telescope and showed me where in the sky to see the stars above all the lights. Afterwards, you talked about being afraid of going to Harbor Park, and I mentioned wanting to disappear." I took his forearm in my hand. "You drew an image of Snake Hill and the stars right here," I traced the image on his skin with my finger, "and you said, 'for if—'"

"For if I accept the scholarship. For if you disappear and come back as something new. Yeah, I remember that," he said, his smile fading. "Yeah, I remember."

"After you did it, I went over it every day with a marker so that it wouldn't fade. When you went to Chicago, it made it feel like someone cared that I was still here and would notice if I vanished. More than anything, though, it made me feel like the person that would reappear would be accepted. But then I left for camp and forgot to bring a marker with me, and after about two days, it faded." I let go of his arm. "That night, you also asked if I'd ever been in love. I didn't answer. But you said 'maybe' because you'd been heartbroken before. I wish I could answer 'maybe,' but I'm numb all over…is this what it feels like?"

His jaw clenched as the brown disks that were his eyes rippled. "It's ok. Here," he rifled through the desk and pulled out a marker, "I'll draw a new one." With the marker in hand, he redrew Snake Hill and the patch of stars on his forearm. "See?"

"It's getting late. I should go."

"Wait! Don't leave."

"I told Herb I would come to his party."

"Text him and tell him you're sick or something. Stay here. I'll ask my dad if you can sleep over. We can talk about it. I don't care that you're—"

"That I'm what?! Say it!"

"That you're you… don't go, please."

"I have to. He's expecting me. I'll see you tomorrow."

"For sure tomorrow?"

"For sure."

"Jacob…," he pleaded. The water in the still lakes pushed past their banks, and tears rolled down his face.

He would never say it, but he had quietly acknowledged the darkness that had engulfed us. We were now bound to the same reality, and with such knowledge, we both knew tomorrow would never come. Not in this timeline.

I smiled, but not because of some epiphany that things would be alright. I just wanted him to remember me smiling.

"Tomorrow for sure. I promise."

CHAPTER 18

The city blocks were empty and dim. I hadn't planned for rain, so the drizzle pooled on my skin until it overflowed and traced lines down my face and arms. Xavier lived only a few blocks away from Herb, but I had decided to just walk. I didn't decide on a direction, but whether I was seeking or running depended on whether I took a left or a right. I hopped over a puddle that reflected the pale glow of the streetlights and continued my aimless roaming around University City. I had briefly caught his reflection as I left Xavier's, but he had since disappeared into the shadows where the streetlights couldn't reach him. He left footprints on the cracked sidewalk and moved through the trees, speaking a language I couldn't understand anymore. His breath rustled the leaves, and blades of grass fluttered with memories of flying. I knew where he would be, but I wasn't ready to find him yet.

Despite having accepted the reality of kissing Xavier, the gravity of the situation never set in—like knowing that a relative had passed but still expecting a phone call on your birthday. It was a reflex. I had promised Xavier I would see him tomorrow, and even though that promise had already grown stale, I could still feel the phantom part of me that was excited to see him. Yet, there was no time to mourn my lost limb or figure out what had grown in its place. Water ran off the sidewalk and collected in the gutter. The resulting flow washed away leaves and carried empty potato chip bags into the sewer. Similarly, disparate thoughts sprung up from all corners of my mind and coalesced into a violent current that exhumed the graves of the Dead and rolled my emotions into one indistinguishable mass. I plunged into the icy flow of the River Styx and floated with the corpses of my only companions. I continued to wander the Philly streets, following the tendrils of the pale moonlight, until I eventually ended up at the top of Herb's block. Trying to resist the current while teetering between life and death was futile; attempting to identify the injured body part was pointless when my entire body was numb. So, I surrendered.

"Ayyy! There he go!" Meat yelled from the patio. "You owe me a dolla'," he said, turning to Eric with his palm out. Eric responded by begrudgingly placing a dollar in his hand.

"Good to see you," Eric said, irked that he had lost the bet, but still happy to see me. Mason approached from the back and gave my shoulders a gentle squeeze to say hello while Meat touted that half his newly gained riches was mine. My body responded warmly, although unconsciously, to these gestures—I greeted them with a smile, but my actions weren't my own. They felt detached, as if I were on autopilot, the outcome of the rushing river that was carrying me closer to entropy.

"I didn't think you was comin'," Herb said. He smiled at me, but there was an unmistakable look of surprise shadowing his face.

"I told you I would."

"I know, but you said you were gonna help set up. Didn't think you could make it."

"Yeah, that's my bad. I got… distracted."

Herb's relaxed posture stiffened, and I became unsure if I should leave. He stared into my eyes, and his look of surprise slipped into concern. He studied me with the same frenzied eyes as Xavier had, unsure of who stood before him, but knowing that the "Jay" who came to his party to do what they had charged him to do wasn't the same "Jay" who he had protected and confided in. I didn't know whether in my eyes he found the person he once knew or he accepted the one who stood before him, but his smile felt familiar as he held out his hand. "It's a dolla' to get in."

"Oh." I reached into my pocket to fish one out.

Laughing, he placed his arm around my shoulder. "I'm fuckin' with you."

"Asshole." I smiled.

<hr>

"…and there's food and stuff in the kitchen," Herb said, escorting me from the basement to the living room.

"Bet. What time Brianna and the other girls gettin' here?" I asked, emerging from the cresting chaos of the river.

"I don't even know if they're comin' anymore." He

glanced at his phone. "Haven't heard from them all day." He coughed to clear his throat and then put his phone back in his pocket. "You can chill up here or go back down to the party or come outside, whatever, up to you. I'm gonna go back out—hold on… Meat!"

"Yo," Meat responded, his voice muffled.

"What are you doin' in here? I told you to watch the fuckin' door!"

"I got hungry," he said, emerging from the kitchen with a chicken wing in one hand, a plate in the other, and his signature goofy smile spread across his face.

"Anyway," Herb said with a hand on my shoulder, "I'm gonna go back outside. Harrison ran to the store to get more ice. He supposed to be comin' back soon. I'll head downstairs when he shows up. If the girls come back before he gets here, I'll come find you."

"Who's gonna watch the door if that happens?" I asked, amused.

Herb looked at Meat, who shrugged and smiled. "I'll find someone." He then pulled me in and whispered, "If you hear the girls are here, you come find me first, ok?"

"Uhm, ok."

"Cool," his voice returned to normal volume, "but yeah, do you, Imma be on the stoop. And you," he pointed to Meat, "you know you're a dickhead, right?"

"What I do?" Meat grinned at Herb as they both walked out.

With a plate of chicken wings in my lap, I sat on the couch and watched the baseball game on tv. The Phillies were playing against the Nationals and were up by two runs. I wasn't a fan of baseball, but I cheered when a player hit the ball. Ryan Howard stepped up to the plate, tapped the wooden bat against his cleats, and swung. "Strike one! Strike two! Ball one… foul ball… foul ball… ball three…" and then, with a poignant crack, the ball went flying into the far leftfield. He ran to second base, and I stood and clapped. In a moment of lucidity, I looked around and was grateful to be the only one in the living room.

Framed photos of Herb's family sat on the mantel. There was an old picture of his dad, Big Dub, dressed in long denim shorts that stopped midway down his calves and a Sixers jersey almost as long. He was holding baby Herb and smiling. Next to it, in a sports-themed frame, was his older brother, Harrison, wearing football gear and grinning with his two front teeth missing. There were several other photos: one with Herb holding a basketball, one with Harrison draping his arm over Herb's shoulder at a cookout, one with his mom and dad at prom, etc., but the one that held my attention was of his parents at their wedding. This was the quintessence of love as I knew it. Whatever I had thought I felt for Xavier, that which had driven me to kiss him, wasn't love. Even as I once again compared my feelings to the fatal love between Romeo and Juliet, it was between Romeo and *Juliet*. Even in the case when that "love" was unrequited—as it was in mine—*Rosaline* had been the object of his obsession. Romeo hadn't fallen in love with Mercutio.

It wasn't love. It couldn't be.

I studied the photos for a little while longer, landing on

the Polaroid picture of a young Herb dressed in his school uniform with another little boy standing next to him. This one was my favorite. When Herb had first shown it to me, I thought it was his dad, which made Herb chuckle. Looking at it now that I realized that the other boy was Xavier. Grinning, they hugged and smiled at the camera with their faces pressed together. The picture reminded me of the many moments that "What's-His-Name" and I shared, where we embraced each other with a loving innocence that would ultimately be chipped away. I wondered whether this picture was of them rebelling against their indoctrination or whether this had been a final act of mercy by the adults in their lives—the memorialization of their youth before they became men. I ran my fingers over my forearm where the "tattoo" used to be and thought of the platitudes shaping the flow of the river that would eventually erode Snake Hill. *Men don't hold hands, men don't hug each other, men don't show emotion unless it's anger, men don't fall in love with other men, men don't kiss other men.*

It wasn't love. It couldn't be.

In my musings, I imagined myself as happy as Herb's parents, which strengthened my resolve to do what needed to be done to realize this future. I made my way to the stoop to wait for Brianna to arrive, but as I reached for the doorknob, something within me stirred. It tingled and hung suspended in my stomach like the feeling when descending on a rollercoaster. It could have been intuition, or the spirits of the Dead, or the rushing river slowing enough for my fear to take form, but something convinced me not to go outside.

Instead, I peeked through the curtains and listened.

"What time you say the girls comin', bro?" Meat asked.

"I don't fuckin' know at this point. Evey texted me earlier today they were gonna meet at her house to get ready and then head over. She said they were gonna be here at ten," Herb responded.

Meat pulled out his phone and checked the time. "It's almost eleven. Text them again."

"Nigga, you text them," Herb replied. Feeling rejected, Meat chuckled awkwardly but didn't say anything.

"You think he gon' do it?" Mason asked, pretending to dribble a ball.

"I don't think so," Eric answered.

"Put bread on it," Meat chimed in. "I could use another dolla'."

"Shut the fuck up," Eric laughed and shoved Meat, who reciprocated by putting Eric in a headlock.

"Yo!" Herb barked. "Y'all niggas drawlin', chill the fuck out, bro!" The two separated and slinked to opposite sides of the stoop like wounded pups, their reticence out of respect as much as embarrassment.

"Damn, what's wrong with you?" Mason asked.

"I'm chillin'. Y'all niggas just annoyin'."

"What the fuck I do?"

"Y'all don't get tired of havin' the same conversation all the time? It's always the same shit with y'all. Why y'all care so much if he fuck Brianna or not?"

"Why else he here then?" Mason responded, dribbling the imaginary basketball between his legs. "Ain't seen that nigga since school ended. Now he just pops up outta nowhere, actin' like nothin' changed."

"For real," Eric jumped in, "I still think he might be gay if I'm being honest." They shook their heads in approval of Eric's assessment, all except for one.

"Nigga, what? He's not gay," Herb said in a deep voice. He almost sounded like his dad.

"Nigga, how you know?" Mason replied with his hands on his hips.

"I just know. Besides, if anybody's gay, it's Meat. That nigga always pullin' his dick out."

Everyone laughed.

"It's not gay if it's funny," Meat said with a toothy smile plastered on his face.

The laughter died down, and the sound of crickets filled the space.

"For real, though," Eric said after a moment, continuing his crusade, "he never be tryin' to hang out with the girls. There's always some excuse for why he can't."

"That's true. He always got a stomachache or headache or low blood sugar or some bullshit," Mason added. Again, the group nodded their heads in agreement, all except for Herb, who only mustered, "Whatever," as a reply.

"Right. And remember that one time where all of us were at my house, and as soon as I said I was gonna invite the girls over, he suddenly had to 'go home to help my mom with somethin'.'" Meat stated, emboldened by the other testimonies.

"Yup, I remember that," Eric said, wresting the reins away

from Meat. "I heard he been hangin' out with that weirdo boul too. Uhm… uhm… damn, what's his name again?"

"Xavier," Meat said. Herb flinched at the mention of his name.

"Yeah, him," Eric continued, "and that nigga definitely gay."

"So, because he doesn't want to do anything with the girls that means he's gay? What if he just scared? Or what if he just doesn't want to?" Herb rebutted.

"If he not gay, why you get him switched out the group?" Mason interjected.

"What are you even talkin' about, bro?" Herb laughed to break the tension. "I didn't." His words came out shaky and unconvincing as he coughed to clear his throat.

"Right. Whatever you say. He's cool, but if that nigga a faggot, I can't fuck with that shit," Mason proclaimed.

"For real," Eric said.

"Real shit, can't have people thinkin' we're like that too. Fuck that," Meat exclaimed.

"I'm goin' on record as sayin' that nigga not gonna fuck her. And when he doesn't, that'll confirm it. After that, you can keep bein' friends with boul," Mason pointed at Herb, "but you'll be the only one."

Herb scowled but said nothing.

"Ard, well, I'm hungry," Meat said after a while.

"Nigga, you just had a whole plate of wings," Eric responded.

"I know," Meat smiled, "but I want somethin' to snack on."

"You fat as shit, dickhead," Eric said, laughing.

"Yo, Herb, the papi store around here still open?" Meat asked.

"It's a jawn around the corner. They close at 11:30, though."

"Bet." Meat pulled out his phone to check the time. "I'm about to go buy some sunflower seeds. E, walk with me to the store."

"Ard. Mason, you comin'?"

"Yeah, I'll slide. You want anything from the store, bro?" Mason asked, resuming the dribbling of the nonexistent ball and taking a fadeaway shot.

"Nah, I'm good," Herb answered.

"Y'all watched WWE last night?" Meat asked, backpedaling down the block while Mason and Eric followed. "That shit was CRAZY!"

***

The moonlight bathed Herb as he sat alone outside. He looked like an ashen version of himself, the unlucky version that hadn't escaped the eruption at Pompeii. "Nah, he's not," Herb said, standing up and pacing back and forth. "He's not. But if he is… nah, he's not."

"If he is…?" was a question that I had pushed away. It was a question never truly considered as the subject itself was totally othered. I wanted to go outside and tell him that the self-interrogation was moot, and I would prove it to him, to all of them, tonight.

"Happy belated birthday."

Herb's head snapped to face the person. "What are you doin' here?" he asked, surveilling the area to make sure no one was around.

"I'm looking for Jacob." It was Xavier. "Is he here?"

"You mean '*Jay*'? If you don't see him, then he's not here."

"You know what I mean. Is he *inside*? I need to talk to him."

"About what? He doesn't have anything to say to you."

"Did he say that to you?"

"He ain't have to say shit to me."

"Look, I know he's here. Can I just speak to him quickly?"

"No."

"Why not? Are you afraid someone is gonna see me? I don't care about your party. I only want to speak to Jacob, then I'll go."

"You're not gettin' in."

"Fine." Xavier sat in one of the patio chairs. "Then, I'm not leavin'." Herb approached Xavier and clenched his fists. "You're gonna hit me?"

Herb exhaled and then took a seat next to him. "Shut up."

"I'm surprised your mom even let you have a party."

"She made me promise to clean up afterwards and to do all the housework for a week. She also said I couldn't have any girls over."

"How'd that turn out?"

"The girls I invited ain't here yet, so promise kept, I guess."

"And your dad?"

"You know him. I didn't have to convince him at all. The cleaning part was a given, and the housework was just a bonus."

They laughed.

"How come you're not inside?" Echoes of the party emanated from the basement and filled the empty spaces between their words. "Sounds like a good time."

"Watching the door. Harrison went to get ice."

"How is he?"

"Good. Still dating Ayana. Leaving for college in a few weeks, too."

"Are you sad about it?"

"Fuck you," Herb said.

They laughed again.

"That's great. Tell him I said, 'congrats.'"

"I will. And I am a little bit."

"I know. So, fourteen… It's one-four the books!"

"That was sooo corny," Herb chuckled.

"Jacob said the same thing," Xavier laughed. "Year older, feel any different?"

"Not really. I don't know. Am I supposed to? Do you usually feel any different?"

"Hmm, I don't think so… actually, I suppose I always get a little wiser."

Herb laughed. "You're an idiot. Mr. C said you won the Harbor Park jawn, so I *suppose* you'll feel different this time around when your birthday comes. Congrats, you earned it."

"Thanks. That means a lot coming from you."

"And you're taking it, right?"

"I don't know," Xavier said. "I was sure it was what I wanted, but now I don't know."

"Don't be stupid."

"Helpful, thank you."

"You're welcome," Herb chuckled.

"Oh! remember that time, I think it was the summer after third grade, when Harrison took us to that carnival in Yeadon for your birthday? We had a contest to see who could eat the most corn dogs and then got on the rides, and we ended up throwing up in the trashcan afterwards."

"I do," Herb said, laughing. "I'm pretty sure I won that contest, too."

"Only because I let you win. It was your birthday."

"Mhmm," Herb responded.

"After that," Xavier continued, "you used all your tickets playing that ring toss game. I can't remember the prize you were trying to win, though."

"It was a huge stuffed turtle. I still have it, too."

"Yes! That jawn was creepy looking. But you were dead set on getting it. You were always determined to get what you wanted once you set your mind to it. It's one of the things I admire about you. Anyway, you ran out of tickets and started crying."

"No the fuck I didn't!"

"Oh, you were *the* biggest crybaby when we were younger." They laughed, and Xavier added, "You wouldn't stop crying, so Harrison played until he won it for you. I have no doubt you'll miss him… I miss my brother, too."

"Xav'…"

"Why do you hate me?"

"I don't hate you." Herb's voice was soft. It reminded me of our night at Snake Hill. I imagined that in this moment he wasn't speaking to Xavier but rather speaking through him, lending his words to the summer air with no expectation of being repaid. "I never hated you."

"Then what? We were best friends, brothers, and you threw that all away because of a dress. My parents just got divorced, you were trying to cheer me up—it was just a dress, a stupid joke!"

Herb looked around to confirm they were alone. "Lower your voice. It wasn't only about the dress. You heard what my dad said to me before he sent you home. You just stood there. You could've tried to explain, to help, but you just stood there. And after he said what he said, you just took the first opportunity to leave. You left me alone."

"I know, and I'm sorry."

"It's whatever. Probably for the best, anyway. I feel like I didn't know who I was when I was around you."

"What does that mean?" Xavier replied. "Do you know who you are now? Because *this* isn't you."

"Grow up, Xav'. We're not kids anymore."

"Just because you say it doesn't make it true. You're the same little boy who cried for a stuffed animal."

"Fuck you," Herb stood up.

"Fuck you too, Herbert."

"Don't call me that," Herb said. The familiar tone towards Xavier became cold, and I thought he would hit him this time, but Xavier didn't flinch.

"Bro, let me get some more and stop being stingy!" Eric yelled from down the street.

"You need to go. The guys are on their way back, and I don't want you to get hurt."

Xavier stood up. "I'm sorry. I know I let you down when you needed me most, but I'm trying not to make the same mistake."

Herb nodded. "I'll tell Jay you were asking for him."

"Will you tell him I don't see him any differently?"

"What happened?" Herb asked.

"Can y'all chill the fuck out?!" Mason reprimanded.

"Never mind," Herb said. "You should go. I'll tell him, I promise."

Xavier descended the stairs and then turned back to give Herb a hug. "Take care of yourself, Herb."

Herb hugged him back. "See you, Xav'."

"Yooo! Look who we found," Meat yelled.

From the couch, I heard giggling. My heart raced. The Phillies were pitching and were up by one run. Bases loaded. Two strikes. Bottom of the ninth.

"I'll go find Jay," Herb said. "Mason, watch the door."

———

"Sorry," I said to Brianna, pulling my hand away from hers to wipe the sweat off my palms.

"It's ok." She smiled and took my hand again, leading us down the stairs to the basement.

We descended into the crowd and was met by the sharp stench of youth. Bodies danced around us as we maneuvered through the crowd. To my left, a couple kissed while his friends cheered him on; and as we passed by the corner under the staircase, I heard, among the indiscriminate conversations, the charismatic voice of Meat.

"Why you actin' scary? You did it before. Come on." We were young, but we weren't kids.

I couldn't hear what song was playing over the sound of my heart, but its rhythm was to the beat of the music and the cadence of our steps. Brianna led me into the laundry room and closed the door behind us. Before I had time to assess how I was feeling, I started to undo my pants and take off my shirt.

"What are you doin'…" she asked, stifling her laughter.

"I—would you believe me if I said I was goin' to do a quick load? It's sweaty as fuck in there."

She smiled and then quickly pulled that warm smile into a straight line, dimming the lights in the room. "I don't know what you *thought* was gonna happen," she said, "but even if it *were*, did you really think it would happen up against the washing machine?"

"Uhm," I said, unsure of whether the question was rhetorical, and equally unsure of what to say. "I didn't think—"

"I know."

"My bad."

"I know," she smiled and then started laughing. "I'm

messin' with you!" She pulled me over to her and gestured for me to help her onto the washing machine. I stood between her thighs and acted as I thought Herb would in this situation. I bit my bottom lip softly and grinned as charmingly as I could, and then, as I slowly ran my hands up her thighs, landing softly on her hips, I leaned in to kiss her. My heart pounded, but I ignored it for fear that trying to slow it down would stop it altogether. Just as our lips were on the verge of making contact, she firmly pressed her index finger into my forehead and pushed me away. "I was messin' with you," she hopped down off the washing machine, "but I'm *actually* not havin' sex with you in a laundry room."

"I know," I said. With my hands still on her hips, I pulled her in and kissed her. Having kissed only one other person in my life, inevitably, Xavier came to mind. Where his lips were smooth and faintly tasted of caramel, hers were sticky from lip gloss and laden with a berry flavor; and although not a transcendent experience, the softness of her lips and warmth of her body pressed against mine slowed my heart rate down until it was no longer perceptible. I knew what was going to come after this, but I wasn't afraid. *WWHD: What Would Herb Do?* was the only thought in my head. It was my mantra. It was the rising action pushing this episode to its finite end.

She broke free of me and grabbed my hand once more, leading me out of the laundry room and back the way we came. "Stop… STOP!" I heard a girl shout as we passed the corner under the staircase. "Why you drawlin'?" Meat's voice was stern and obstinate, a stark difference from his goofy lilt and demeanor. To my right, a group of girls consoled one of their own as the boy she made out with not too long ago danced with another girl. We were young, but we weren't innocent.

Herb sat slumped in the chair but corrected his posture when he saw us emerge from the basement. In his eyes was that same look of concern, but he didn't try to hide it this time.

"Where y'all goin'?" he asked.

"Upstairs," I said, climbing the stairs, "which room can we use?"

"Hold on, let me talk to you in the kitchen right quick."

"I'll be right up," I said to Brianna. She nodded and continued walking.

"What're you doin'?" Herb asked with raised eyebrows.

"What do you mean? What does it look like?"

"Are you sure you want to do this? You don't have to. Tell her you changed your mind and hang out downstairs."

"I know. I want to."

"Why?"

"Huh?"

"Why are you doin' this?"

"Because I'm not…," I responded.

"You're not what?"

"I heard you and Mason and them talkin' outside. I know you switched me out of your group because you think I'm… but I'm not."

"I didn't switch you out the group," Herb's voice cracked. I turned to leave, but then he grabbed my arm. "Wait. Ard, I did switch you out, but it's not because I thought," he made sure no one was coming and then brought his voice down to a whisper, "not because I thought you were gay. I did it because I was tryin' to keep you away from this. You always make up these excuses why you can't hang out with the girls, but I know you be scared. The day of the trip, I saw it. And it made me mad you were about to be forced to do somethin' I knew you didn't want to do. I was lookin' out for you.

"Remember how I told you that Xavier and I used to be friends?" I nodded. "I said that we stopped bein' friends because you grow out of certain things, but that was only part of it. Before the incident with Xavier happened, I had sex for the first time. I know the guys and I talk about girls and stuff all the time, but we never talk about how it changed us. I don't know how to explain it, but it unlocks somethin' in you that changes how you see everything. When that thing happened with Xavier, it was to try to put it back in the box—but that's the thing, once it's out, you can't put it back. I lost my best friend because the world changed. I didn't want the same thing to happen to you. You're the smart one. This shit not for you."

There was that look of concern again. It made me feel good to know Herb cared so much, but it also made me sick to my stomach. "This shit not for you," he had said, but who was he to determine that. I was tired of being the bearer of everyone's expectations and hopes. Herb warned of the world changing, but my world had changed years ago, and I'd never stopped trying to put it right again.

For the final time, I thought of the home that "What's-His-Name" and I had had together, our home that was cut down and uprooted. We hadn't chosen to love each other the way we did, yet we were castigated for our expressions of said love, albeit as pure and innocent as it could be for two third graders. As I got older, what would the punishment be? The loss of friends was evident as my friendship with Xavier lay drowned and broken on the banks of the River Styx. Even so, what more could this world inflict on me, and, more importantly, how much more pain and punishment could I endure? Dismissal from family and community? Violence? Isolation? Death? The price seemed steep for fleeting experiences of vulnerability, as we were taught in elementary school. "Boys, don't…" The price seemed steep for authenticity, as we showed to Malcolm, leaving his soul bare and body bloodied. The price seemed steep for "love," whereas my experience fit no known reference, yet for a moment believed existed beyond that patch in the sky and in that fatal moment on Xavier's lips. The price seemed steep for happiness that wasn't guaranteed, as I had come to learn the truth of the Dead wasn't reality. The world had changed when I learned love was conditional and could only exist in certain forms. Doing this wasn't breaking the world apart but rather putting it back together. This was making it right.

"Condoms?"

"You don't have to do this," he answered, concern etched on his face.

"I do, Herbert."

Herb recoiled and then scoffed. "'I don't see you any

differently,'" he said, fulfilling his promise. It wasn't his truth to tell.

"Do you have any condoms?"

"Jay…," he stared into my eyes and searched for any softness that still existed in me but found none. "In the nightstand with the lamp on top, there's a black bag in the bottom drawer."

I nodded and then went upstairs to meet Brianna.

"Run me my money, nigga!" I heard Meat exclaim from downstairs.

CHAPTER 19

"Yo," Meat called to me from across the table, "did you hear me, nigga?"

"Huh? Nah, my bad. What'd you say?" I asked, pulling my gaze off the entrance of the cafeteria to respond to Meat.

"I asked if you wanted your tater tots."

I picked up one of the tots, which was brown and crunchy on the outside and cold in the middle. "Nah...," I said as I dropped it back onto the tray, "you got it."

"Good looks," he said, pushing his empty tray out of the way and pulling mine over.

"You good?" Mason asked from Herb's seat at the head of the table.

"Yeah, I'm good." Months had passed since Xavier's text messages and calls stopped, and I hadn't seen him since that night at Herb's party. Months had passed, yet the small, burning hope that he would walk into school one day still flickered like the lantern in the pasture. I glanced once more at the entrance and then turned to Mason. Maybe tomorrow.

"I'm good, just thinkin' about next year. Where Herb at?"

"I think that nigga in the library again." Mason scanned the room to confirm his hypothesis and then sat up straight. "What is there to think about? We all goin' to West."

"I know," I said, "but we really gonna go without Herb?"

"He movin' on without us, so why wouldn't we do the same?" Mason answered with a disapproving scowl while Eric nodded in agreement and Meat shoveled half-baked tater tots into his mouth. I smiled in accordance, but the gesture arose from self-preservation, not from agreement with Mason's reasoning. To him, Herb's deviation from the plan made their extensive history seem worthless, erased the value of their present and the possibility of a shared future. He and Herb had been friends since preschool—it must've been difficult for him to imagine them living separate lives. "Besides," he continued, "it's too late to apply anywhere else. Decisions about eligibility come out early next year, I think, and we'll be goin' to West, anyway."

Soon after the school year began, Herb received a letter from a scout at a private school in Lower Merion, stating they wanted him to attend on a basketball scholarship. The offer, however, was contingent on Herb finishing the first semester of eighth grade with a B- average; so, every day during lunch, he studied in the library and then was off to the suburbs for practice. I had barely seen him since the start of the school year as a result, but I knew this was only his excuse and not his reason.

After the party, things between us appeared to remain the same, but gradually I noticed the uniqueness of our relationship was vanishing. First, it started with our conversations, which flattened and came to center on only a few topics like sports, girls, the newest Jordans, or whatever other immediate need or desire we sought to be met. Although Herb was never very verbose, there had been nights—like the one at Snake Hill and others that occurred after we watched a movie or on long walks home after a day at the courts—where he was vulnerable about his fears and interests, where our conversations occupied four dimensions and had access to the past, present, and future. Those ended. Then, as studying and practice occupied more of his time, we transitioned to only hanging out in group settings. The most cogent sign that our relationship as I had known it had ended was that Herb stopped putting his arm around my shoulder. Even when his touch felt different, he still endeavored to shield me, but with my full membership in the group, his protection was no longer warranted.

I had strived for full acceptance, yet I didn't know the price of belonging. I used to think that the guys were the ones that held me at arm's length, that they were the reason I never felt I fit in, but after his party, I realized that Herb's protection wasn't an attempt to help me assimilate but to preserve who I was. Xavier's statement to Herb about missing his brother came to mind, and it made me think about my relationship with Christian and how I hadn't been able to relate to the new person my brother had grown into. In the same way, Herb could no longer relate to me as he once had. But just as kung fu films and video games had reminded Christian and me of our shared history, I still had hope that Herb would remember Snake Hill.

Sitting at the table—Mason our de-facto leader, Eric his right hand, and Meat blissfully oblivious—I realized that both Xavier and Herb wanted the same thing for me. Although they approached it from differing perspectives—Herb from a prescient standpoint warned of giving into the current, while Xavier demonstrated the outcome of bucking against it—they both wanted me to hold on to that stubborn piece of myself that didn't fit the mold, to hold on to that remaining bit of self-determination and curiosity, to hold on to that last shred of guileless whimsy, to hold on to being a child, just for a little while longer. I looked once more at the entrance of the cafeteria, hoping for either Herb or Xavier to walk in. I wanted to tell Xavier that I was sorry and Herb that he was right, but the sound of the bell jolted me back to reality.

Maybe tomorrow.

"Jacob," Mr. Castor called to me as I exited the classroom, "Sorry… *Jay,*" he corrected. "Hang back a minute."

"Jacob is fine," I said, and he nodded.

"How're you doing?"

"I'm good."

"Yeah? You've been pretty quiet since the year started." I glanced back at the empty desk where Xavier had sat and nodded. Mr. Castor saw this and said, "I miss him too." He shuffled through the papers in his brown leather satchel, weathered by age and peeling at the straps, and pulled out a stack of papers. After rifling through graded assignments and those yet to be assessed, he pulled out a single page. "I read your essay and made some edits." He handed me the sheet. "It was good."

"Are you sure?" I asked, scanning the document, which was covered in red annotations.

He smiled and handed me a clean version. "I'm sure. You can see that it's largely unchanged from what you wrote. You're a talented writer." Uncomfortable with accepting the compliment, I scoffed. "I'm serious. That's why I submitted it to the President over at Central." Before I could respond, he added, "I know you said you changed your mind about going, but I want you to reconsider the decision."

I glanced again at the empty desk and clenched my jaw to hold back the tears that were forming. "What about the deadline?"

"You gotta know the rules before you can break them," he said as he gathered the scattered sheets into a neat pile and placed them in his bag, "and after twenty years of working in the school district, I would say I'm somewhat familiar. You also don't make it this far in life without friends—the President and I were both class of 244—and without support." He pulled a crimson and gold brochure out of the front pocket of his bag and handed it to me. "Don't let anyone tell you any different. Who you are and who you want to be are among the few things in life that you can control. I've done what I can. The rest is up to you."

"Thanks, Mr. C." I looked at the Bible on his desk and something propelled me to ask, "Mr. C, what do you think about Revelations?"

"Decent allegorical text. Not my favorite. A bit too fanatical for my tastes, which I feel detracts from the greater message of the New Testament. The metaphors are very on the nose. Story's a bit predictable, too. However, that's to be expected. Really, it's just a derivation of traditional Mesopotamian oral folklore—but basically everything was back then. I like to think of it as a kind of apocalypse version of the telephone game."

I looked back at Xavier's empty desk and smiled.

After an unseasonably warm fall, the cold had set in. The kind of cold that seeps into your bones and chills the marrow, the kind that strips the trees bare, leaving nothing to be desired from their scraggly bodies—neither shelter nor inspiration.

It was early February, and snow had replaced the rain, covering the ground in white and obscuring the sky in gray. The stream had slowed to a trickle and froze in some places. I tossed rocks at the frozen spots to break up the ice, relishing the sharp cracking sound when the rock landed. Stones littered the sheet of ice but did nothing to influence the flow of the water. The bank had eroded some since last coming with Xavier, and I imagined that in a few short lifetimes, the gentle stream held at bay by the remaining shore would be a rushing river at the foot of the hill. With no more rocks to throw, I set my sights on the summit and saw him standing there. I removed the glove from my right hand and dipped it into the river to confirm my reality. The water was clear and smarted to the touch.

My feet slipped with each step as the gradient of the hill increased. I kicked my boots into the hillside as I had seen mountain climbers do on tv, grunting and playfully blaming my shallow breathing on the change in altitude, while I pulled out frozen blades of grass from under the freshly fallen snow. As I got closer, I saw him staring up at the sky and drawing circles where the patch in the sky had been.

When he noticed me, he brought his hand down to his side and turned to look at me. I took a step forward, and he took one toward me on the opposite foot—a step on the right, and here he came. We moved closer to one another until we were face-to-face. So much time had passed between us, but it was him. His cheeks were full and round, he was missing his front teeth, and he donned a bald fade because his mom didn't want to deal with the hassle of his hair. I flipped my palms upward, and he did the same, revealing his bloody hands embedded with gravel. Tears streamed down his face as he looked up at me, so I reached to wipe them away—yet there existed something irreparable between us, like space-time had ripped in two and we existed on opposite sides of the rift. I brushed my hand across my face, and he did the same, wiping the tears from his eyes. I smiled and said, "Hi, Jacob."

Lying next to each other in the snow, we looked up at the blanketed sky. "I got into Central. Just found out today. Should I go?" I asked him directly, knowing he couldn't understand me but wanting to speak to him anyway. "I haven't told Mason and them yet—not sure if I should. What's the point, right? I probably won't go. It's a solid opportunity, but it wouldn't be right. Herb transferred schools last month. He finished the semester with all As and got onto the basketball team, so the scout at the private school thought it would help him adjust better if he finished out the year there. I knew he could do it, but can I tell you a secret? I wanted him to fail. I know that makes me a bad person, but I didn't want him to leave. Before he transferred, I overheard a teacher talking about moving Herb to the gifted program. He could've had the seat right next to mine. So yeah, Herb's gone. I can't leave the guys too, even though Mr. C pulled some strings to get me in. I wish he hadn't. I feel guilty for wanting to turn it down, but I'll feel guilty if I go. Central was part of a vision that Xavier and I created together. It's broken now, though," I pointed my right hand to the sky, and he his left. His breath staggered out in a cadence complementary to mine, inhaling when I exhaled with precise timing and angst. Where the portal had been, where it still may have been, behind the clouds.

"But what if I did leave and start fresh? Imagine me outside of this place, under a different sky. Who would I be? Would you be there? I thought you were gone, but you've always been there, haven't you? It was you at camp, and you the night of the party, moving through the trees. It was you who pushed for truth. It was you who promised happiness. It was you when I fell in love with Xavier, even as I denied it was love. It was you when I kissed him. It was you who I saw in Malcolm's eyes, and you who I tried to kill. It was you who sought acceptance. It was you when I didn't feel shame for just existing. It was you who Grandma Junie talked about when she said, 'softness.' It's you who remembers that Mom is trying even as I shut her out. It was you who pulled Christian in for a hug even after I pushed him away, and you who Herb protected when he placed his arm around my shoulder. It was you who broke that cold, hard thing even as I rebuilt it. It was you who shed tears for What's-His-Name even after I burned our home down, and you who preserves his memory even as I forget his name. It's you who grieves even as I carry the sadness in my heart."

A biting wind blew in response, but I couldn't understand him.

Snow began to fall. I could feel the cool snowflakes touch my face before melting against my waning body heat. My feet and hands were numb, and I could feel the cold congealing my blood. The howling wind caressed my face, penetrating my clothing and prickling my skin. My body trembled in its attempts to maintain homeostasis, but I held it steady, wanting to listen to him speak for just a little longer.

"I knew you would be here," I responded, "but I'm a man now, so I can't come looking for you again." I placed a finger on my forearm, and he did the same. With it, I traced a triangle that was missing a third side and drew a circle at its peak. "For if you disappear…," I said to him and closed my eyes. The trembling quieted and became fainter as my heartbeat slowed to a muted thump. A warm tear escaped my clenched eyes and rolled down my face.

Xavier... Herb... Xavier... Herb… Xavier... Herb. Their names circled my mind as I promised to commit them to memory.

I searched for the skyline, but the winter air obscured the city's glare. I searched for stars, but the clouds swallowed the night. The heavens above were empty —an act of God had changed the composition of the sky.

The cold's tender touch caressed my face until it numbed, the only sensation emerging from the tears no longer dammed by the lifelong adage, "men don't cry." I had made my decision, but just a little longer I wanted to be coddled, to let go and feel like something would catch me, to fall and have someone pick the gravel from my hand, to be me and be loved, to cry and have the dirt wash off, to be a child and feel hope for the future. Snow continued to fall until it encased me in a white coffin.

Without sound and without warning, I felt his presence ebb until there was none. A parting gift, on the wind, Jacob whispered his name, "Andrew."

The End.

Acknowledgements

"Think of the parents you're born to, the family you're born into, the person you're born as, and all the chance encounters that happen in a lifetime."

To know me is to know how sentimental I am. I'm a hopeless romantic for whom every moment—from the mundane to the momentous—is equally steeped in serendipity. I'm thankful for the person I am and the person I'm constantly becoming. But, for a long time, I wish I wasn't who I was. Unhappy with the person who looked back at me in the mirror and even more so with the feelings and thoughts that I couldn't rid myself of, like Jacob, I wished to be someone who didn't live in fear and shame. With time, grace, (lots of therapy), and the support of my community, though, I've come to fully recognize the value of these experiences and the beauty of artificial roses. So, thanks to childhood me, teenage me, young adult me, and all past iterations of myself that hurt in secret but never gave up. I love you.

I want to thank Love, Universe, and all other manifestations of God for our paradoxical, yet wholly unique and personal, relationship. I love you.

Thanks to my mom, who has loved me unconditionally, even when I didn't love myself. It's because of her that I keep moving forward when the road ahead disappears. It's because of her that I have an indelible forgiveness for those of have intentionally wronged me, knowing that the guilt is theirs to carry not mine. It's because of her that a guest in my home will eat before I do and that I'll share my last, even as I mask my hunger with a smile. I love you.

Thanks to my family, by blood and by choice, who taught me what it means to be deeply human—imperfect but enough—and to laugh, especially, when life hurts the most. I love you.

Thanks to my friends, whose presence is a constant reminder that I'm blessed. I love you.

And a special thanks to my beta readers, Aaron, Advait, Helena, Kuria, and Rebeacca. Your participation was invaluable in this process. I'm grateful for your friendship and the insights you provided. I love you.

About the Author

Linton Taylor is a Chicago-based writer and debut novelist who fell in love with storytelling at a young age, penning his first short story in seventh grade. In college, he experimented with short vignettes, but it was a senior-year fiction writing course that sparked the idea for *The Gesture That Fit*. Born and raised in West Philadelphia, Taylor draws on personal reflections about identity, queerness, and the survival strategies learned in child-hood to craft intimate, unflinching narratives exploring belonging and masculinity.